A NEW SEASON

The Fortunes of BLUES and BLESSINGS BOOK TWO

KAREN SLOAN-BROWN

BROWN REFLECTIONS

A New Season
The Fortunes of Blues and Blessings
Book Two

Copyright © 2014 by Karen Sloan-Brown

This book is printed on acid-free paper.

ISBN: 978-0-9915517-2-9

Library of Congress Cataloging-in-Publication Data on file.

Editor: Maxine Thompson

MANUFACTURED IN THE UNITED STATES OF AMERICA

A NEW SEASON

The Fortunes of BLUES and BLESSINGS BOOK TWO

KAREN SLOAN-BROWN

A New Season

The Fortunes of Blues and Blessings
Book Two

Ecclesiastes 3

1 To every thing there is a season, and a time to every purpose under the heaven:

[2] A time to be born, and a time to die; a time to plant, and a time to pluck up that which is planted;

[3] A time to kill, and a time to heal; a time to break down, and a time to build up;

[4] A time to weep, and a time to laugh; a time to mourn, and a time to dance;

[5] A time to cast away stones, and a time to gather stones together; a time to embrace, and a time to refrain from embracing;

[6] A time to get, and a time to lose; a time to keep, and a time to cast away;

[7] A time to rend, and a time to sew; a time to keep silence, and a time to speak;

[8] A time to love, and a time to hate; a time of war, and a time of peace.

Chapter One

"Mama, our whole family is nothing but one bastard after another. The only legitimate one of us born from love was Apollo, and he's gone to glory."

"Diana, why are you so bitter? You've always been blessed," Maia said as she rocked in her chair on the veranda.

"If that's true, how come I've never got what I truly wanted?"

"You've been given more than most. All of us have," Maia answered, watching Caesar and Roman wrestle in the grass.

It seemed as if the sun had risen again when Roman showed up at the front door. His unexpected arrival brought new life into the house after Aaron died. Looking like the reincarnation of his father, Roman's youth and energy seemed to lift all of their spirits. The day after he got arrived, Maia took him with her to buy a buggy for her horse, Pegasus, and then he taught her how to drive it. With the reigns in her hands, she felt as if she was free from the all the weights of grief and regret. Her long-lost smile found its way back to her face as she took much pleasure in Roman's company. It was like having a second chance to see Aaron as a young man in the flesh.

For Caesar, Roman was better than a chocolate candy bar. He was thrilled to have another man around to look up to and to play ball with as they took turns pitching and batting in the front yard. A month later, when Roman told them over supper that it was time for

5

him to get back to Chicago, Diana was the only who wouldn't miss having him around.

Diana didn't have anything against him, she was just torn. On one hand, she had been pleased to see her boy having fun. But on the other, she couldn't help feeling jealous of how Caesar was drawn to Roman. She had tried her best to get closer to her child, but whenever he needed or wanted anything, he always called for his Grammy. There were many days when Diana wondered why she had even come back to Savannah. No one seemed to really care that she was there.

Late in May, when school was out, Maia sensed that Diana was at loose ends.

"You know, Di, it's not too late for us to put the garden in."

"I don't know if that will help me, Mama. I just don't have a life here. I love you, and I love Caesar, but there's nothing else here for me," Diana said.

"Baby, you have to make a life for yourself. It doesn't just happen out of thin air. What would you like to do?" Maia asked.

"There's only one thing I can do, and that's sing," Diana answered.

"Well you can start a choir with some of the youngsters around here or at the church. They would love it," Maia suggested.

"Mama, I thought I could make it staying here in Savannah, but I'm empty. Now that Caesar is out of school, I don't even have a reason to get up in the morning. I'm ready to go back to New York. That's my home, and Caesar is old enough to come with me now," Diana said.

"You're his mama, so I won't tell that you can't; but it's not fair to take that boy out of the only home he's ever known while you run around looking for your big break."

"He would be fine if you came with us, Mama. There's nothing keeping you here in Savannah either," Diana replied.

"That boy is happy here, and so am I. If you need to leave to be happy, my dear, then that's what you should do. But, remember, contentment comes from within," Maia said angrily, as she got up and pulled open the screen door so hard the spring snapped.

Diana sat outside on the back porch relieved that they'd finally had the conversation; it had been building inside her for a long time. She wanted to be there for her son; but deep in her soul, she must have known she wasn't going to stay since she'd only packed her small bag of clothes when she left New York.

"I have a surprise for you," Diana told Caesar that evening when he came home from playing with his best friend, Vernon. "We're going to Lincoln Amusement Park this Saturday."

"Yay, Mama! Caesar said, "I can't wait. Can I bring one of my friends?"

"Sure you can, baby. We're all going," Diana said as she looked up and saw her mama standing in the doorway shaking her head in disgust.

Diana got up early on Saturday and spent the morning preparing a picnic lunch for them to take to the amusement park. She fried chicken and shrimp and baked a peach cobbler, and Maia made red rice. Diana packed all the things she knew Caesar liked: apples and grapes; along with pickled cucumbers and okra; and his favorite, pralines.

"Don't forget your swim trunks," Diana yelled as she filled up the familiar basket that her nana had made for them out of sweetgrass when Diana was just a girl.

They loaded up the buggy, and Maia held the reigns while Pegasus carried them down the block to pick up Caesar's friend, Vernon. The two of them were the same age and spent a lot of time playing outside together since Vernon had four sisters who were all older than him.

The boys were so excited that they just laughed out loud at nothing as Pegasus trotted down the street, but Maia's heart sank when she saw the how many blacks were still riding the trolley down to the park. Aaron had given his life trying to lead the boycott. She let it go. It wasn't her fight anymore, and she wasn't about to let anything ruin this day for Caesar.

"Mama, when can we ride the Ferris wheel?" Caesar asked as soon as they saw it towering above the park.

"Oooo, I want to go swimming first," Vernon said when he saw the other children swimming in the pool.

"Let's find us a good spot to set our things down before we do anything," Diana said.

They found a shady spot near a large tree away from all the rides and other excitement.

"Are you boy's hungry?" Maia asked.

"Not yet, Grammy. I want to go swimming," Caesar said as he pulled off his shirt.

"Wait for me," Diana said. " I want to keep an eye on you two."

"Last one down there is a rotten egg," Caesar said before he took off running.

Diana couldn't keep up with them as they raced down and splashed into the water. It made her feel good to see him having so much fun.

"It's time to go back over to Grammy and get something to eat," Diana said after watching them for an hour. "We can go and ride on the Ferris wheel after lunch."

Back at the picnic spot, the boys wolfed down the food and played catch until Diana finished eating.

"You two go on down there and give Pegasus this apple," Maia said, trying to get a private moment to talk to Diana.

"Yes'm, Grammy," Caesar said happily. The two boys took off, tossing the apple back and forth between them until they got down to the horse.

"You know, baby, there are days that we can make very special, but there are regular days that just turn out to be the most special days of our lives when something unexpected happens. Are you willing to take the chance of missing out on those days with your son?" Maia asked.

Diana looked over at the boys rubbing Pegasus and said, "Mama I'm going to take this day and make the most of it."

Then she stood up and went to join the boys. Later in the afternoon, they walked to one of the pavilions in the park and saw some people dancing in a cakewalk contest.

"I used to dance up a storm," she said to Caesar, watching them carrying on.

"Could you really dance that good, Mama?" he asked as he bounced up and down.

"I sure could, son," she said as the music flowed around them.

A rush of memories from *The Creole Show* clouded Diana's head, and she was almost tempted to take the floor and show them how it's done,.But this day was for Caesar.

"Let's get on the merry-go-round," she told them.

"Yay!" they yelled out in agreement.

Diana sat on one of the horses near the boys and thought about how much this amusement ride was like her life: beautiful to look at, everyone seemed happy, the music kept playing, but it was just a bunch of ups and downs and going in circles. When the ride stopped, the boys jumped off and ran under the large tent of vendors and played some of the games, hoping to win prizes. They got bored with it quickly when they didn't win.

"Mama, can we ride the Ferris wheel now?" Caesar asked again.

"You certainly can," Diana answered as she savored the sound of him calling her Mama.

Most the of the time, he still called her ma'am, and she didn't know if it was because he was being respectful or if he didn't feel like she was a mama to him.

"This was the best day," Caesar said to Vernon as they helped Maia fold up the blanket when it was time to go home.

"I'm glad you boys had a good time," Diana said.

"When can we come again?" Vernon asked.

"Hush, boy," Maia said with a laugh. "We haven't even left yet."

They rode back home, tired and content, under a red-orange sunset that reflected off Pegasus's coat as he trotted in front of them. Maia broke the silence.

"How long before you're on a train out of here, Di?" she asked, looking straight ahead.

"Mama, I'm not trying to rush off. It's just that the theater season starts in late August, and the casts for new shows are already coming together to begin rehearsals. If I want to get a decent role, I need to get moving as soon as possible. It's a good thing that I've known the guys who're producing the show for years."

Maia stopped Pegasus in front of Vernon's house, and his mama came off the porch to meet him.

"I missed you all day, Vern!" she exclaimed as he climbed down out of the carriage.

Caesar, Diana, and Maia watched as he ran into her arms for a hug. They could feel the love between them from across the yard. Then they waved back at carriage before they went inside.

***

Typical for June, it had been hot all day, and Diana had not yet ventured out into the sun. She wanted to protect her skin from its darkening rays, knowing she was about to return to the stage. She watched Maia out there tending to the garden that they had planted so many years ago, and she thought about the times when it was the three of them, with Nana, out there planting the first seeds. So much had happened since then.

Diana could hear the rubber ball bouncing against the tree and knew it was Caesar. That's what he did whenever Vernon wasn't home or couldn't come out to play. She had decided to wait a few days before she talked to him about leaving, but it couldn't be put off any longer. It was time for her to go back to New York. She went in to the kitchen and poured two glasses of lemonade and went out on the veranda.

"Caesar," she called out.

He turned and saw the pale yellow liquid in the glasses and came running. Diana was so proud of her son. He was beautiful, tall and strong for his age, and smart, too. Watching him run she longed for just a little more of that youth and vitality, the freshness, the energy that she missed more every day. She handed Caesar the glass and watched him drink, seeing each thirst-quenching mouthful pushed down his throat. She took a sip from her own glass and pulled him to the settee to sit down beside her.

"This is hard for me to say baby, so I'll just say it quick. I'm going back to work in New York," Diana said, looking into his face.

She waited for a response, but he just sat there quietly.

"I love you so much, and I have loved being here with you. I don't want to go, but I feel like I can't breathe here sometimes. Do you understand what I'm saying, son?"

"Yes, ma'am," he answered.

"I wish I could take you with me. Would you like to see New York, baby?" she asked.

"No, ma'am," he answered, "I'm all right here with Grammy."

Diana could feel her stomach starting to burn and her head beginning to throb. This wasn't going the way she had wanted. She wanted him to show more emotion for her, she wanted to give him something precious, but this goodbye was void of any of that.

She kept talking. "I wish your father and I could have made a life together and raised you, but I made some mistakes."

"Grandy and Grammy looked after me," he said matter-of-factly.

"I know that, and I am thankful for that, but I just want you to know that my leaving doesn't mean that I don't love you. It hurts me to stay where I can't be the person I was born to be."

After a few minutes of uncomfortable silence between them, Caesar asked, "Can I go back to play now?"

"Sure you can, baby," Diana said as her mama stood in the distance, shaking her head.

**

This time Maia insisted that they drive Diana to the train station, telling her, "If you are going to leave this boy, you're not going to sneak away."

There wasn't much luggage to put in the buggy, so Maia let Caesar sit between them where he could hold Pegasus's reigns on the way.

"You don't have to do this, Di," Maia said. "You didn't even try to make a life for yourself or do anything here."

"It's over, Mama," Diana whispered. "Let it be."

"Chile, you better stop and count your blessings like I told you," Maia warned.

On East Broad Street, a horseless carriage passed them, and Caesar hollered, "Look Grammy, look at that."

"It's an automobile," Maia said.

Diana saw how impressed he was with it, so she put her arm around Caesar and said, "I'm going to buy one for us when I get to New York. What color do you like?"

"My favorite color is blue," he answered.

When they got to the train station, Diana gave both of them tight hugs and a kisses on both cheeks and stepped out of the buggy.

"I love you, Mama. I love you, Caesar," she said as she waved and then turned and walked away.

Chapter Two

D iana found her townhouse very much like she had left it, and she was happy to be back in her place away from the judgmental looks of her mama. The first thing she wanted to do was get a copy of The New York Clipper and catch up on what was going on in town, and who was doing what and where.

She walked down to the newsstand at the end of the street. Earnest Hogan lived a couple houses down the block, and she was tempted to pay him a visit in her anxiousness to get back to work. They'd met casually at a few parties, but they weren't friends, so she thought better of it. She paid the nickel for the paper and kept walking to get some much-needed exercise. Later, she read that Belle was doing a show at a theater in Midtown. She got dressed up that evening and went down to take a look.

After the show, she made her way backstage to say hello.

"Hey, Diana," she heard someone calling behind her.

She turned around to see it was her old friend Belle. She took long strides to meet her so glad to see a familiar face.

"Belle, how you doing, honey? I enjoyed the show," Diana said, wrapping her arms around Belle's ample body for a warm hug.

"I can't complain, chile," Belle said, stepping back to get a look at her friend.

"So what's going on in town now?" Diana asked.

"I'm back here making the rounds with my pickaninnies on the Keith-Albee vaudeville circuit."

"I heard you got married," Diana said.

"Yeah, I tied the knot with Henry Troy. You remember him; he was in the cast with us for *In Dahomey*.

"We need to catch up, Belle," Diana said, feeling like so much had gone on without her.

"Let's paint the town red this weekend. My show closes on Thursday. We can celebrate you coming back home," Bell said, walking away to the dressing room.

Diana met Belle on Friday at the Marshall House Restaurant in Lower Manhattan at a few minutes past seven o'clock. She prayed that her old friend might have some good news for her. She had made a big sacrifice to come back to the city, and so far it hadn't been worth it.

"It sure is good to see you, ole lady. I was getting worried about you," Belle said, standing up and giving Diana a quick hug around the neck before she sat down.

"You know me, Belle, I don't miss a curtain call," Diana answered.

"I thought you were letting this shit get to you, gal," Belle said.

"I can't lie," Diana said. "It was taking me real low, and I went home to get my bearings."

"You gotta understand, Di, it's all about the money. If you got food on your table, then the rest is just gravy."

"I ain't ever been hungry, so food don't mean that much to me. I was in it for the glory. I wanted to be at the top, the greatest singer there ever was."

"I hate to be the one to tell you, but that wasn't gonna happen in our lifetime, baby. You light, but you still the wrong color. And by the way, food might not mean nothing to you, but I'm hungry as hell.

Let's get something to eat," Belle said, patting herself on the tummy.

"Now I didn't say I don't appreciate a good meal," Diana said as she motioned for a waiter to come to the table.

They both ordered steaks with all the fixings and enjoyed themselves talking over old times. Then Diana ordered apple pie and told Belle all that had happened with David and about Caesar.

"You have been busy, Di. I didn't know you had a baby," Belle said.

"He's seven years old now and I feel terrible about leaving him but I was dying there."

"Well, my friend, ain't nothing more complicated than love but some more love. Nothing we can do about it now except get you back out there while you still got your teeth, get you another dandy, and let the good times roll," Belle said as she scooted her chair back from the table. "Now get yourself up, chile, we got some scouting to do. Things are jumping in the Tenderloin District."

The two of them caught a ride to Ike Hines's Professional Club and got a table close to the piano and ordered drinks. The lights were dim, and Diana had to strain her eyes as she looked around; it had been a while since she had been to Black Bohemia. Nonetheless, she didn't see any new or interesting faces that she might like to become acquainted with.

Belle tapped her arm to get her attention. "You see that tall, dark, hot cup of coffee walking over to the piano? That's Scott Joplin, the new composer in town that everybody is raving over. He can play the keys off that thing," Belle whispered to Diana.

They watched him sit down and begin to play. For nearly an hour, Diana allowed her mind to be hypnotized by the movement of his hands, the sound of the music, and the drinks that kept flowing to the table. When Joplin's set was over and he walked over to the bar for a drink, Diana followed him.

"Hello, Mr. Joplin," Diana said as she extended her hand.

"Hello, I haven't had the pleasure," he said.

"My name is Diana Portunus. I just wanted to tell you how much I enjoyed you music. You're very talented."

"Thank you," he replied, looking closer at her. "I believe I've seen you perform in a show in St. Louis."

"It's possible," she said. "I have an ear for melodies, and your compositions are extraordinary. Have you ever thought about writing an opera?"

"No, I haven't," he said with a facetious smile.

"Well, think about it," Diana said, touching his chest. "I'm waiting to sing in it," she said as she walked back to her table.

They stayed for about another hour before Belle stood up and said, "Let's get going, honey, I got a husband to get home to." She clutched Diana's hand at the door and spoke in her ear, "There's a new production going into rehearsal for midseason, Henry's got a part in it. Go see George about it."

"I will," Diana said as they left the club going in opposite directions.

It was hot and muggy outside, but Diana couldn't complain. The electric lights twinkling in the city were like stars, and soon her name would be on the top of a marquee. She caught the trolley train home, feeling like she had made the right decision to come back. This was her home.

Diana was tired when she finally got into bed, but even after being out among people again, she felt so lonely inside. She got up and poured herself a small glass of brandy and drank it down. It was only a moment before she felt mellow and her thoughts went back to the two perfect weeks she spent in Ocean City with David. Then she fell asleep.

***

Over the next few weeks, Diana couldn't catch a break. Work was scarce. Feeling a bit restless and worried, Diana put aside her pride and, after an early breakfast, took the short walk to Ernest Hogan's front door.

"Well, hello there," his wife, Louise, said, surprised by the unexpected visit when she answered the door. "Please come inside. We just finished eating."

Diana trailed her through the front of the house. Ernest was sitting in the kitchen reading the paper when Diana followed his wife in.

"I don't mean to disturb you this morning, but I heard that you're going into rehearsal with a new musical," Diana said. "I just got back in town, and I need to get working. Has your show been cast yet?"

"Good morning, Miss Portunus," Ernest said, putting down the paper. "I know what that's like. I've been there, but unfortunately the show has been cast, and all the roles are filled."

"Well, that's my luck, but no harm in trying though. Sorry for disturbing you both so early on a Saturday," Diana said as she walked to the front door and let herself out.

Diana did her best to stay busy for the rest of the day. She took a long walk, went shopping and bought a new dress and hat, and got her hair fixed.

On Sunday morning, Diana got up and went to church; she needed some of the help that comes directly from the Lord. Wearing a pink dress covered in tiny flowers, she moved to a pew close to the front of the Abyssinian Baptist Church sanctuary. It had been years since she had graced the doors of the church on a Sunday, so she knew she was reaching the end of her rope.

"Brothers and sisters, come to the altar for prayer," the pastor said, raising his arms in an invitation.

Diana walked forward and kneeled down on the red carpet.

The pastor began to pray, "Father, we come humbled before you, knee bent and head bowed. Lord, we are your people and we are in need of your blessings. Touch all the lives that are represented here today for we need your protection, Lord, we need your provisions, Lord, and we need your peace, Lord, that passes our understanding.

Forgive give us, God, for all our sins and shortcomings. Father, we hunger and thirst for righteousness, help us to do thy will and not our own, Lord, and grant us all a double portion of your mercy and grace. Amen."

Diana returned to her seat, and the choir began to sing "Count Your Blessings," and she knew it was God. She raised her arms in praise. Her mama had prayed for her, and the Lord had heard it, and He was showing her that she wasn't alone.

"Thank you, Lord Jesus," Diana cried out.

The pastor moved to the pulpit and began to preach,

"Brothers and sisters, I know that you are tired of struggling, tired of working as hard as you can and never getting ahead. Well, today I want to remind you about Moses and the Israelites. Even after they were set free, their trials and tribulations kept coming, they wandered for forty years in the wilderness and many of them didn't make it to the Promised Land. Brothers and sisters, we too have been brought through much misfortune, and we have been freed from slavery, but the struggles are not over. The sun comes out and then the storms start again. We take two steps forward and then are pushed back. Like Moses, many of us won't get to the Promised Land in our lives, but I've got good news for you today. It's not about the Promise Land, or fame and fortune, it's about the journey brothers and sisters. We are blessed when we learn to put our trust in the Lord. Just like the Israelites, we have witnessed so many miracles on this journey. So don't get down and discouraged, the Lord has brought us a mighty long way and blessed us in a mighty way. Rejoice and give Him all the praise!"

The pastor took his seat, and the choir sang the closing hymn. The words were tailored-made for Diana, and she was filled with the

Holy Spirit.

> Why should I feel discouraged, why should the shadows come,
> Why should my heart be lonely, and long for heav'n and home,
> When Jesus is my portion? My constant Friend is He:
> His eye is on the sparrow, and I know He watches me;
> I sing because I'm happy, I sing because I'm free,
> For His eye is on the sparrow, and I know he watches me.

Diana felt the comfort and reassurance that rang out from the song, and she stood on her feet and shouted, "Thank you, Lord! Thank you for your many blessings in my life!"

She began to cry and an usher placed a tissue in her hand to dry her tears before she lifted her arms in praise again.

> "Let not your heart be troubled," His tender word I hear,
> And resting on His goodness, I lose my doubts and fears;
> Though by the path He leadeth, but one step I may see;
> His eye is on the sparrow, and I know He watches me;
> His eye is on the sparrow, and I know He watches me.

Diana sang the chorus as if it were the last time she would have the opportunity to sing. She sang from her gut, from her heart, and from the very depths of her soul.

"I sing because I'm happy, I sing because I'm free, His eyes are on the sparrow and I know he watches me."

The choir continued to sing, and Diana heard the message from heaven.

> Whenever I am tempted, whenever clouds arise,
> When songs give place to sighing, when hope within me dies,

I draw the closer to Him, from care He sets me free;
His eye is on the sparrow, and I know He watches me;
His eye is on the sparrow, and I know He watches me.

Diana joined in and sang the chorus and let her heart soar with the joy that filled the sanctuary. She felt encouraged and empowered, and for the next few months Diana kept the faith.

Chapter Three

"Hey, chile, what's shaking around here?" Belle hollered, coming into Diana's townhouse for a visit before she left on tour.

Nothing, and it's getting me down," Diana said, pouring another drink and inviting Belle to join her on the sofa.

"Keep your head up, ole gal. Henry says the music for the new musical is done, and the company is coming together to start rehearsals. Get your ass down there in the morning."

"Belle, you always looking out for me," Diana said, feeling grateful.

"Shit, get yourself a man, and I won't have to," Belle chuckled, taking a big sip of her drink and rising to her feet. "I can't stay, chile. I got a train to catch."

"Thanks for the tip," Diana shouted before she closed the door.

This was the opportunity Diana had been waiting for. She took extra care getting dressed after breakfast. She picked out her bright gold dress with the green sash and the matching hat that brought out the glow in her skin. She stood in front of the mirror and felt confident. She colored her lips the shade of fresh peaches and set out for the Marshall Hotel, where Bert Williams and George Walker stayed whenever they were in New York.

Diana had hoped to catch them eating lunch, but she was told they were in rehearsal at the West End Theater on 125th Street. Diana jumped on a trolley car and headed there, praying that the cast for *Bandanna Land* had not been chosen yet. She didn't know what it was about, except that Belle had told her it wasn't going to be the same "back in Africa" theme. She was sure that Aida would probably have the lead again since she was married to George, but she knew no one could top her singing. They could write her a part if they had to.

Bert saw Diana walk into the theater while the chorus was rehearsing. He walked over to say hello. "Long time no see, babe. How you been?"

"I'm feeling good and ready to go to work," Diana answered.

"Sounds good. What you got on your mind?" he asked.

"I came down here because I hear you're working on a new musical called *Bandanna Land,* and I need something to get me back out there again."

"I'd love to have you out there, babe, but there isn't anything suitable for you in this one," Bert said.

"I'm not being choosy right now. I just want to sing. Anything is fine, even the chorus," Diana said, trying not to appear desperate.

"You can see them up there. We already have too many, and I'm going to have to cut some of them. It's getting harder and harder to make a decent profit once we get out of New York City," he said, avoiding her eyes.

"Well, you know where to find me," Diana said as she walked to the exit. At the door, she looked back and yelled to him, "Break a leg."

Diana headed home in disbelief. She had prayed, she had trusted, and she had felt so positive that her fate was moving in an opportune direction, but she had been turned away again. She couldn't believe that there was no role for her, not even a bit part in the chorus.

Looking at them on the stage, she should have known better. All the chorus girls were just that, girls. She was over forty-five years old, a has-been before she really got her chance to shine. She shook her head in despair. If it wasn't one thing, then it's another. First racism, now her age. Diana felt low, lower than she had ever felt in her life. There was nothing she could do, and there was no place to run.

Diana had stopped trying to drown her troubles in the bottom of a bottle, but right now all she wanted was a drink. She started walking, and before she knew it, she was at John B. Nail's Saloon. She saw a few familiar faces, but she didn't want any company. She just wanted to be alone with a glass of whiskey. The bartender recognized her and brought her a glass.

"To you," she said to him as she lifted it to her lips.

The first swallow tasted like honey from a honeycomb to her and took away the chill that she felt on the outside and the inside.

"Thank you, God," she said. "That was just what I needed."

After a few more drinks, Diana found some happiness and peace in the bottom of the glass. She picked herself up and took a carriage ride back to her townhouse and went to sleep.

The next morning--or more accurately, the next afternoon--when Diana woke up, the long hours of rest had strengthened her resolve. She wasn't weak, and she didn't give up that easy. She would just have to stay determined and keep looking for that next opportunity. It was fall, and the theater season had already started, so Diana thought about trying to get some work singing in supper club until the new season. Unfortunately, she found most of them hired only white singers.

When the holidays rolled around, Diana considered going to Savannah to spend them with Caesar, but it would only be harder for her to leave again. Besides, she couldn't bear to see her mama's disapproving looks, especially since she hadn't been working since she left almost six months ago. By the time the new year came, Diana couldn't think of anything to celebrate. Her anxieties were overwhelming her, and every morning she stared at the mirror, looking for more lines around her eyes and mouth.

Diana would talk to her reflection, saying, "My mind is young, my desires are young, my dreams are young. Why must my body get old? I'm not ready."

There were days when she thought she would explode; she didn't have an outlet for the pent-up emotions. She needed a confidant or her friends to tell her troubles too, but she was too embarrassed to let anyone know what she was going through. She would spend most of the day pacing back and forth across the floor of her townhouse, so tense she couldn't sit still. The nights, she would spend in the Tenderloin going to nightclubs and drinking to amuse herself. The more she drank, the less she thought about the hurt and disappointment she felt, so she drank more.

Diana was losing her confidence. She needed attention. If she couldn't get it on stage, she would have to get it elsewhere. She started socializing with more men at the nightclubs. Some of the younger ones who were new in town thought she might be able to help them get started, unaware that she was looking for a break of her own.

Diana sat nursing a drink in a nightclub in the Tenderloin when a new band began to play. In one quick glance toward the musicians, she noticed a cornet player staring back at her. When the set ended, he came over to her table.

"Can I buy you another?" he asked, pointing at her drink.

"As you can see, I can buy my own drinks."

"It's only a small cost to make the acquaintance of a lady as lovely as you," he said, bowing before her. "My name is Franklin. Franklin Jefferson."

"Pleased to meet you, Franklin. I'm Diana Portunus, and you sure play a sweet horn," Diana said, looking him up and down.

"Once I saw you sitting over here, every note I played was just for you."

"Have a seat, Franklin. I love listening to a sweet talker. Besides, you remind me of someone who was very special to me."

Franklin pulled out a chair and sat down. He bore a similarity to David, tall, well-built, and the golden brown of fresh-baked bread. When Diana grew tired of his talking, she stood up.

"Are you coming or not?" she asked, putting on her coat.

"Definitely, I can't have you go out into the cold alone."

Franklin went home with her and only left when his band had a gig. He was attentive and made her feel attractive. For Diana, it felt good to have a handsome man on her arm when she went out. She could see all the eyes on them when they walked into a restaurant or a club. Whenever Franklin's band had a job, Diana got a front-row seat. Franklin kept her warm for the rest of the winter; but by the spring, she was already losing interest in him. He was a struggling musician, and most of the time, he didn't have any money. At first, Diana didn't mind footing all the bills, but she didn't grow up like that. In her world, a man worth anything took care of his woman.

When the temperatures got hotter in July, Diana felt smothered and no longer wanted to be bothered carrying Franklin's extra weight. She looked at him sleeping in her bed, on her sheets and pillows, and had enough. Enough of him eating her food and drinking her liquor.

"Frank, where did you stay before you came here?" she asked as they headed out for an evening on the town.

"Wherever I could. I was trying to make some big connections."

"I can respect that. I'm looking for my next break, too, but I can't carry you."

"I got real feelings for you, Diana, and it won't be long before I have my own band."

Diana didn't respond. She only gave him a smile and nodded her head. She knew how that story went. They had a good time that night. He bought the drinks, and she held him tight against her breasts on the dance floor, feeling his energy and smelling his scent. When the band took a break, they walked back to their table to finish their drinks. Franklin lit a cigar, and Diana concentrated on the swirls of smoke.

After a few minutes, Diana put her hand on Franklin's arm, pushed herself up from her seat, and said, "This show is closing, baby. I earned my money to take care of me, not a grown man." Then she left him sitting at the table in John B.'s.

Diana stood at the door for a few minutes to smooth over her edge when she saw an automobile roll down the street. She thought about Caesar and how impressed he was with the one they saw on the day she left. She got up the next morning and ordered a blue model T. It took over a month before it was delivered, and when it came in, Diana didn't even know how to operate it. It took her more than three weeks before she was comfortable enough to drive it alone.

Diana found that driving the automobile got her as much attention as walking around with Franklin. Behind the steering wheel, she felt young and independent. The vibration of the engine under her feet made her feel powerful. She took a ride in it almost every day.

On a mild Saturday evening in September, Diana grew agitated as if she was suffocating in her own house. She got up and put on one of her finest dresses, despite the fact that she was in the mood to go slumming. She drove out to a club in Brooklyn known for the having some of the most risqué entertainers and the strongest liquor. Catching eyes along the way, she knew she looked good, with the silver-gray dress shining in her blue automobile. She pulled the car around in the unpaved lot and tiptoed to keep her shoes clean.

The music was floating around outside the tavern, even before Diana got to the door. She walked into the darkness of the smoke-filled room and sat down at the bar. The small band was playing some ragtime as the crowd cheered them on. She ordered a drink from the bartender and turned on her stool to face the quartet.

A large copper-colored woman wearing a purple satin dress, with her short hair laid in waves around her head walked slowly to the front of the stage and into the spotlight. The music slowed down, and subdued applause could be heard across the room. The woman stood there for a minute, looking from the ceiling down to the floor, and then she began to moan with the music. She closed her eyes, balled up her fists, held her arms out wide, and began to sing.

Born in March with my mother's love, showered in April, blessed from above,
Life served to me on platter in May, I danced at the party till the end of the day.
In June I fell in love with a dandy, in July it was all sweet tastes of candy,
Like a clean new suit just pressed, I was young, fine and so blessed.
It all burned in August, the passions and the prospect, fate was mean, and had no respect.
Blessed, the world, a balloon on my string,
Now my man's gone and I aint got a thing.
I was the doll, the queen in this town,
Damn the fortunes, the blues have run me down.

Diana felt as if she was drowning in the words, and ordered another drink to lift her up. She could feel the hurt and pain that the woman placed behind very word and tone. It made her feel self-conscious, as if people were staring because it was about her.

> September came, my troubles were deep, October, like a
> fool, I gambled, losses were steep.
> I prayed to Jesus all alone in November, and if I got an
> answer I just don't remember.
> December, with all its joy I was sad, January found me
> broke, gone was all I had,
> Father time won't give me a break, my flowers have wilted
> and both hands shake.
> February is cold and heartless you can bet, and I'm tired, so
> discouraged and full of regret.
> Blessed, the world, a balloon on my string,
> Now my man's gone and I aint got a thing.
> I was the doll, the queen in this town,
> Damn the fortunes, the blues have run me down.

Diana downed the rest of her drink in one gulp, grabbed her coat, and strutted out of the club, with the music fading behind her.

"That's not me," she shouted in the air outside. "I'm Diana Portunus Liberty."

Diana hopped into the Model T and drove away. She steered onto the open road, feeling the cool clean air of the night blowing in her face, and it refreshed her. She needed to get as far away from that place as quickly as possible. She pushed the pedal down further to go faster, and the speed of it was exhilarating. She started to feel so happy that she laughed out loud. Then she realized she was lost and didn't know where she was headed but she didn't care.

The feeling of the wind was amazing, and she drove faster. Unfortunately, the further she drove, the more rocky the road became; but Diana pressed on and went faster, and with each bump, she felt light and young. Her laughter became hysterical, and then the road ran out. Diana plowed through the field with her foot solid against the floorboard and careened straight into an evergreen tree.

When Maia received the telegram Sunday morning, she was shocked but not surprised. She shook her head again at her daughter, not knowing if it had been an accident or on purpose. She couldn't understand why Diana had been so determined to be unhappy. When Maia last waved to her at the train station, she knew there would be no fairytale ending. Diana's eyes were closed to all the blessings she had been given, always wanting something other than that which was on her plate. It was only what she couldn't have that intrigued her.

"*September again,*" Maia thought, the time of transition when the seasons changed. It was the same month that she lost Apollo. Maia fell down onto the couch as her heart broke again for her baby girl. "At least she's at peace," she mumbled quietly to herself. "If only this boy didn't have to inherit her unhappiness."

Chapter Four

Caesar seemed to adjust to the news better than Maia thought he would. The greater truth was he didn't know how to react. He loved his mama, but he had never really known her as his mother. His greatest pain was seeing the sadness in the eyes of his grammy every day.

Albert Jackson, who handled the business for Maia after Aaron's death, went to New York, packed up Diana's things, wrapped up her finances, and brought her body back to Savannah. Her townhouse was sold, and between the proceeds and the income that Diana had earned over her career, there was a sizable amount of money to be put into trust for Caesar. Maia took this time to also make him the primary beneficiary of her estate, which would also be put in trust until he was twenty-five years of age, with a portion to go to Roman on the event of her death.

On January 1, 1909, Caesar's ninth birthday, Maia sat him down for a talk.

"Caesar, it wasn't my place to tell you about your father until now. His name is David Mallory. He and your mother met in Nashville when Diana joined the Fisk Jubilee Singers. They were together for seven years while they toured around the world. Your father asked your mother to marry him and settle down in Nashville, but she had big dreams of being a famous singer in New York. Ten years later, she decided she had made a mistake and wanted him back, but he was married by then. They did get together for a short time, and that's when you were conceived. Diana came back to Savannah, and you were born here in this house and have lived here since then.

"Caesar, I'm old now, and you're gonna be a man soon. You need your father in your life now that your mama's gone. We are gonna take a trip to Nashville and find him."

Caesar's ears filled up with the words his grammy spoke, and he covered them with his hands, unable to hear anymore.

"Grammy, I'm almost a man myself. I don't need no father now," he said.

"A boy always needs a man to be an example for him to follow."

"Grandy was the example for me. Since he's gone, and you say you old, I need to be here to take care of you."

"No, Caesar, I've made up mind, and there's no changing it."

Maia packed everything that Caesar owned, along with a scrapbook she made of Diana's career, into one of the trunks his mama had carried around with her for twenty years. For herself, Maia needed only a small bag and some food for them to eat on their expedition. She had Vernon's father ride with them to the train station so he could take Pegasus back home and care for him while they were gone.

Caesar was excited and apprehensive as they boarded the large train; it was his first trip out of Savannah. He spent the whole day looking out of the window, absorbing all he saw as the world he knew grew bigger and bigger. When the train made a brief stop in Atlanta, Maia's mind drifted back to the time she and Aaron spent there before Caesar was born and how much she missed her husband. She and Caesar two occupied the evening reading to each other and eating until they both nodded off to sleep. The train arrived in Nashville the next morning just at daybreak.

"Do you know where we might find a place to stay?" Maia asked one of the porters at the Nashville train station.

"Ma'am, there's a lodging house on Spruce Street. It's run by Preston Taylor and his wife, Georgia; he's the pastor of Lea Christian Church," the porter replied. "Take the streetcar to the east end of Edgehill and walk one block down to Spruce."

Maia decided they should leave the trunk at the station until they found out exactly where David lived. They walked up from Union Station and rode the streetcar as the porter told them. And after asking for directions a couple more times, they found the Taylor rooming house. Maia climbed the stairs as quick as she could, anxious to get Caesar out of the colder air of Tennessee. She tapped the door knocker twice and waited. It was opened by fashionably dressed woman.

"Come on in here out the cold," the woman said as she smiled warmly, inviting them in.

She was pretty, with a full-figure. Her complexion was light, and her eyes were dark. Maia figured she was less than forty years old.

"Hello, I'm Georgia Taylor. How can I help you two today?" she asked, her eyes bouncing between the two of them.

"Good morning, Mrs. Taylor, my name is Maia Liberty, and this is my grandson, Caesar. We just got here from Savannah, and we need a place to stay for a few days."

"Call me, Georgia, and welcome to Nashville. We'd be happy to have you here as our guests."

"Thank you, Georgia," Maia responded and tapped Caesar on the shoulder.

"Thank you, ma'am," he added.

"What brings you two to Nashville at this time of year?" Georgia asked, smiling.

"We're looking for David Mallory. Would you happen to know him?" Maia asked curiously.

"I certainly do. I have known him for years. We were both Fisk

Jubilee Singers before I got married. He lives here in Edgehill. He has a furniture store downtown and a grocery store about a half mile away," Georgia said.

"My daughter, Diana, was a Jubilee singer too," Maia said, "That's where she met David."

"This world gets smaller every day," Georgia said. "I'll show you your rooms where you can get settled, and then I'll tell you where to find David."

Maia and Caesar walked the four blocks to the grocery store as Georgia had told them. Maia had never met David, but when she saw the man inside, she knew immediately who he was. Caesar favored him from his facial features to his stance.

They went inside, and Maia said, "Caesar, I want you to stand over here near the door for a few minutes. I won't be long."

She walked over to the counter where David stood beside the cashier and said, "Excuse me, Mr. Mallory, I need to talk with you privately about a personal matter."

David was puzzled. He didn't know who this woman was, but he sensed something about her.

"Come into my office," he said, leading her to the door on the left in the back. He pointed to a chair and took the seat behind his desk and waited for her to speak.

"Mr. Mallory, I'm Maia Liberty; Diana Portunus Liberty was my daughter."

Maia hesitated and let the words sink in as she watched the shift of emotions pass over David's face. She could see the surprise and confusion over her coming to the store and the disbelief of hearing Diana was dead.

"Diana and I were very close, Mrs. Liberty. Please, call me David."

Then she continued, "I'm aware that you never responded to Diana's telegrams and letters, and I don't presume to know your reasons for not doing so, but I'm here because your son needs you. He's young, and I'm old. I love him with all my heart, but I can't give him the care that a boy needs."

"Mrs. Liberty, with all due respect, I don't know what you are talking about. I haven't seen Diana in ten years."

"It was nearly ten years ago that Diana tried for months to tell you that she was pregnant. She sent telegrams and letters before and after the baby was born, but she never heard from you."

David mulled over everything he heard before answering.

"I'm sorry to tell you that I didn't receive any letters or telegrams from Diana. Had I known about this situation, I would have responded accordingly," David said, realizing that they had probably been intercepted by Grace.

"That is unfortunate, David. Not hearing from you caused her a lot of pain and grief, and your son has spent these years without knowing his father. My husband, Aaron, and I raised him as our own; but he is dead now, and I am close to it. His name is Caesar, and I've brought him here with me. He's waiting outside," Maia said.

David got up and walked ahead of Maia out of his office and into the room of the store. He didn't see him at first, and then he noticed a boy outside throwing rocks against a tree. He stood there bewildered, trying to absorb the fact, this boy was his son.

Maia moved around David and went to the door and called him. "Caesar, come inside and meet your father."

David's legs went numb as he watched his son run over to him and reach out his hand.

"Hello, sir," Caesar said.

David mustered a hello as he looked into the boy's face and saw a reflection of his own youth. "I'm glad to meet you."

There was a moment of awkward silence before David said, "Mrs.

Liberty, I need this evening to speak with my wife, but tomorrow I will bring you to my house. Where are you two staying?"

"We're at the Taylors' rooming house," Maia said. "Caesar's trunk is at the train station."

"I'll be there first thing in the morning," David promised.

Maia and Caesar left and walked back to the rooming house, and David went back into his office. He felt as if he was having a strange dream. His whole life had changed in a matter of minutes. One hour ago, he was an honorable man with a trustworthy wife. Now he was a neglectful father married to deceitful woman with a son who didn't know him. He decided he would wait for a while before he went home. He needed time to calm down and gather his wits, but he couldn't stop wondering how Grace could have done something so evil and despicable when there was a child involved.

Finally, he couldn't take it another minute. He grabbed his coat and headed out the door. He got into his car and drove full speed all the way home.

Grace met him at the door as she usually did, but the reception that she got let her know that something was wrong.

"A woman came by the grocery store today, and she had a boy with her that she says is my son. What do you know about it?" David asked angrily.

Grace turned her back, trying to think quickly. Was there a lie that could get her out of the line of fire? It was useless; the truth had already made itself known. She turned around and looked him in the face with no explanation.

"How could you do that, Grace? How could you steal my letters and destroy the telegrams?" David demanded, wondering what kind of woman he lived with.

"How could you do what you did to me? I've never loved anybody else, and you were unfaithful to me."

"Yes, I was wrong, but I came back to you, and I've been here ever since," he replied. "You deceived me for years; you knew I had a child for all this time, and you never told me."

"I couldn't take the chance of losing you. I forgave you for you did to me, and now you have to forgive me for what I've done," she said.

"No, Grace, what you did is unforgivable. You hurt an innocent boy."

"So you're just gonna leave me for her now?" Grace hollered out.

"No, Grace, she's dead. But my son is coming here to live, and I'm going to be the father I should have been when he was born," David said before he stormed out of the room, disgusted by the sight of her.

Grace sat down to think, but her thoughts ran in two paths. She had lived with the fear of this day for a long time. After the first telegram came, she spent months running to the stores in the mornings to catch any telegrams and checking the mailbox every afternoon. She was relieved when they finally stopped after a year, but for a while, she thought Diana might come to town with her baby in her arms and tell him in person.

Now Grace's worries were over. She was glad that David wasn't going to leave her and that Diana was dead, but she didn't want the constant reminder of his love for another woman living under her roof. It would be difficult for her to tolerate, especially since she hadn't been able to have a child of her own.

David spent the night in the spare bedroom and left the house with his buggy early before breakfast. He went to his furniture store and picked out a new bed, a dresser, a table, and a chair for his son. He had one of his helpers load the furniture on his buggy and took them to his house. He cleared out the bedroom next to his and Grace's, and he and the workers placed all the furniture he had bought for Caesar inside. Grace kept her distance, but she watched all the activity in silence. Once the furniture was in place in the room, David headed over to the Taylors' rooming house, where Maia and Caesar were finishing their breakfast when he came in.

"Good morning, Georgia," David said. "I want to thank you for the hospitality that you have shown my son and his grandmother, but they'll be leaving today and coming to stay with me at my home."

Georgia's eyes opened wide at his unexpected announcement, and then the resemblance between the two was obvious.

"They are always welcome, David. I hope you all can come to dinner with Preston and me soon."

Their first stop was to pick up the trunk at the train station, and then David took them on a ride around town to show them his furniture store downtown and some of Nashville. He took them to Centennial Park to see the Parthenon, and Maia held them there for ten minutes while she let her mind travel back to the myths and stories that were a large part of her youth. And in that moment, in her head, she forgave Richard Bailey.

When they got to the Mallory's home, David said to Caesar, "Help me carry your things up to your room." They each grabbed a handle on the end and climbed the stairs.

When they set it inside on the floor David said, "I didn't know about you, Caesar. If I did, I would have come for you."

"I've been fine," Caesar replied. "My grandy and grammy looked after me good."

"Well, I'm gonna look after you from now on," David said.

"Yes, sir," Caesar said.

Grace was polite to Maia and chose her words carefully.

"Would you like some hot tea or coffee, Mrs. Liberty?" she asked.

"No, I'm fine, dear, but a little water would be nice," Maia answered.

Grace poured her some water and said, "I know you probably think badly of me, but I honestly didn't believe that there was a child. I thought she was trying to find a way to get David's attention."

"Grace, you don't owe me anything. I'm not the one you hurt, and I've learned over my life not to judge anybody for their actions. You've got another chance to make things right, which is more than most. Caesar's a good boy and easy to love. Don't make more problems for yourself. You still have your husband."

Grace raised her glass to her lips and held it there without drinking. There wasn't anything left to say.

David was happier than he had been in years; he had the family that he had always wanted. He spent every minute he could spare away from work with Caesar. One day, he even took Caesar with him for the whole day. David introduced Caesar as his son to all his neighbors, the folks he worked with, and his business associates without clarification. It felt good to Caesar, too; he finally had a father of his own.

Maia went David when he enrolled Caesar at Napier Elementary School. Caesar was ahead of the children who were his age, and he was bigger, too, so he was put into the fifth grade class. David was so proud that he walked with him to school for three days. Maia watched them for a week, and all of her doubts about bringing Caesar to Nashville were smoothed away. Her only worry was that Caesar had come between David and Grace. David avoided looking at his wife and he spoke to her only when it was necessary. But Maia felt sure that in time David would see that Grace wasn't the only one to bear the blame for what happened.

At the end of seven days, Maia took the walk with Caesar to school.

"It's time for your grammy to go back home, baby. They're gonna take good care of you here, I can see that. I want you to know that I loved you from the beginning, and I always will. You gave me and Grandy joy that we thought we would never see again. It's hard for me leave without you, but I know you are going to be fine. I'm proud of you now and the man you'll become. Promise me that you'll study hard in school and always count your blessings," Maia asked him.

"I promise, Grammy, and I'll always love you, too," Caesar said, feeling the burn of tears coming to his eyes.

"When you get home from school, I'll be gone, but I'll always be here and in here," she said as she tapped his chest and the side of his head.

Maia didn't have far to lean over to kiss him on the cheek and forehead before she said, "Give your grammy one last hug."

Caesar wrapped his arms around her neck and held on tight. After a while, Maia pulled his hands down and kissed them.

"Learn something for me today," she called after him as Caesar walked slowly into the school.

Maia had packed her bag before she left to walk Caesar to school.

When she got back to the house, she asked David to drive her to the train station.

On the way, he said, "I don't know how to thank you."

"That's easy," she said. "Take care of my grandson."

***

That evening at dinner, David talked about some things that had happened at the store. Then he turned his attention to Ceasar.

"What did you do at school today, son?"

"We took turns reading, and then we had a spelling test."

"How are the black dolls in the store selling?" Grace asked, trying to interject herself into the conversation.

"Finish what you were saying, Caesar," David said, interrupting Grace.

"That was all, sir," Caesar said, seeing Grace sneering at him.

Caesar felt sorry for her. He knew what it felt like to be ignored, so he tried to be extra helpful to her. When they finished eating, he helped clear the table, and in the kitchen, he rolled up his sleeves to help wash the dishes. When he reached his arm over the sink, Grace pinched it tight and twisted his skin hard before she let go. Caesar looked at her with eyes that asked why as he stood stunned at what she just did.

"Get out of here!" she hissed at him in a low voice so Davis wouldn't hear.

Caesar ran out of the kitchen and up to his room. He laid across the bed and wished he had gone back home with his grammy.

Caesar did his best to stay away from Grace when David wasn't home, and most of the time, he walked to the store after school to ride home with his father after work. David loved the way it seemed that Caesar was drawn to him; there was nothing he wouldn't do for the boy. He dressed him in the best clothes and shoes and had Caesar's hair groomed whenever he did his own.

When the seasons changed, Caesar stayed after school to play baseball with the other boys. He was built taller, but he had a gentle disposition. They treated him well enough, but none of them dared to become close friends. A lot of it had to do with social class and means. Most of the families didn't have what the Mallory family had, and money built a fence that very few ventured across.

On Easter Sunday, Grace was livid as Caesar sat between her and David.

"Why do I have to bear such humiliation, sitting here in front of everyone with the bastard child of some floozy who tried to break up my marriage?" she asked herself silently.

As the service continued, her angered simmered like a pot poised to boil at any moment, but she did her best to contain it and kept a smile pasted on her face. Whenever they stood for prayer or for a selection, she pressed her balled fist into the boy's thigh with all of her weight. Caesar grew steadily uncomfortable.

"Dad, I need to go relieve myself," he told David in a whisper.

"Go ahead, son," David said.

As Caesar crossed over in front of her, Grace stuck out her foot and pulled it under his back leg and tripped him. He stumbled awkwardly through the aisle but caught himself. He looked back and saw her looking smug and satisfied. Caesar knew that she didn't like him, and he knew why. He just didn't know what to do about it.

Toward the end of the school year, Caesar started dreading the coming months that he would have to be around the house with Grace.

"I was thinking that maybe I would go back to Savannah to visit my grammy for the summer," Caesar said one afternoon at the store.

David wasn't sure about that. He had just gotten to know his son and wanted to keep him close, but it was hard for him to deny Caesar anything.

"I guess a few weeks will be all right, but I really want you to work with me at the store," David said.

"Yes, sir," Caesar answered.

"There is another thing. I don't want you to keep calling me sir all the time," David added.

"What would you like me to call you?" Caesar asked.

"Well, you could call me Papa, Paw, Dad, or Daddy," he answered, "because that's who I want to be, I mean, that's who I am."

"I want to call you Dad," Caesar said.

"That's good, son, real good," David said, patting him on his shoulder.

Caesar was so happy about going back to visit Savannah, but he wasn't the only one glad about it. Grace couldn't wait to be rid of his face for a while. Caesar sat down and wrote a letter to Maia to let her know he would be coming home.

Dear Grammy, I have good news to tell you. Dad says that I can come to visit you this summer. It's all right here but I like it better in

Savannah. I miss Vernon and my other friends at school. I have been doing very good in my lessons and I work every day after school at the grocery. I'm glad I finally got to meet my father and I like him a lot, but I'd rather stay there with you. I don't want you to be by yourself, Grammy, I can take care of you now. I will see you very soon. Love Caesar

***

When Maia got Caesar's letter, it gave her chest pains. She loved him and wanted to see him so badly, but she knew he had to go on with his life. She couldn't bear seeing him and having to say goodbye again. She could feel how weak her heart was from being broken so many times. In the quietness of the night, she could hear its slow and faltering beat. There were moments when she placed her hand on her chest and willed it to continue. Maia went to her neighbors and got Pegasus and rode over to *The Tribune*.

"It's good to see you, Maia. What brings you out today?" her friend and editor asked as he gave her a gentle hug.

"I came to see if you would do me a favor?" she asked.

"You know I'll do anything for you. Are you ready to get back to work?"

"No, Sol, I want you to arrange a benefit where I can do my final public reading of a story."

"I get on it right away; it'll be a good opportunity to promote the new NAACP."

Having been a well-known and respectable storyteller, people came from Charleston and as far as Jacksonville, Florida, to hear Maia's last recitation. In the midst of the crowd of blacks and whites, men, women, and children of all ages who filled the room, she saw friends, neighbors, her pastor, Aaron's business associates, and then she saw Daphne, and beside her, there was Joseph Elliot and his family, Juliette and her family, and Jack with his wife and family. Maia nodded to them in recognition.

"I want to thank you all for coming today. It has been my greatest pleasure to tell my stories, and it has been a great blessing to me to have found an audience that appreciated them. To see you all here it gives me hope for the future that one day we will come together and live in harmony in this land and around the world.

It causes me to reflect back on a time nearly a thousand years ago on this continent, where the animals had free reign, and the roamed from the Atlantic to the Pacific, and from the gulf below to the plains high above. In the northeast part of the land, it was overcrowded and the animals had to be strong and hardworking. The seasons were rough, they had to work through the spring and harvest through the summer. In the fall, they had to prepare for the brutal winter, and it seemed like they never got a change to frolic around and be happy. Sometimes it was so difficult that it created discord between them. They got mad at the fat cattle, who were greedy and ate more than their share. They got mad at the sly fox, who stole and ate from the others. They were disgusted with the lazy bears, who wouldn't do any work.

"Life went on like this until a couple of yearlings named Rebel and Hope were grazing in the field and were approached by an eagle named Winston, who told him about the land out west where the seasons were mild and life was easier. They ran back and shared the tale with the others. The hens didn't believe them. The mule was stubborn and didn't want to go. The pigs liked how they lived, and the deer were scared and wanted to be left alone. Rebel and Hope decided to strike out on their own.

"They left early one morning with only an oil lamp, excited to find the place with no raging heat, bitter cold, or other dangers that plagued them. In the beginning, they made good progress, but the sun, the moon, the wind, and the rain wanted to make it interesting and have some fun with them. The sun began to hide from them behind the clouds to confuse them and make them cold, but they kept warm with the lamp and moved forward. The moon refused to rise, and if not for their lamp they would have been blinded in darkness, and they moved forward. The wind blew with a strong force to blow out the light, but they kneeled down and circled their lamp to protect the flame. And when the wind ran out of breath they moved forward. The rain took over and sent a torrential downpour to douse the flame, but good fortune led them to a cave for protection from the rain. And when the clouds were empty they moved forward. Rebel and Hope finally got to the beautiful coast on the southwest. They had battled all of the elements together with the comfort of their light, and now they were content. The two of them spent their days running along the beach with the warm waves splashing on their hoofs and were happy. They had found their peaceful place."

The room filled with applause when Maia finished her tale. Then a line formed, and they presented her with flowers of every variety. There were so many that she couldn't hold anymore of them, and they were laid on the carpet beside her.

Daphne came up and they exchanged a look that said more than ten thousand words, then they embraced, and Maia could feel the genuine love that flowed between them. Joseph and his family came next in the line, he gave her a quick hug, and his children shook her hand. Juliette and her family did the same; but when Jack came through the line, he gave her a long hug and a kiss on the cheek, and his children also gave her hugs. Maia thought her heart would burst. When the procession had finished, she thought she had been given more hugs, kisses, and handshakes that evening than she had received over her whole lifetime.

Sol gave Maia a ride home, and she waved at him from the veranda. When he had driven away, she went around to the back to her garden, walked into the center of it, and then laid down. She could smell the fresh vegetables close to her nose. With her hands, she dug into the soft earth, and she felt God. She looked high into the sky at the wonder of the stars, and then she closed her eyes and gave her heart its rest.

Chapter Five

Caesar took the news of his Grammy's death very hard. She was really the only mother that he had ever known. He was hurt and angry, thinking that he should have been home with her instead of in Nashville. With school being out, he did his best to stay out of Grace's way.

"Get on out of here, bastard," Grace said when she pushed him in his back as he stepped out of the door on his way to the store.

It was all Caesar could do to keep himself from turning back around and knocking her down. He thought of his grammy, relaxed his shoulders, and gave her a dirty look of his own. Grace rolled her eyes at him. Her frustration had grown even more after Maia died; she knew that now she would never be rid of the boy. She desperately needed a way to make her husband love her again. An idea came to her while she was making dinner.

The way to her man's heart was through his son. She made up her mind that she would let David see her being sweet to Caesar, and it would soften his grudge against her.

"David, why don't you take Caesar fishing. It might cheer him up some?" Grace suggested when he got home from work.

"That's a fine idea; I hate to see him feeling so bad and disappointed. He was really looking forward to spending the summer with his grammy. I'll take him on Saturday."

Grace smiled to herself; her campaign of good deeds was off to a good start. David woke Caesar up early that day, and they went fishing on the Cumberland River.

David broke the silence asking, "Do you want to hear about how I met your mama?"

Caesar smiled shyly and said, "Yeah, she never told me much about you."

"You might not believe it, but once upon a time, I was a real good singer. I sang solos in the church choir, and all the girls would clap for me."

Caesar laughed, and David did, too, as the memory flashed in his mind's eye.

"When I finished school at Meigs, my aunt Lilly wanted me to go to Normal school, but I went over to Fisk University, and there I joined the Jubilee Singers. I had been singing with them for a year when your Mama joined. I saw her walk into the room, and I knew then I wanted her to be my wife. Diana was a beauty; to me she floated above everybody, no matter where she went. She let me walk her home that first day we met, and I followed her like a puppy dog for eleven years. If I could do anything differently, I wouldn't have let her get away from me so easily. It was my pride that robbed all of us."

Caesar dug up a rock from the ground and threw it into the water. David and Caesar didn't catch one fish that day, but they bonded in a way that they hadn't done before. Every Saturday, they did something together.Greenwood Park was Caesar's favorite. They would watch the baseball games; go swimming in the pool; and whenever he rode the merry-go-round, it made him think of his best day when his mama took him, Vernon, and Grammy to Lincoln Amusement Park.

"Y'all mind if I come with you two today?" Grace asked them one weekend.

"I don't mind," David said, thankful that she had begun to warm up to Caesar.

"What do you think, C?"

Caesar shrugged his shoulders; he didn't want to cause any more problems.

"I'll get a blanket," Grace said, rushing up the stairs.

Surprisingly, they had a good time at the park. They looked at the animals in the zoo and bought barbecue for a picnic.

By the time the summer had ended, they were all feeling better. Caesar started hanging out with his friend Edward from school, and he started to laugh out loud like a boy should. David was happy and pleased with the way Grace was trying to be good to Caesar, and Grace was much better since David had come back into their bedroom.

"Things aren't the same as they had been before but I'll keep playing my game and wait," she said to herself.

Caesar was glad when school started again. He could be around more kids his age. He would meet Edward halfway on the walk to Napier School. Edward was a year older than Caesar, but they were in the same class. Edward lived in the Black Bottom with his mama; two younger brothers; and an uncle, who worked at the bottling company. Edward first made friends with Caesar because he secretly wanted to trade places with him and live his life. From the outside, it looked like it was all he ever wanted. As the months went by and they grew closer, they shared the truths about what went on behind their closed doors.

"My stepmama is crazy as a bed bug; she's always hitting, kicking, and pulling my hair, or scratching me," Caesar told Ed. "My Dad don't know anything about it."

"Where's your real mama?" Edward asked one day as they sat on the steps in front of Edward's house.

49

"She died in an automobile, but I don't know if it was an accident or not," Caesar said.

"That's sad, man. Least you got a daddy, though, and nice place to stay," Edward said. "My 'uncle' is not really my uncle. My mama waits on him hand and foot, even though he's mean to her, while me and my brothers have to fend for ourselves. She always feeds him the best food from the table first and then gives me and my brothers his scraps."

"Don't worry, man. As long as I got something, you gonna have it, too," Caesar assured him.

This was why Caesar always brought him food and treats out of the store to share with his brothers. When they all went to the Negro State Fair that was held at Greenwood Park in October, Edward came, too. There wasn't one black person in town who didn't "dress to death" and catch the Fairfield-Green streetcar and enjoy the horse-driven wagons that would bring them to the entrance.

"Dad, let's get on the rollercoaster," Caesar said as soon as they got to the outside gate.

David paid the twenty-five-cent admission for them all, and the boys ran straight to the rollercoaster.

"I'm not getting on that thing, it looks dangerous, and I don't want to mess up my hair. I just got it pressed," Grace said as they hopped into the seats.

She walked over to look at one of the produce exhibits and saw two women from the church watching David and the boys. She moved closer so she could hear them talking.

"That David Mallory is so fine, and his boy looks just like him," one of them said.

"His mama musta sho' been pretty," another one said.

"I don't know what he sees in Grace. She's almost black as coal and skinny as a rail," one said with laugh.

Grace felt hot heat rush to the top of her head, and the vein on her temple began to pulse. What did she have to do to satisfy these people? She dressed well and used Madam Walker's Hair System to keep her hair smooth? Her rage was building, and all she wanted to do was to pull Caesar off that ride and beat him upside his head. She couldn't get to his mama, so he had to take her punishment.

***

That trip to the Negro State Fair marked the end to Caesar's reprieve. Grace was careful and covered Caesar with sugar in David's presence, but she used one of David's belts to wake him up for school in the mornings. Sometimes she even poured cold water on him. Caesar had to pay for all the times that someone called her ugly or black. He had to pay for the day he was born, and he had to pay for every time David turned his back on her in their bed.

Caesar started sleeping on the floor and sliding under the bed whenever she came in his room. He even thought about telling his dad what was going on, but he was afraid of what he might do. School would be out over the holidays, and Caesar wasn't looking forward to being in the house with Grace.

"Dad, can Edward could come over and stay until after my birthday?"

"Sure, son," he said. "Whatever you want."

The two boys had a great time. Edward got to eat all that he wanted, and Caesar got peace from Grace's abuse. On January 1, 1910, his tenth birthday, David bought him a new red American Flyer bicycle.

The closer the father and son became, the greater were Grace's resentments and insecurities. One part of his life was a dream come true, and the other was a never-ending nightmare. For every reward and compliment he received from David, he was delivered a slap or a kick from Grace. She was getting more vicious in her attacks on Caesar, but he was getting better at avoiding her. It was their private battle, and David's love and attentions were the spoils of the war.

One day when Caesar came into the store after school, David said, "Would like to see a show, one like your mama used to do on Broadway and when she was on tour?"

"Yeah, Dad, you bet! When can we go?" Caesar asked, eager to see what took his mama away from him all the time.

"Very soon. I want you to see the woman your mama always used to talk about, the one she wanted to be like."

"No fooling, Dad?" he asked, getting more excited.

"Uh-huh, the Black Patti Troubadours will be coming to the Bijou Theatre next week, and we're going. Do you want anyone else to go?"

"No, Dad, I just want us two to go," he answered, knowing Grace would spoil it for him.

David smiled and shook his head with satisfaction; he loved doing things together as father and son. Grace stood in the background and frowned like she had a bad taste in her mouth. It was just more of the boy pushing her out of the picture.

Caesar counted the days until they would go to see the show. He was curious to see the magic that had captured his mama and wouldn't let her go. He looked through the scrapbook that Grammy had given him, and his mama looked so pretty in the pictures. He had heard her sing at Grandy's funeral, and her voice had made everybody cry. He wished he could have seen her on the stage, but this would be just like seeing her up there for him. Grammy had told him that it was in her blood. He wanted to see if it was in his blood, too.

On the night of the show, David and Caesar dressed in their best suits.

"We're going to be the best looking guys in the theater," David said to Caesar.

"You two do make a handsome picture," Grace said when they

came down the stairs, despite her wanting to go in the boy's place.

"One dollar tickets, please," David said when they reached the theater ticket booth. He wanted to get them the best seats in the house.

"It looks like a castle in here," Caesar said, impressed with the building on the outside. But it only got better once they went inside.

Once they were seated, Caesar's eyes traveled around the room, taking in all the beauty in the auditorium, the colors painted on the wall and the ceiling, and the gold trim. He could feel the excitement that hid behind the curtain on stage; and he didn't know why, but he felt a little nervous. He read the playbill he had been handed to calm himself. The show was called *A Trip to Africa*, and it had three acts.

From the moment the stage curtains were drawn, Caesar could understand why his mama wanted to be up there in the spotlight. It was another world with no problems or sadness; it was music, laughter, and make-believe. He could almost see his mama up there in the character of Princess Lulu, the teacher who had been kidnapped and taken to Africa by the Zamboo tribe to be their queen. The dancers made him want to dance, and the other characters tickled him until he cried.

When Sissieretta Jones sang "Suwannee River," you could have heard a pin drop. And then when they applauded, you couldn't even hear your own thoughts. Princess Lulu was rescued in the end, and the audience stood on their feet and clapped for all the cast.

Caesar turned to David and asked him, "What does it feel like to have so many people clapping at your feet?"

"It feels good, son, real good. You're on top of the world."

"Thanks, for bringing me, Dad," he said.

"There will be other shows, son. The music never stops," David said as they walked out of theater.

Chapter
Six

For the next few years, life for Caesar had taken on a rhythm that he was used to. Things weren't always the way he wanted them to be. He still had to dodge the licks and kicks of his stepmother, but he had managed to find a measure of happiness with his Dad and with the city. It was the spring season, when all that had been contained during the winter breaks through with new growth, but blacks in Nashville were in mourning. Georgia Taylor, the lady who had given a room to Caesar and Maia when they first came into town had died, and there was going to be a large memorial service at her church. She had been one of the original members of the Fisk Jubilee Singers, and Rev. Preston Taylor, her husband, was one of the richest and most prominent business men in the community.

"Let me straighten up your tie, Caesar," David said before they went inside the church for the funeral service. And even though Caesar was only thirteen, when he stood toe to toe with his father, he looked him straight in the eyes.

There were over a thousand in attendance, and former Jubilee Singers were on the program. Inside Lea Christian Church, every pew was filled, and even the standing room was taken. More than half of the people had to pay their respects from outside the sanctuary.

Most of the young people took advantage of this opportunity to hang outside to socialize. The younger ones played tag, and the older ones divided into groups of girls and guys and stood back and sized each other up. Caesar was finishing up his freshman year at Pearl High School, and he was popular with the girls there since a lot of the older boys had to leave school and go to work to help their families.

There was one girl in particular that he liked. Her name was Rose, and to him she was prettier than the flower. They were in the same grade, but she was one year older, and that was the one thing that kept her from paying Caesar the attention he wanted. She and the other girls preferred the older boys who they thought were more mature. However, Caesar was fortunate enough to have something that leveled the playing field: money to spend.

"Rose, you want to go get a pop at the store?" Caesar asked as he moved closer to the group of girls.

She smiled and said, "Not today, but another I day I would."

"Maybe after school?" he added.

"Sure," she said, and as far as Caesar was concerned, this day of sadness had just taken a turn for the better.

"Dad, I talked to Rose today, and I think she likes me," he said when David and Grace got home from the burial at Greenwood Cemetery.

"Is that right, son?" David replied, resisting the urge to tell him not to worry about girls for a while.

David had missed Caesar's younger years, and to him, it seemed like the boy was growing up too fast. But he knew from his own experiences that you'd have more luck stopping bees from making honey than keeping the boys from chasing after the girls.

"I don't know how much time you'll have for the girls. I'm gonna need your help more at the store. I know you already know how to stock the shelves and work the cash register, but I need to teach you when to order more produce and order dry goods."

"Don't worry, Dad. I can make time for Rose and work."

"You've got to keep your grades up, too," David urged, even though he knew Caesar always did well in school.

David gave Caesar more responsibilities, and that cut into a lot of his free time; but Caesar never minded because it kept him from being around Grace. By the end of the year, David had taught him how to tally up the day's sales and make the deposit at the One-Cent Savings Bank.

Caesar changed with the seasons as he became a young man. Through the winter when he wasn't at school or working at the store, he played basketball at the colored YMCA. He loved to run, jump, and shoot the ball into the hoop until he was drenched with sweat. The game freed him of all the tensions and aggravations of his life that had become as regular as the sunsets and the moon risings.

When spring came, Caesar played baseball at Hadley Park. He loved to pitch. Standing up on the mound and throwing his fast ball, he was the one in control. The summer gave him time to go to the picture shows at the Bijou, where he would sit by Rose and hold her hand and lose himself in fantasies. He grew taller, and shoulders broadened. His muscles thickened, and his voice deepened.

***

The Fourth of July celebration at Greenwood Park was coming, and Caesar was going to get to go to his first dance.

"Do you wanna go to the dance with me, Rose?" he asked when she came to the store on an errand for her mother.

"I guess I do, but can you even dance?" she answered, giving him a questioning smile.

"Not now, but it won't take me long to learn," he answered confidently.

All the black folks in town were at Greenwood Park for the celebration. Caesar and Rose met up after leaving their parents at the main tent, where they had eaten. The beat of the music and the blaring horns lured them inside the hall where the dancing was.

"We gonna start with the camel walk," Rose said, leading Caesar out on the dance floor.

"Okay," Caesar said, "I'll try not to show you up."

"Fat chance!" Rose said, limberly moving her arms and feet.

Caesar followed Rose's lead and popped his knees back and forth as he shifted his feet. He was true to his word as they went through the kangaroo dip, and the foxtrot. The danced until they were drenched in perspiration.

"Let's go get a cold drink to cool off," he said, pulling her by the hand.

They stopped by the refreshment stand and then followed the procession to go watch the fireworks show. When the thunders lulled and the lights stopped flashings, Rose gave Caesar his first kiss. When the night ended, he practically danced all the way to David's car.

Caesar's joy always made Grace sick to her stomach, and the next morning she was in a bad mood. After David left for work, she went straight to his closet and picked out a thick belt.

"I'm not putting up with it!" she yelled as she stomped down the hallway into Caesar's room, swung open the door, and struck him hard across the back as he lay in bed.

"What the heck?" Caesar shouted, waking up in a daze.

When he saw it was Grace, he jumped out of the bed, snatched the belt out of her hand, and raised it over his shoulder. Grace froze, wondering if he was about to hit her. At that moment, Caesar knew he was stronger than her, and he could hurt her if he wanted to, but he hadn't been brought up to raise a hand to a woman. He gave her a look of disdain and threw the belt to the floor.

"Get out of here," he said, looking her in the face.

Grace turned on her heels and rushed out of the room and down the stairs.

"Oh my God!" she said, looking at her hands. She was shaking like a leaf in the wind, but she wasn't scared.

The whole scene had given her a rush. Caesar's reaction, his quickness, and his strength had excited her. Most of the time, David barely acknowledged her presence, and Caesar ignored her; but this time, she had gotten a response.

Unfortunately for Caesar, his actions didn't discourage Grace from bothering him. Instead of pushing him in the back of the head when he sat at the table, she started rubbing it all the way down to his neck. Instead of kicking him in the leg when he walked by, she would grab him around his waist and try to hold him. Grace still couldn't keep her hands off of him, but her attitude had drastically changed.

Grace looked at her reflection in the mirror and said, "If his mama could have my husband, then I have a right to take her son." She would still come into his room some mornings, and he could feel her watching him in the bed. He started to think that she had gone crazy.

"That crazy witch keeps coming in my room and watching me," he said to Edward on their way to school.

Edward shook his head and said, "At least she's not hitting on you all the time, man."

But if Caesar could have his choice, he would prefer her strikes and jabs.

Caesar strained his brain, trying to think of a place to go where he could get out of the house during the holiday season, but he knew his Dad wouldn't give him permission. He used to be able to count on Edward to be there with him, but now he thought it was boring at their house. His so-called uncle had long since moved on, and there was plenty to eat in his own house, not to mention there was so much more going on in the Black Bottom at Christmas. Caesar and Ed would sneak into house parties and try to sip a little of the bootleg that flowed from Thanksgiving to New Year's Day.

"Man, it's no fun hanging in Edgehill. You need to come down to the Bottom," Edward told him.

"I would if could, Ed. I'm tired of her trying to touch me with her ugly claws. I'm living with the 'wicked witch,'" he laughed, trying to make light of the situation. "I need you to come up to the house for a few days."

"I'll come for a while. I like older women myself," Ed joked. "But you got to try and get out of there, C."

"Well, Ed, if they looked like your next-door neighbor's sister, I wouldn't mind."

"Which one are you talking about?" Edward asked.

"The sassy one who wears the hats all the time," he answered.

"Ain't it the truth," Edward said. "I asked her what her name was, and she told me, 'Zora Neale Hurston, and don't forget it'."

Caesar was home on Christmas Eve and Christmas Day as he promised. The stores were closed, and they were all home together.

"Thanks, Dad, it's just what I wanted," Caesar said after he opened the gift from his Dad in the morning.

It was the Kodak camera he had asked for. While he looked through the eyepiece and pretended to take shots, Grace came over and handed him a gift box. He opened it, and inside was a beautiful pocket watch with a chain on it.

"Thank you, ma'am," Caesar said, placing it back under the Christmas tree.

David was pleased that Grace had made such a nice gesture, but Caesar knew that it meant that it was only a matter of time before this situation exploded. He thanked them both again and grabbed his coat and headed out into the cold December air. He walked toward the Bottom with his fists clenched in his pockets. He tried to count his blessings like Grammy had told him, but living in that house with all its secrets and madness was giving him the blues. He spent the next week trying to escape by running the streets the streets and having fun with Edward and Rose.

Halfway through the month of March, David planned a trip to Highpoint, North Carolina to make an order for goods and furniture. His other manufacturers were taking orders from the federal government since the World War started over a year ago, and his inventory in the stores was down. He was anxious to tell Caesar his plans when he got there after school. He had taught him most everything he knew about running the store, and he wanted to give him a chance to take on the responsibility while he was out of town.

"Hey, son," he called to Caesar when he came by in the afternoon, "I need to discuss something with you."

Suddenly, Caesar had the urge to relieve himself, and butterflies took flight in his stomach.

"Yes, sir," he said as he warily went into the office.

"Sit down, son," David said as Caesar's mind raced, wondering what he knew. "I'm going to be traveling to North Carolina on business, and I want you to take over the store for me while I'm gone."

David waited for what he expected to be enthusiasm and his eagerness to show how well he could do the job, but there was none.

"I'd really like to go with you on the trip, Dad. I think I could learn more there," Caesar said earnestly.

"I wish I could take you, but I need you here. Your stepmom is going to have her hands full with the downtown store and helping the Red Cross women's group make bandages for the war. It'll be a good experience for you. After all, it'll be yours one day anyway,"

David said, giving Caesar a pat on the back on his way out of the office.

On the evening before David was leaving for Highpoint, Caesar said, "Dad, wake me up in the morning. I want to go with you to the train station."

It really made David feel good. They had come a long way as father and son. Now he couldn't even imagine his life without Caesar; he was truly his pride and joy. The next morning, thetwo walked side by side and caught the streetcar to Union Station. David bought his ticket and gave Caesar a big bear hug.

He noticed the strain on his son's face and said, "Don't worry, son, I won't be gone that long."

Caesar had a plan to get through the days while David was away. He wouldn't even see Grace. He was going stay at the store until it closed, and then he would eat at Ed's house and hang out until it was time to go to sleep.

Caesar felt more comfortable after a few days. He hadn't seen Grace, and everything was business as usual at the store. He laid in his bed exhausted and drifted off to sleep. Except, bad dreams of Grace touching him and the feel of her cold fingers down his back woke him in the night. But his horror had only begun when he became conscious that she was actually in the bed with him.

"Get out of here!" Caesar hollered as he struggled to get free from her terrible grip.

Grace fought her way on top of him and put her lips on his in a kiss. He pushed her away with disgust.

"Kiss me, you no good bastard!" she yelled.

"You're crazy!" he said, screaming his words at her as he tried to push her away.

Grace pulled at Caesar's chest and ripped his sleep shirt. After that, any reservations he'd had about not hurting her dissipated, and he threw her down hard against the wooden floor and spat on the rug next to where she fell.

"Leave me alone!" he shouted at her as he grabbed his clothes and ran out of there like a bat out of hell. Grace sat on the floor dejected, humiliated, and too weak to even shed a tear for herself. She knew she was wrong to go into his room, but she couldn't stop herself. She was so empty and desperate for a human touch.

***

Caesar went to the store and slept in his dad's big chair in his office for the rest of the night. The next day, Ed came by after school.

"Hey, C, what's the good word, another day, another dollar?" he asked as he reached in the ice box for a pop.

"It's over, Ed. My life is shit, and I don't have anywhere to go," Caesar said to him.

"What's wrong, C?" Edward asked with concern.

"That evil witch got in my bed last night while I was sleeping," he answered and went through every detail of what happened.

"That's crazy," Edward said. "What are you going to do? Are you going to tell your dad?"

"I don't think so. They don't get along that well, and I don't want to cause any more problems. One thing I do know is that I'd rather sleep in a ditch than go through that again."

"You can stay with us until your dad gets back," Edward said. "Then tell him you want a lock on your door."

"Thanks, Ed. You've been a friend whenever I needed one."

"You for me, and me for you, C."

David returned to Nashville on April 1, All's Fools day. He went by the store, and Caesar was there sweeping up.

"Hey, boss," he said when he saw Caesar.

"Welcome back, Dad," Caesar said, walking over and giving him a hug and then going back to his sweeping.

David noticed that Caesar was jumpy and avoiding eye contact with him.

"Everything go all right while I was gone?"

"Sure, Dad, no problems," Caesar heard himself answer, but in his mind, he was saying, "If only you knew."

"Let's go home early today," David said. "I missed y'all."

When they got to the house, Grace was all smiles, acting as if though nothing had happened. She knew Caesar hadn't said anything because he never had before. Sometimes she wondered who he thought he was protecting. The only thing she was sure of was that the hell they all lived in was caused by him and his mama, and she was justified in doing whatever she needed to do to survive in it.

Caesar's back was against the wall, and he didn't have many choices. The one thing he knew was that he couldn't stay under that roof much longer. He would have already gone, except he promised his grammy that he would finish his schooling, and he was very close to keeping his word. He was ahead of the students when he moved to Nashville, and he was a fast learner. He didn't have many friends in the beginning and had spent most of his time on his lessons.

When this school year ended, Caesar would have all the credits he needed to graduate. After that, it was goodbye, Grace. He didn't want to leave his dad, but if he stayed, somebody was going to get hurt or even killed, and he didn't want to be a part of any of it. He sat at the desk his dad had bought him when he first moved in, and he counted the days before he would leave. It was seventy-two. He had done his best to get along there, especially after his grammy died. But if he had learned anything from his mama, it was if you can't stand the heat, get out of the kitchen, and he couldn't stand it anymore.

On Easter Sunday, while David and Grace were at church, Caesar went into his dad's closet and got one of his smaller suitcases. He took it to his room and opened it on his bed. He looked through his dresser and closet and packed it with some clothes for all seasons and his best suit. He gathered his pictures of Grammy and Grandy, him and Vernon in Savannah, and the scrapbook of his mother's life in show business and packed them, too. He filled the suitcase with all the important things from his life and left some room for his camera, and then he slid it under the bed. Now he just had to figure out where he was going and what he was going to do when he got there. He tried to fill as much fun as he could into the days he had left in his present life because he knew everything in his future was about to change.

"Dad, can you teach me to drive?"

"Sure, son, I think it's about time you learned."

Caesar learned quickly and loved to speed down Spruce Street. He went to parties at Greenwood Park, where they danced the Black Bottom, ate barbecued pork, and snuck drinks of cold beer. He went to the picture shows with Rose, and they kissed and touched each other in the dark instead of watching the actors on the screen. He spent a lot of time hanging around in the Black Bottom with Ed learning how to play cards and gamble. One afternoon at Ed's house, after a stroll down Second Avenue, they saw Zora sitting out on the porch with her nieces and nephews. Caesar went over and asked her, "If you could leave here today, where would you go?"

"Hmm, that would be a place where I could speak my mind and someone would care to listen. I would have to go to the big city," she said with a grin.

"Which one?" he asked.

"Just choose one," she said.

The weather had turned hot during the last weeks of school, and the students in Caesar's class were getting excited about the end of the school. He and Edward listened quietly to all of the different plans the other students had for after graduation simply for the reason that Edward still had another year to go before he could finish, and Caesar wasn't sure what his plans were. At home he never let his guard down and Edward came over for dinner whenever Caesar wasn't eating at his house. Ed was the only person who knew his days there were numbered.

"Ed, I'm going in the service to fight in the war," Caesar told his friend as they sat in his room on the night before his graduation.

"C, why you wanna do that and get killed in the white man's war. It's not our fight," he said upset at the news.

"Ed, all I know is I am fighting for my life, 'cause here I don't have one."

Chapter Seven

It was the proudest moment of David's life, to see his own flesh and blood graduate from high school. As he watched Caesar get his diploma, he could see that he was a young man now and not the boy he had met six years ago. He wished he could serve him all the good things that life had to offer on a silver platter and protect him from all its pitfalls and make sure he got all the happiness that he deserved, but he knew that if there wasn't a cloud in the sky today, surely there would be one there on another day.

Things had worked out all right, David thought to himself. Maybe he had even been too hard on Grace over what had happened. He felt so fortunate to have had this time in his son's life. Those other things were in the past, and they had both made mistakes. He reached for Grace's hand and squeezed it as they watched the students' processional leave the auditorium.

They had a big party for Caesar at the house, and David gave him an envelope with twenty-five dollars in it.

"A man needs to have some money in his pocket," he told him.

When the party was over, Caesar walked outside with Edward to say goodbye.

"I'm gonna miss you, Ed. If it wasn't for you, I wouldn't have made it through."

They shook hands, and Edward pushed him on the shoulder and said, "You better take care of yourself, C, or I'll tell your stepmama where you are."

"I'll be fine, Ed, and I'll write you when I get settled."

Caesar went inside, took the money his dad had given him, and added it with the rest of the money he had saved. He counted it and divided it into three parts: One third he packed in the suitcase with his camera, another he put in his pants pocket, and the last third he put in his shoe. Then he sat down at his desk and wrote a letter:

Dear Dad, The first thing that I want to say is that I love you very much. I'm grateful that I got the chance to know you as my father. Thank you for all you have done for me and bringing me into your home as you son. There have been things going on that you haven't known about from the first day that I came to live with you, and they have gotten to a place where I can't stay. Sometimes I feel like I have been a problem since I was born, but I don't want to cause any problems in your life. I know you might think I'm too young to make this decision, but I've had to grow up fast in my life. I can take care of myself and I'm ready to be on my own. When you read this letter I will be a soldier in the U.S. Army. Love, Caesar.

He sat up his bed for the next few hours, and when he saw the light of day coming into the window, he picked up his suitcase, walked down the stairs and out the front door, breathed in the fresh air of his freedom, and exhaled a sigh of relief. He went to the store and placed the letter in the mailbox and walked toward Union Station.

***

For the first few days, David didn't worry when he didn't see Caesar around the house. He thought he was hanging out and celebrating with his friends. It wasn't until Monday morning when he got the mail at the store and read the letter. He was devastated. Questions and confusion about the problems that the boy had had in the house swirled in the conflux of his emotions. He ran out of the store and drove straight to Black Bottom to find Edward; he would have to know what was going on and why his son felt his only answer was to run away. David found Edward tossing a ball outside with his younger brothers.

"Hey, Ed, I need to talk to you," he called out, hanging back from the group.

David could tell by his short glance that Ed knew why he was here.

"Just a minute, fellas," Ed said as he tossed the ball and walked over to the vehicle. "Hey, Mr. Mallory," he said, leaning into the driver's window.

"Good morning, Ed. Have you seen Caesar today?"

"No, sir, I haven't seen him since the party at your house," he answered.

"I got a letter from him at the store today, and it says he was leaving because of some problems in the house, but he didn't say what they were. Do you know what they were, Ed?"

"Yes, sir, but I don't think it's my place to say."

"Well, somebody has got to tell me what's going on, and Caesar's not here. You're his friend, aren't you?"

"Yes, sir, I am."

"Well prove it. I can't fix it if I don't know what's wrong," David said, frustrated with all the mystery.

Edward didn't want to get involved, but he thought that Caesar should have told his dad a long time ago. He looked down at the ground, where he had drawn a line in the dirt and started talking.

"It's Mrs. Mallory, sir. She started beating on him as soon as he got here, every time you turned your back. He let it go on for years because he didn't want to cause a fuss in the house. She kept on, and he just took it. Then it changed, sir. She starting touching him funny like, like she wanted him to touch her back. And when you were out of town, she got in his bed. He didn't touch her, sir, but he said he couldn't stay there no more."

David felt the vein on the side of his head begin to thump.

"Thank you, Ed," David said calmly. "Come on up to the store if you want a job. I need some help."

David drove a few blocks and then he pulled over to the side of the road, overwhelmed by what he had just heard. How could he have not seen all of this? How could he have not known? It hurt him that he had let his son down again; and for the first time since he was a boy, he leaned over the steering wheel and cried. He cried over the mistakes he had made with Diana, he cried over his marriage to Grace, he cried over the son he had not known about for so long, and he cried over the misery that he had brought his son into. He cried until his shirt was soaked and his eyes were swollen, and his whole body was drained. He was empty. He wanted to kill Grace, but he was too tired. He drove back to the grocery and closed it. Then he drove to the furniture store on Cherry Street downtown.

"Close the store, and go home, Mr. Andrews," he told his salesperson. Then he laid down on one of the beds on display and went to sleep.

It had been two days since Grace had seen David and four since she'd seen Caesar, and she was starting to panic. It was dinner time, and neither one of them was around. Sitting at the table, she wondered if they were together and if Caesar had decided to open his mouth. Abruptly, she stopped eating and rushed up the stairs and went into Caesar's room. She saw that a lot of his clothes and things were gone. She rushed down the hall to her bedroom, but all of David's clothes were still neatly arranged.

Grace stood there thinking back over the last few days, and then from the upstairs window she saw David coming home. She rushed down the stairs to see what was going on. When the door opened and she saw his face, it was obvious that he knew everything. She didn't know what to expect; she held tight to the banister to brace herself for whatever was coming.

"It's over, Grace. He's gone, and it's over. I never knew you could do the things that you've done to that boy. I can't even stand the sight of you," he said in a low voice.

"It's not all my fault!" she screamed. "Why couldn't you just love me? Somebody's got to love me."

"I tried, Grace. I tried for a long time," he said.

"No, you didn't. You were in love with that whore the whole time."

"I was committed to you, Grace. I married you and came back to you. But now you're a snake full of venom, and you bite everything that comes near you."

"You're the one who made me this way. I wasn't like this before," she said.

"No, Grace, you let yourself get like this. You had a choice from the time you saw that first letter addressed to me. I was wrong, and I admit it. I should have never married you, and now I'm leaving. You can have this house and everything in it, and after I get some of my things, I'm never coming back here."

"After all the mess I put up with, that's it?" she said, agitated

"Don't think I didn't make sacrifices to stay in this marriage," he said firmly.

"I loved you too much, David, and I didn't want to lose you. It made me crazy," she said, changing her tone and pleading with him.

"I guess it did because you turned our house into a hell hole for my son," he replied, turning away.

"He was gonna take you away from me like his mama did!" she yelled.

"You didn't give him a chance, Grace. You didn't give me a chance. I never said I was going to leave you. Now I can't stay. I don't even know who you are," David said, going up the steps.

What Diana couldn't do, Grace had accomplished it herself. She had torn up her own home because of her jealousy and anger. David grabbed a suitcase and stuffed it with as much of his things as it would hold, and then he stormed out of the house. He could still hear her screams halfway down the street as he headed for the Taylors' rooming house.

Gossip spread around town like a wildfire. Most of the talk said David left Grace because she'd turned mean from not having babies. Some said he left because Caesar ran away. Others said she threw them both out because they treated her badly. David didn't care what they said. His only concern was to find his son and bring him back home. Unfortunately, when he went to the army recruiting station, they didn't have any records of his signing up. David was tortured, and there was nothing he could do except wait for word from Caesar.

***

Caesar had decided to take Zora's advice and head off to a big city. The one he chose was the one that drew his mama back time and time again, New York City. He stood in line at the ticket counter. Tall, with traces of hair above his lips, he looked older than his age. He paid the fare for his ticket, boarded the train, and was on his way.

Caesar wanted to see what his mama had seen and go to the places where she had gone. He chose a window seat in the rear of the colored section and settled back for the ride. Looking out as the sights of the city were being left behind, he felt nervous inside, but he couldn't wait for his adventure to begin. Tired from being up with no rest for two days, he laid over the top of his suitcase and went to sleep.

Caesar woke with a shot of adrenaline to his heart when an older gentleman tapped him on the shoulder.

"Sleep any longer like that, and you gonna get a crook in your neck. I'm T. Howard, headed to Baltimore," he said as he sat down on the seat beside Caesar. "What's your name, young man, and where you headed?"

"My name's Caesar Portunus, and I'm going to see my mama in New York before I volunteer for the army, sir," he answered.

"That's good, son. It ain't nothing wrong with fighting for your country. I was a Buffalo soldier in the 10th Cavalry Regiment and proud of it. I fought in the Indian Wars for twelve years, stationed in Fort Concho, Texas, and won a Medal of Honor. Our people need young black men to join the fight for democracy in the world. If we fight for it there, they got to give it to us back here."

"I'm gonna do my best, sir," Caesar said.

"Only one thing, young man, don't mess with the army. When you get to New York, join the National Guard, they treat black men in the army like slaves."

"I'll remember that," Caesar answered as he straightened up.

T. Howard spent the next three hours telling Caesar all about his exploits out West and how his whole family was moving north to find work.

When Caesar's second train finally pulled into the Grand Central Terminal in New York City, his long legs were stiff from being cramped over the lengthy ride, and his shirt and jacket were sweaty and wrinkled from the early June heat. He was hungry for a good meal and anxious to find a place where he could change out of the clothes he'd been wearing for four days and eat.

When he stepped off the train into the terminal, it was as if he had gone to another country. There were more people than he had ever seen in one place, and so many of them were speaking languages he didn't understand. He had felt so conspicuous in Nashville, that everyone knew more about him than he wanted them to. But here, it was as if he was invisible as he walked across the great hallway. No one stopped or looked his way.

He saw a black man sweeping absent-mindedly near the front of the entrance. Caesar walked over and asked him, "Is there someplace close I can get a room and some food?"

The man looked him over, noticing the quality of his clothes, shoes, and leather suitcase and said, "Try the Marshall Hotel over on West 53rd Street. You can walk there from here.

The man swept his broom closer to the large double doors where he pointed the way to Caesar and gave him directions on how to get there.

The young man found the building without any trouble and walked up the stairs into the lobby and stood at the front desk. A small man with kinky white hair sat at the desk, and a tall, thin dark-skinned man stood beside him.

"I need a room," Caesar said to the man sitting there.

"How long will you be staying?" the clerk asked.

"I'm not sure. Maybe a week," Caesar answered.

The front desk clerk showed him the costs for the rooms and meals printed on the desk. Caesar reached in his pocket and handed him ten dollars.

"Are you a musician?" the tall thin man asked as he took the money.

"No, no," Caesar replied with a smile. "But my mama was a singer."

"Oh really? What's her name? I might know her?"

"Her name was Diana Portunus."

"Yeah, son, I did know your mama," the man said as he thought back. "She came in here a lot. She was a classy lady with a voice like an angel, but show business can be the devil in disguise. Not many of the good ones left. Things change."

Caesar nodded in agreement.

"I'm Jimmie, and this here's my place. Here's your key. Your room is up the stairs to the right, and the restaurant is through the two doors," the clerk told him.

"Thank you, sir," he said and headed up the stairs.

Caesar looked around the room, put his things away in the closet and drawers, and then he put the portion of his money that he kept in his suitcase in the back of the frame of the picture on the wall. He walked back down the flight of stairs to the dining room to get something to eat, and when he got to the double doors, he could smell beef cooking in the kitchen.

There were twelve tables in the dining room, and two groups were already eating. Four men sat at one table, and three women and a man sat at the other. Caesae figured them to be in show business. They were all dressed to death: the women in brightly colored dresses, high-heeled shoes, and matching hats; the men in suits, with fresh white shirts, ties, and sporty shoes that shined.

Caesar sat down at an empty table and watched them as they talked and ate. They laughed with exaggerated expressions and it was as if they were performing on stage. They looked special to him, just like his mama did, and he could smell their fragrances mixing with the aroma from the kitchen. He knew that each of them was blessed with a gift.

"We got fried chicken and corn, liver and onions, or pot roast," an older waiter said after coming over to his table without a menu.

"I'll have the pot roast and corn bread with a glass of lemonade," Caesar said.

When his meal came, it tasted so good, and Caesar gobbled it down like the hungry young man he was. When he was finished, he sat a little longer, watching the others enjoying themselves. He started to wonder if he had a gift like they did. His grammy could write good stories, and he had heard that Hercules could make anything grow out of the ground. Grandy could build anything from the foundation to the roof, and his mama could sing like a bird. But what was his gift?

He liked sports, but he didn't run the fastest, hit the ball the hardest, or jump the highest. He couldn't play music, he didn't know how to write stories, and he had never even tried to sing. He thought about the Black Bottom, there he couldn't win at cards or dice.

I guess I don't have a gift, he thought. *I'm probably not the only one either.*

The men saw him watching their table, and they signaled for the waiter, who stood at the door to the kitchen.

"Who's the young man eating alone over there?" one of them asked.

"Jimmie says it's Diana Portunus' boy from down south," the waiter whispered.

Caesar saw the men talking for a minute, and then they waved for him to come over to the table. He stood up and walked over to their table. He hoped that they had known his mama.

"I hear you're Diana's boy. I'm Bert Williams," one of the men said. "I worked with your mama for years. What's your name?"

"Caesar, sir," he said, realizing that he had seen Bert in some picture shows.

"Well, what brings you up to the big city?" Bert asked.

"I guess I just wanted to see what goes on up here," Caesar answered.

"Is that right? What do you do, Caesar? I know you don't just walk around looking good for a living."

The other men laughed, and Caesar felt embarrassed. "No, sir, I worked in a store with my dad. I just graduated from high school, and now I'm going in the army."

Two of the men laughed again, and one said, "Son, you too young to throw your life away. Can you sing, play music, dance, or anything?"

"No, I can't," Caesar answered agitated.

"Uh, all that pretty wasted," the man said as he shook his head.

"Meet me out front at 11:00 in the morning," Bert said. "I'm gonna take you around town."

Caesar smiled a toothy grin, something he hadn't done for a while, and said, "I'll be there, sir."

He turned and walked slowly out of the dining room, and then he darted up the stairs at full speed. He had a lot to look forward to: lying down in a bed to sleep and getting up in the morning to meet Mr. Bert Williams.

***

The next morning, promptly at 11:00, Caesar flew back down the steps to find Mr. Williams parked out front in a fancy automobile.

"When we get back, I want you to pack your things up son; this isn't the place for you. I want you to stay with my wife, Lottie, and me."

"I can take care of myself, sir. I don't want to be no trouble," Caesar said.

"How old are you, son?" Mr. Williams asked.

"I'm almost sixteen," Caesar answered proudly.

"I was just about your age when I first left home, raggedy with nothing but my wits. You may have a cushion to shield you from rock bottom right now, but being black still has its disadvantages. One word of advice: When good fortune smiles at you in this life, don't turn your back. It doesn't happen often."

"I'll think about it, sir," he said, but Caesar was leery of moving into a house with perfect strangers again. He had just gotten out of a bad situation.

"Hurry up and get in. I don't like to wait."

Caesar jumped into the passenger side, and Bert pulled away from the curb.

"Caesar is a helluva name. What do your friends call you?"

"They call me C."

"Good, I'll call you C, and you can call me Mr. B."

The two of them rode through Manhattan, and Bert showed him the Statue of Liberty.

"Do you know anything about that?" Bert asked as he pointed to the statue.

"Not much," Caesar said.

"I wasn't born here," Bert said. "I'm from the West Indies. My family came here to find the Promised Land, the American dream. I've memorized the words that are on that statue, 'Give me your tired, your poor, Your huddled masses yearning to breathe free, The wretched refuse of your teeming shore, Send these, the homeless, tempest-tossed to me, I lift my lamp beside the golden door.' Beautiful. Only thing, they forgot to say, as long as you're not black."

"That sounds like something my grandy would say," Caesar added, "His name was Liberty."

"No kidding?" Bert said.

"Nope. My mama's was, too: Diana Portunus Liberty."

"Impressive names you got there in your family, C. Let's go see where your mama lived; it's not far from here."

They drove to Harlem, and when they got to 371 West 125th Street, Bert pulled the vehicle over and said, "This is it, C. That was your mama's townhouse. She and Ernest Hogan were among the first black folks to live out here. I don't know your family situation, but take it straight from the horse's mouth: You should be proud of your mama."

Caesar got out of the car and gazed up at the building. *She was happy here*, he thought to himself. He tried to imagine her face smiling and looking at him from the upstairs window. After a few minutes, he got back in the automobile, and he and Bert headed to Broadway.

"This is where your mama and I performed many times; we even made history here playing in *In Dahomey*. Is there anything else you want to see or anyplace else that you want to go?" Bert asked Caesar.

"No, Mr. B, I guess that's it."

"Take a breath in your running, C, and give yourself some time. A black man in the army ain't nothing to write home about. Take six months. The sun is out, and it's time for a young man to play" Bert said as they drove.

"My money won't last that long, sir," Caesar said.

"Work for me. I owe your mama a favor. Lottie's always got a house full of kids, and she could use some help around the house."

Caesar thought it over. The army wasn't going anywhere. He might as well wait, see some more of New York, and have some fun. He wished Ed could have come with him, and he thought about writing home to his dad, but he still didn't know what else to say.

They stopped at a restaurant in the Tenderloin to get some food, and everywhere they went, Mr. B was treated like he walked on water. By the time they got back to the hotel, Caesar had decided he was going to stay at the hotel. But he did think that waiting for a few months before going into the service was a good suggestion.

He walked into the lobby to a different clerk at the front desk and said, "I need to speak with Mr. Jimmie Marshall in his office."

The clerk nodded his head, and Caesar walked behind him, opened the door, and went inside. Jimmie was sitting at his desk smoking a fat cigar.

"Mr. Marshall, I think I'm going to stay longer, and I need a job," Caesar said as he stood with his arms at his side.

Jimmie looked at him and wondered why a good-looking kid who appeared to be well taken care of was out on his own. He didn't look like trouble, and Jimmie sensed that he could use a break. "It just so happens that I could use some help in the kitchen. Is that up your alley?" Jimmie asked, holding the cigar between his teeth.

"Yes, sir, it is," Caesar said anxiously.

"I'll speak with my cooks this evening, and you can start tomorrow."

Caesar went up to his room and let his body fall down tired in the chair.He wasn't physically tired, but tired of wrestling with his past. He had seen that there was nothing left of his mother in this town. The world had kept turning and life had moved on, and he was going to have to do the same--no more looking back.

For so long, Caesar felt like he had been rejected, then he had felt abused, but that was over. He wasn't going to be a victim or somebody's whipping board. He was Caesar Portunus, the ruler of his own destiny. Tomorrow was going to be a new day.

Chapter Eight

C aesar thought it was early when he made his way down the steps toward the kitchen, but he could already smell the comfort of country ham, eggs, and hot biscuits. His mouth watered, and his stomach grumbled, but he was going to work, not to eat. Jimmie was sitting there in the dining room area drinking a smoking cup of coffee.

"Good evening, youngster. You're already late for the party," he joked, "We're going to have to get you a clock."

Caesar thought about the expensive watch from Grace that he had left on his bed in Nashville. There was no way he could have ever used it.

"Come on with me," Jimmie said as he raised his long, thin legs up out of his chair and led him to the kitchen.

The hotel kitchen was a huge room with a big stove and a grill on one side, and the other half of the room was a cleaning area with three large sinks. Caesar saw that there were three people working: a heavyset man wearing a short white coat and a tall white hat, a petite woman wearing an apron and her hair tied up in a scarf, and another man, who looked to be in his twenties, washing dishes.

"Morning, crew," Jimmie said. "This here's Caesar; he's going to be working with y'all starting today. He probably don't know the first thing about working in a restaurant, so show him the ropes. He's here to help everybody."

"Welcome to the heart of the Marshall Hotel, Red," the heavyset man said after Jimmie left. "The lounge might be the blood that runs this place, but without the heart, it's dead. My name is Adam; that's Ruth," he said, pointing to the woman. "And that one over there is Johnny."

"Glad to meet y'all," Caesar said as he shook their hands.

"Oh, we finally got somebody in here with some home training, thank the Lord," Adam said. "Do I detect a Southern drawl there? Where you from young man?"

"I was born in Savannah, but I been in Nashville for about six years," Caesar said.

"Well, most of the people up here are from someplace else," Adam said.

"It's about time we got some more help around here. Y'all breaking my back around here," Johnny said.

"Uh-uh, you gon' and do what you been doing. I'm gonna teach this one how to cook," Adam said, waving his hand at Johnny.

"You can't teach what you don't know," Ruth said under her breath as she went back to kneading some dough.

"Remember this, Red, if you don't remember nothing else," Adam said, "A woman really don't have no business being in a restaurant kitchen, they lack the temperament, finesse, and creativity that's needed to prepare a digestible meal."

"Nothing but nonsense," Ruth grunted as she hit the dough hard with a rolling pin.

Breakfast for the guests had already been prepared and after about an hour, the morning rush was over. It was time to set up for the noon meal.

"Now, Red, the way this place is run is like this: I'm the chef, I cook the food with a little help from Ruth here. We give the waiters the menu for the day, the waiters bring in the orders, Ruth makes the plates, the waiters serve them and clear the tables, and Johnny over there cleans the dishes. Our meat is delivered every other day. The staples like flour, corn meal, and sugar are brought in twice a month. Ruth makes the pies and cakes for dessert after breakfast. Now, a fine restaurant serves only the best quality food. The main ingredient in a well-prepared dish is fresh, the fresher the better, so every day I go to the street market under the railroad on Eighth Avenue and over on Lenox. Today you're going with me," Adam said.

"Yes, sir," Caesar answered with enthusiasm, following Adam to the rear door.

Out in the back of the kitchen, there was a truck with the words *Marshall Hotel* printed on it. Adam lifted himself up into the front seat and Caesar hopped in beside him. They drove down Fifth Avenue until they got to Harlem. When they reached 132nd Street, Caesar smelled the cozy aroma of roasted peanuts wafting through the air. Adam pulled the truck over a few blocks down, and they got out. Caesar could see yams roasting and he was reminded that he hadn't eaten.

Adam went to a vendor selling potatoes and said, "Load me up, Jim, and I don't want no eyes on em. Now, you pick your food by the smell, young man. Onions got to have a strong onion smell, a peach got to smell like the juice will burst out from the skin, cheese got to have a good stink on it. And it got to be pretty, boy. If it don't look good, it don't taste good."

"I know some things about food, sir. My father owns a grocery store," Caesar said.

"Is that right? Well, that's good, 'cause it don't pay to be ignorant in this business."

Adam bought fresh green beans and collard greens, and he bought apples and bananas from other street vendors along the street.

Caesar saw to it that everything was loaded in the truck. Down on 135th Street, Caesar could see a crowd around one of the vendors. In the smoke rising above the table next to the newsstand, he saw the biggest woman he had ever seen, with a face that was round and pretty, and when she spoke, he heard a voice that was even bigger.

"What she selling?" Caesar asked.

"Are you hungry, boy? That's Pigfoot Mary, but since we're gentlemen, Mrs. Lillian Dean. She's got the flavor for the folks who's craving a taste of down-home. Hot pig feet, chittlins and hogmaws, and some fried chicken and corn. Her pockets have gotten fat up here; she's one smart woman. Go get you some, son, if you hungry. I prefer to eat higher off the hog myself," Adam said while he waited in the truck.

Caesar stood back and waited his turn in line; he could feel the energy of the people surrounding him as he stood there, the hum of all the sounds blending together and the pungent smells coming from the pots.

"What you want?" Pigfoot Mary's heavy voice bellowed out toward him.

"The chicken," Caesar answered.

Pigfoot Mary wrapped up a leg quarter and a breast in wax paper and put them in a brown paper sack, "Two-bits," she said as she handed him the bag.

Caesar put the money in her hand, and her ruby red-painted lips gave him a quick smile and nod. He climbed into the truck and felt the steam heat in the bag as he reached in to pull out the chicken, even before Adam started to drive. One bite and he was in a temporary heaven. It was crunchy and spicy on the outside, juicy and tender on the inside, with a touch of honey.

He heard Adam chuckle to himself as he watched him eat. "I ain't said the woman can't cook."

They'd just gotten everything unloaded off the truck and into its proper place and made the menu for the day when the butcher came with the meat delivery. Most of it was placed in the ice box, except for a big hunk of beef that Adam placed on the counter. He grabbed a huge knife and began to slice it down into steaks.

"Now, first thing you need to know is meat is like a woman, son. A little fat around the edges ain't gone hurt nobody. If it's too much where I can't find the meat, then I can't use it. If you got quality meat, no matter if it's young or aged, you slice at it gently and handle it carefully. You don't want to disturb the juices and lose the flavor. With some cheap, cantankerous piece of meat with a lot of gristle, you got to beat it to get it tender. Same with fish. If you can smell it from two feet away, it ain't no good, boy. Leave it alone. It'll get you sick.

"Lastly, you don't want no mean old chicken. The meat will be dry. You choose your chicken just like you that Goldilocks. You don't want it too big, muscle meat is tough. If it's too small, you gone be left unsatisfied. You want the one in the middle that's just right."

Caesar worked hard in the restaurant. He hung on Adam's every direction in the kitchen, and on many days, the chef directed him from a chair at the small table and let him do the work. Caesar had also gotten closer to Ruth.Her gentle spirit reminded him of his grammy, and he loved to help her roll out the dough for the pies and stir the batter for the cakes. After he had been working there for a couple of months, she began to ask him questions about his family.

"You are a real gentleman, Caesar," she said. "Whoever raised you, they did a real good job."

"My grammy raised me while my mama worked up here in New York and when she was out on the road," he answered. "When my mama died, Grammy took me to live with my Dad in Nashville. I left as soon as I graduated from high school."

"Do your daddy have a wife?" she asked.

"Yeah, he does," Caesar said in a low voice.

Ruth could see the tension grip in his arm as he beat the batter and the change in his face, and she knew the wife was the reason he had run away.

"You got a girl you sweet on in Nashville?" she asked to ease the strain in the air.

"Yes, ma'am, her name is Rose, but I don't think she gonna wait on me to come back."

"That's all right, man," Johnny interjected from across the room. "There's plenty of girls waiting right here in Midtown. I'm gonna take you out on the town one night."

"Leave him alone," Ruth said. "He don't need none of your trouble."

***

The summer season turned into the fall, and Caesar had adapted well to being on his own. He didn't hang out, and he didn't waste his money. He worked all day and went to his room when the restaurant closed. Johnny really liked him and acted like a big brother to him since he always helped with the clean-up, even though he didn't have to.

Whenever they finished, Johnny would say, "You all right with me, C."

Caesar had mastered his cooking lessons, and with a knife he was as adept as any Japanese warrior. He sliced, diced, and carved a masterpiece within each meal. He could take the leftover scraps from the previous day and make them into soups or sauces that he seasoned with cheese or potatoes. All the food he helped prepare looked like artwork and tasted better. He loved to mix things that would awaken all the taste buds--sour, sweet, and spicy--and treat the mouth to crunchy and smooth textures. Caesar had found out what his gift was.

Business at the Marshall restaurant had picked up, and Jimmie had noticed. In the mornings when Caesar came down to work, Jimmy would say, "Work your magic, son." When the holidays rolled around, they all wondered if he would want to go back home, but Thanksgiving went by with Caesar eating in the dining room with some entertainers who were on the road.

As Christmas closed in, Adam said, "Don't you wanna go home and see your folks, Red?"

"No, sir," Caesar replied. "I closed that door behind me."

"Now don't think that I don't want you here, but somebody there is worried about you and want to see you," Adam told him.

Caesar picked up the large trashcan to empty it, anxious for a reason to get away from the questions. He stood out in the cold and watched the cloud of his hot breath blend in with the cold air. He did miss his Dad and didn't want him to be worried, but he didn't want him to know where to find him. That night after work, he wrote home.

Dear Dad, I'm sorry about not writing you before now but I needed some time to find my way here. I'm doing real good and I have a job cooking in a restaurant. I'm learning a lot and I like it, maybe one day I can have my own restaurant. I haven't joined the service yet and I don't know if I changed my mind about it. I'm writing because I don't want you to worry about me and I hope everything is all right for you. I don't know when I'll be back but I miss you very much. Love Caesar.

David got the letter from Caesar on Christmas Eve, and it was the greatest gift that he could have received. He had been worried sick and had spent many days at home in bed, unable to go to work in his stores. There were several women in town who were trying their best to be a comfort to him after he had left Grace, but he wasn't interested. The last thing he needed was the company of another woman professing her devotion.

From the letter, David could see that his boy was becoming a man, and he was proud of that, but he wanted him home. He had already missed more than half of his life, and now he was missing more. In a week, Caesar would be sixteen years old, and it was another birthday he would miss. He saw the letter was marked in New York, and he wasn't surprised the boy would go there. He thought about going there to look for him, but he knew that even if he found him and brought him home, he couldn't stop him from running off again. Caesar was getting old enough to make his own decisions; and after what he had been through, David didn't blame him for wanting to stay away, he blamed himself.

***

"Tonight is the night, my man," Johnny said to Caesar on New Year's Eve.

He was taking Caesar out on the town for his birthday. The two had planned it for days, and Caesar had even bought himself a new suit of clothes to celebrate. John Reese Europe and The Tempo Club Orchestra would be playing, and it was the place to be that night. It was just past 9:00 as they walked with hunched shoulders in the frigid cold down to the dancehall in the Tenderloin District and when they stepped through the tall red doors into the dimly lit room, Caesar knew he had entered another world.

"Yessir, the ladies are looking good tonight. Let the good times roll," Johnny said as he gave the room a onceover. "Let's check our coats and have some fun."

Everyone in the room was dressed to the nines from the bandstand to the back wall. The band was playing the latest mixture of ragtime with the new jazz sound that was becoming the new rage. The piano set the time, the drums carried the beat, the banjos churned out the melody, but it was the trombones and other horns blowing that seemed to raise their spirits to the roof. The dance floor was filled, and Caesar could fill the beat reaching into his right leg, making it bounce as he stood near the entrance.

"Come on in, man," Johnny said with a grin. "This party is going to last all night."

Caesar watched Johnny go up to a pretty girl in a green dress and lead her out on the dance floor by the arm. His eyes scanned across the room, and he noticed a girl he thought might be around his age in a dress with red and yellow flowers. He was always partial to bright colors, so he went over to her.

"Hello, my name is Caesar," he said politely. "Do you wanna dance?"

She nodded her head, and he took her hand and walked deep into the crowd. Out in the center of the floor, as he began to move, he remembered how much he liked to dance and the feeling of freedom that it always gave him. He danced with her for almost half an hour. They did the cakewalk, the crab, and the foxtrot; and she taught him how to do the snake dip. They danced until the heat of their bodies radiated off of them, erasing all memories of the winter season that lingered at the door.

Caesar didn't know how long it had been since he had so much fun. He didn't have a worry in the world as he moved to the intoxicating beat of the music and felt the exuberance that filled the hall. Caesar could have danced all night. Every girl he asked wanted to dance with the tall, good- looking young man in the blue suit.

"I'm going to get us a coupla beers. It's almost 12:00," Johnny shouted in his ear.

When midnight came, they raised their glasses to the New Year in celebration.

"Happy birthday, C, and Happy New Year!" Johnny hollered out to the ceiling before he grabbed the girl next to him and gave her a kiss.

Caesar followed suit and gave the pretty girl in the flowered dress standing next to him a midnight kiss. Caesar felt like he was truly a man now. Tired and exhausted a few hours later, he and Johnny walked back to the Marshall Hotel.

"Thanks, Johnny, I had a bunch of fun," Caesar said, his breath swirling with the white frost in the darkness.

"Good, my man, that's how it should be," Johnny replied.

Even at the late hour, the streets were alive with people walking and cheering, feeling the hope in the fresh cool air that comes with each New Year. Caesar wished he could have shared this night with Vernon or Ed, the only best friends that he'd had growing up.

***

"My bones are aching something awful today," Adam said on a bitter cold Friday morning in February. "Can you make the market run on your own, C?"

"No problem, Mr. A, I can do that."

Caesar had never been an idle child, and hard work never bothered him. He stayed disciplined and worked long hours in the restaurant, experimenting with flavors and creating new dishes.

"Miss Ruth, I can make the biscuits for you if you want to get your kids off to school before you come," Caesar offered, knowing she had a husband and four kids to take care of.

"Thanks, C, you are a godsend. You baking pies and cakes now as good as I can."

The work became easier for all of them in the kitchen, with Caesar filling in so they could all have days off and spend more time with their families.

"I'm gonna need you to work late on the weekend, Red," Adam added. "You think you can run this ship on your own?"

"Don't give him everything to do," Johnny said, breaking into the conversation. "Boys got to go out and play, too, you know."

Even though Johnny was older and had other friends that he liked to hang with, he always saved some time on the weekend to do something together with Caesar. Most often his favorite thing was to go dancing. Sometimes Caesar forgot how old he was because he didn't get to meet many people his own age at the Marshall. He had always been mature beyond his years, but even more so since he had come to New York.

"Here's your pay, Caesar," Jimmie said, coming in the kitchen as he always did at the end of the week. "I took the rent out already."

"Thanks, Jimmie," Caesar said, pocketing the money.

Caesar planned to save it all this week. Last week he had bought a larger coat, clothes, and shoes since he was still growing taller and bigger. He kept his old habit of splitting his money and putting it in three places, even though he had not had any trouble with anybody stealing from him. Another consequence of his upbringing was that he basically kept to himself, not wanting to become close to people and then have to say goodbye.

"Have you met any girls you sweet on down at the dancehall?" Ruth asked him again.

"I've met a few," Caesar answered. "But not the future Mrs. Portunus."

"Take your time, Red; it ain't no need to rush into that," Adam warned.

Caesar liked the girls that came to the dancehall, and he knew many of their names, but he wasn't looking to get to know any of them. He remembered his grammy telling him that women were gifts from God for men to love, but after Grace, he didn't trust them that much.

The weather broke early that year, and the early spring was bringing more than just a change in the seasons. Caesar liked the job that he had, but he was still a restless young man. As the temperatures got hotter and the days grew longer, he started to lay awake at night, he had the longings of youth, feeling like he was missing something that he needed, and he craved excitement and adventure. When he felt himself tempted to get closer to one of the girls he met at the street market on Lenox Avenue, he knew it was time for him to move on again. There were days when his emotions overwhelmed him, and he even considered going back to Nashville.

On one of the nights that he and Johnny hung down at the dancehall, Caesar saw a giant recruiting poster on the wall for the first Negro National Guard of the State of New York that would be formed in Harlem. His head felt clear, and all of the angst he was feeling was lifted.

"That's it, Johnny!" he exclaimed, looking at the poster. I'm going to join up next week."

***

On June 29, 1916, one year after he graduated from high school, Caesar Portunus went up to the old Lafayette Theatre on 132nd and 7th Avenue to volunteer for the National Guard. The dance hall area was being used as an armory, and there was a very short line of men there to sign up. Caesar lied on his enlistment paper and gave his age as nineteen.

"The men in this regiment will be officer candidates, so you'll have to pass a test before you can be admitted," the registrar said to him when he reached the table.

Caesar was slightly worried as he was led to the table in the rear where the test was to be taken, but he had a good head on his shoulders and was smart with words and numbers. He finished the test within one hour and turned it in.

"Come back in three days, and we'll let you know if you'll be accepted," the registrar stated to Caesar on his way out.

Caesar caught the elevated train for a quick ride back to Midtown. He felt good about his decision. He knew it was something his grandy would have done. He had always told him that a man fights for what is right, and this felt right to him. Back at the restaurant, Caesar went into the kitchen, cleaned up his hands, and put on his apron.

"Where you been all morning?" Adam asked curiously.

Caesar had never stayed away from the kitchen for long during the day.

"I went and did what I came here to do a year ago," he answered.

"What was that?" Ruth inquired, as she peeled the apples for her pie.

"I enlisted in the National Guard," Caesar said proudly.

Ruth bowed her head lower into her pan filled with apples and held her tongue, and Johnny stood at the sink with his elbows deep in the soapy water, shaking his head.

"Well, since it's too late to talk you out of it, let's get some work out of you before you go marching off to war somewhere," Adam said, disappointed with the news.

Caesar had become more like a son to Adam over the last year, and he thought the boy was too good to waste out there fighting the white man's war. For the rest of the day, the only noise heard in the kitchen were the clanging of pots, the clinks of glass against glass, and the sound of stirring or chopping. No one was in the mood for their usual conversations, jokes, or songs.

Two days later, Caesar couldn't wait to get back to the administration office and check on his status. He smelled the tobacco as soon as he walked inside from when the building had previously been a cigar store.

"I'm here to see if I passed the entrance test," Caesar announced when he reached the front of the line.

It didn't take long for the man at the desk to go down the list and find his name. "Yes, Caesar Portunus, welcome to the National Guard," the attendant said.

Caesar held in his jubilation when he first learned that he was now Private Caesar Portunus, a member of the 15th New York Infantry Regiment in the New York National Guard, along with 300 other men. His initial enthusiasm was tempered when he discovered it wasn't exactly the situation that he had imagined. There were no barracks or uniforms for the men, and they were told that they would meet at the armory in the evenings, starting next week, to begin their drills. Caesar went back to the Marshall to make further arrangements with Jimmie since he wouldn't be leaving his room right away after all.

"I can't say I'm disappointed young man," Jimmie said happily after hearing the news. He would accommodate to whatever Caesar needed. "You know I can pull some strings if you change your mind and want to get out of it," he added. Besides, he suspected that Caesar wasn't old enough.

From the time Caesar started working in the restaurant, all of the Marshall's tables stayed full and on many days, some guests had to wait, not to mention, that the number of his fat-wallet white clientele that came in for dinner had doubled. Adam, Ruth, and Johnny were also relieved and glad that he would still be around, at least until the late afternoon. The only person dissatisfied with the circumstances was Caesar. His youthful energy was building, and sometimes he felt like he would explode. He didn't necessarily want to be in the war, but he needed a way to burn off his frustrations.

For the next few months, Caesar worked in the kitchen in the mornings. And then after an early dinner, he went to the Lafayette, where the regiment met.

"Soldiers in formation!" the drill sergeant would bellow once they were all assembled.

"Yes, sir," they responded, taking their places in the squad.

"We don't have our rifles yet, so we're going to practice with these broom handles," the sergeant said as they were handed out.

"These are probably all we'll get!" somebody yelled in the back. "Brooms and shovels."

Some days, Caesar felt foolish as they drilled on the floor of the dance hall and marched with broomsticks. And on many mornings, he woke with stiff shoulders from the trenches they dug in the backyards of houses in Harlem. Most of the men hadn't previously served in the military. And as the numbers grew, they were divided into units, and Caesar was assigned to the machine-gun company.

On the weekends, Caesar volunteered to help his commanding officer, Napoleon Marshall, with the recruiting campaign to enlarge the regiment. He loved it because on those days he got to wear a crisp uniform. They would travel down the streets of Harlem and stand on the busiest corners and hand out fliers. Caesar loved the admiring looks he got from the young women on the street. Their recruiting efforts were working, and the regiment had outgrown the dancehall floor, so their nightly drills moved to the streets.

It was midway through September when Jimmie came into the kitchen with big plans for a shindig at the Marshall Hotel.

"I need y'all to prepare a feast fit for a king on Thursday. There is going to be a big celebration for James Reese Europe here at the Marshall. He just enlisted in the National Guard, and I want to send him off right."

Caesar was thrilled at the news and proud that Mr. Europe was going to be part of his regiment. He thought that maybe it might help them get noticed.

The first of the week, the kitchen looked like a food factory. There were only three days to prepare the meal, and Caesar couldn't work a full day.

"Look here, Red," Adam said early on Wednesday, "We got to carve down half of a cow, cleaned ten chickens, and dress a hog that's gonna be roasted whole. Then we got to go pick up white potatoes and sweet potatoes, turnip greens and collard greens, baked beans and green beans, corn bread, French bread and Italian bread, and all kinds of fresh fruit."

"I got it covered, sir," Caesar said. "Easy work for a soldier, Captain."

"We'll see," Adam said, feeling some doubt.

On Thursday morning, Caesar helped Ruth work on a cake that was five layers high and three flavors. Johnny stayed busy handling all the deliveries that came all through the day and washed up all the dishes. The kitchen was so hot with all the boiling and baking that they stood out in the back whenever their hands weren't busy. Jimmie hired extra help to host and serve; he wanted everything to be at its highest quality.

The celebration spread throughout the Marshall, including the restaurant and the lounge. Caesar put on his uniform, but he was amazed at how fine all the black people were dressed in their tuxedos and formal gowns and at how many whites had come out to support Mr. Europe.

The liquor and wine was in as great abundance as was the food, and the music from the small orchestra was superb. Caesar could tell that the man they called Reese was held in great esteem by more than just the entertainment community. When Mr. Europe came forward to conduct the band, the crowded room cheered, and exhilaration filtered through the smoke in the air, and even Caesar was buoyed and ready to go off to war.

When folks stood up from their tables to dance, Caesar saw Bert Williams across the room and went over to speak. "Hello, sir," he said with a handshake.

"I see you went on and signed up. Good for you. Your mama would be proud of you, C. Just don't give them all you got," Bert said with a squeeze to his hand before dancers on the floor stepped through and separated them.

The party went on for hours, and Caesar could sense hope in the room from everyone there. What they were really celebrating was the idea that black people defending their country was going to change things for the better. At the end of the evening, he didn't want to say goodbye to Adam, Ruth, and Johnny. He was tired of so many goodbyes.

"I'll see them when I come back," he said to himself as he packed his things and went back to the armory.

Chapter Nine

"Attention, troops," Colonel Marshall said, addressing the 15th Regiment after blowing his whistle. "As you all may have noticed, our supplies are slowly but steadily drifting in. We now have rifles, even though they are without bayonets."

"I guess they're afraid we might hurt ourselves going through all these drills in the dark," someone in the back heckled.

"I want to commend you men on the adeptness in your drill maneuvers and announce that donations for sports equipment, a record player, and magazines have come in. In spite of all of these encouraging developments, our enlisting numbers are falling off target. Colonel Hayward, in an effort to lift morale and increase recruitment, has commissioned James Reese Europe to form a military marching band."

"That ought to really make a difference!" the heckler yelled.

It took some time and effort but soon they formed a small regiment band that led the platoon in military parades in Central Park and around Harlem.

"Man, this is embarrassing," a fellow soldier yelled as the newly formed band screeched through the tunes.

Caesar didn't think they sounded that good either as he marched behind them, but for him it felt good enough just to belong and to be a part of a group. He had felt so alone for a long time, and now he had a new family.

By the end of 1916, things were coming together for the 15th Regiment marching band. More professional band musicians, including Noble Sissle, had been recruited, and their numbers had grown to 65 members, and it was like night went into day. They sounded like they were ready to lead an army whenever they played. Yet, the only action the enlisted men had encountered was the cold temperatures as they drilled on the freezing streets of New York City. Caesar gritted his teeth to keep from shivering in the bitter air of December as he marched on, unaware that things were about to drastically change.

***

When the winter season gave way to the spring in 1917, the 15th Regiment numbered around 1,400 men. At the beginning of April, President Wilson declared war on Germany.

Colonel Marshall addressed the troops, "The 15th regiment has been recognized by the War Department as a viable unit, and we have been instructed to raise our numbers to war strength. We are even more pleased to announce that even Bill 'Bojangles' Robinson has also enlisted and will be performing with the band."

A few weak cheers rose from the troops; most were resigned to their present conditions. Nevertheless, the extra 600 men needed were recruited in only five days from Harlem, Manhattan, Brooklyn, and the Bronx, even after submitting to more stringent physical examinations than those for admission in the army.

"Portunus, you are assigned to distributing the uniforms and equipment to the men," Colonel Marshall said to Caesar.

"Yes, sir, Colonel," Caesar said, going into the equipment room.

When the line formed, he took note of more young guys around his age who'd enlisted, and he couldn't help but feel that they all might have a lot in common. After they all received their uniforms and supplies, they were called to order.

"Attention, men. On Sunday morning, this regiment will be marching first to the elevated train, where we'll ride to Grand Central Station, and then to New York Central Railroad, on our way to the New York Military Reservation near Peekskill for boot camp."

Caesar made a mental note of the day. It was May 13, 1917. He got up early, dressed, and lined up with the other young men in the regiment. They shared kindred looks of pride as crowds of family and friends cheered them all along the route. Caesar felt like a man among men as they stepped high behind the inspiring music from the band.

At the camp, they drilled and trained there for the next 18 days. While they took direction, the men sized one another up to determine the pecking order: who was the strongest, the smartest, the weakest, who looked like trouble, who you could trust, and who might be a good friend. Caesar would look around him and wonder what different circumstances brought them all to the point where they would volunteer to risk their lives. Were some running, like him, or did they have something to prove?

"Come on, pretty boy, show us what you got," a cocky guy named Jones said, throwing short jabs in the air at Caesar.

"Why you picking on the young boy?" one of the other older fellas asked.

"What's your problem?" Jones snapped. "They man enough to enlist. That's why they here, to fight. He shouldn't have no problem with a little sparring match."

Charles Jones was from Brooklyn. He had enlisted after losing his job at Grand Central. He loved to be the center of attention, and they all called him Jones. He wasn't that handsome. He was skinny, short, with bumpy skin; but he thought himself a pretty boy and wore his hair parted down the middle. Caesar didn't trust him because whenever he laughed or talked, because he only used one side of his mouth.

"I can take care of myself," Caesar said, getting up on his feet.

Jones threw a jab before Caesar planted his feet. His chin felt the hard feelings of Jones behind the punch. He countered with a hit to Jones's jaw.

The punch staggered Jones. "You got one in, young boy. Come on and get another," he sneered, bouncing up and down and coming forward swinging high.

Caesar had all the good looks that Jones felt he should have been born with, and somewhere in his mind he hoped he would leave a scar or bruise on him that would disfigure his pretty face. Fortunately, Caesar was nearly a foot taller and was twice as fast. Jones's fist never made it to its target again.

"I couldn't tell if it was all in sport or if you two was actually fighting," another one of the young guys said to Caesar when Jones finally backed off.

"We ain't never been friendly, but he don't bother me," Caesar said. He had been up against a tougher opponent than him in his own home.

In nature, like goes with like, the young men gravitated to each other, those from the South related to each other, the religious prayed together; and those who liked to smoke, drink, and gamble communed together. In Caesar's circle, they were all less than 20 years old, and most were already working and on their own. They all became more familiar with each passing day; and the more Caesar listened, the more he realized every black man there had his own story to tell. By the time they came back to New York for a military parade of the National Guard, they had been unified.

"I'm looking damn good in this uniform," Jones said, strutting across the floor in the makeshift military base inside the dancehall.

"If you say so," Caesar said as he rolled up his blanket roll, and made sure it was properly placed on his shoulder, and positioned his rifle at his right arm.

They all looked good in the regulation uniforms as they marched down the streets behind the band, and they knew it.

"We're all dressed up with nowhere to go," Caesar heard someone behind him murmur.

Halfway through the month of July, they were sworn into the United States Army and then sent to Camp Whitman in Poughkeepsie, New York. Bonds were formed between the men as they realized that they were really soldiers; and if they ever made it into the war, they would carry each other's lives in their hands. Caesar had spent most of his life as a loner with few friends, and now he was surrounded by hundreds of men who had sworn to fight to the death for their regiment.

Back at the barracks, Caesar walked up to introduce himself to some of the new recruits to whom he had issued uniforms.

"Hey, fellas, my name's Caesar Portunus," he said, holding out his hand for a shake. "You guys are the only ones here who look younger than I do."

"Needham Roberts is my name," the youngest looking one said, smiling at his remark.

"Henry Johnson," the shortest one said, shaking hands.

"Can anybody come to this party?" another new recruit asked in a heavy Southern accent as he stepped into the group. "I'm Stormy Robinson."

"Glad to meet all y'all," Caesar told them. "I'm from Nashville by way of Savannah. Where y'all from?"

"I was born in North Carolina, but I'm from Albany. I got a wife and a baby boy there," Henry Johnson answered.

"I'm from Newark, New Jersey," Needham added.

"I'm a country boy right out of Mississippi," Stormy Robinson said, pulling on the waist of his pants. "But we might as well make ourselves at home right here and get our bunks before we end up sleeping outside."

Caesar and Stormy became bunk mates and after they got their belongings situated, they went over to the mess hall to eat.

"You got much family in Mississippi?" Caesar asked Stormy.

"I guess I still do. There's my mama and daddy, my twin sister, and two younger brothers."

"That's sounds okay. I wish I had a brother or a sister. Things would have been a lot easier," Caesar said.

"When you daddy is a dirt-poor sharecropper growing cotton in the red dirt of Tunica, it just amounts to another mouth to feed," Stormy remarked, shaking his head. "What made you join up? You don't seem like you need room and board."

"You'd be surprised," Caesar said. "Everybody's here for one reason or another."

"I was running up north for my life," Stormy joked, but it was the gospel truth. "This white girl smiled at me one day when I was at the general store with my daddy. I smiled back, and, unfortunately, the storekeeper spotted me and ordered us 'black niggers' out of the store. When we got outside, my daddy gave me the last few coins in his pocket and told me to get as far away from Mississippi as I could."

"We do what we gotta do to survive. Sometimes it's running," Caesar said, thinking of himself.

By the end of the meal, the two were best buddies. To Caesar, Stormy was just fun to be around. He got up in the morning with a smile, no matter how bad things were, and he ended the day the same way, no matter what they went through. They had little in common in the way they were raised but they were similar in many ways. They were both tall and strong, intense young men searching for something. They pushed themselves hard in whatever they did, work or play. They rarely got tired of all the drills, platoon maneuvers, and combat tactics that they ran through all day and favored rifle practice, where they trained in the attack and defense of the enemy. They only thing they didn't like was all the manual labor they were called to do.

The confidence among all the recruits was growing, along with their defensive skills, when word spread about an attack on a colored National Guard unit in Houston, Texas.

"I hear thirteen soldiers was hanged, and forty-one others were sent to jail for life," Stormy told Caesar as they laid in their bunks.

"I don't know if we training to fight them white folks down south or the ones over in Germany," Caesar commented.

The morale at the Whitman Camp fell like a brick; and with less than thirty days training under their belts, they were ordered back to New York for construction work and to guard tunnels and bridges around the city. In October, the 15th Regiment got orders from the War Department to report for training at Camp Wadsworth in Spartanburg, South Carolina.

"Oh, hell," said Stormy. "I done worked my ass off to get up here away from them hoogies, and now they gonna send me right back."

"It's not just one of us now, Storm," Caesar said. "We an army now."

"It don't make no difference to them, C," Stormy replied.

There wasn't one black infantry man in the 15th who wanted to go down South. The protests from the mayor of the city and the whites in the town had gone out loud and clear.

"We not even soldiers to them; they think we just some uppity niggers," Jones said.

The men who had lived in the South knew firsthand that Jim Crow was crazy, and the others didn't even want to meet him face to face. The only combat they wanted to see was overseas against the Germans. The enthusiasm in the regiment drained to a new low as the train traveled south, and qualms of confrontations with their native enemy preoccupied all of their thoughts.

"Let's play some music," Lt. Europe said to the band to lighten the mood.

The music distracted them for a while, and the men took turns showing off their best steps.

When the troops finally got to their provisional station area, all they found was a partially cleared field in the middle of a pine forest.

"See, man, I told you," Stormy said.

"Yeah, I guess it's business as usual," Caesar said as they looked for a temporary place to pitch their tent.

The troops were divided up into teams for cutting down the small trees and brush, building the camp, and digging ditches for drainage. The younger men, which included Caesar and his pals, were assigned to the digging. They had energy to burn after being cooped up on the train for two days.

"Fellas, I don't think I need to worry much about getting shot by them Germans. It's my back that's killing me in this army," Stormy joked.

"Back and feet!" somebody else yelled.

Then Henry added, "It's these damn mosquitos," and they all laughed.

Once the camp was set up, the supplies came in, and the men were issued heavy underwear and trench shoes for taking overseas.

Still, the whites in the town were looking for trouble, and the men had been advised by Colonel Hayward to ignore any insults that would be used to provoke them.

"I'm going stir-crazy out here in these woods," Stormy said to Caesar while they were on their weekend break.

"Let's go into town and look around," Caesar suggested.

A small group that included Caesar, Stormy, Henry, and three other soldiers walked through town that evening.

"Let's find somewhere to buy a beer," Jones said, tagging along with the young guys.

"We don't serve niggas in here," was the response they got from the first little joint they ventured in.

They soon discovered that everything was closed to them, and they couldn't get any service or buy stuff anywhere. They gave up their hope of having a good time and were headed back to camp.

"Get outta my way, boy," a white man passing by with a woman said as he pushed Caesar off the sidewalk, making him stumble into the street.

"Don't get hot under the collar," Stormy said as Caesar stepped back on the walk.

Henry and the others tensed up, waiting for an angry response, but it didn't even faze Caesar. He had been used to ignoring physical attacks for a long time.

"It takes more than that to get me riled up," he assured them.

Nonetheless, all hell broke loose when Noble Sissle was attacked by a hotel owner for not taking off his hat when he went inside the lobby to buy a newspaper. Fortunately, the white National Guard soldiers standing around closed ranks and were ready to fight in their fellow infantry man's defense, and any plans for rioting and lynching were quickly put to rest. Needless to say, the atmosphere in the town was like a powder keg, and as a precautionary measure, the 15th broke camp on October 24, after only twelve days.

Even in their precarious position as soldiers going to war, the 15th Regiment breathed a sigh of relief on the train back up north.

On the long train ride, while most of the troops were sleeping, Caesar noticed another man who reminded him of Johnny back at the Marshall restaurant writing in a tablet. Watching him, Caesar decided that he should write a letter to his dad back home since it looked like they would be finally leaving the States and going overseas. In a few swift motions, he slid closer to the guy to ask if he could spare some paper.

"Who you writing to?" Caesar asked.

"Not writing," he answered. "I'm drawing."

"Are you an artist?"

"I don't make a living at it. I do whatever I have to do to get by, but it's what I do best," he answered. Caesar moved to his side and watched him for a while as he created life on the paper, sketching the other soldiers as they slept.

"My name's Caesar Portunus. My buddies call me C," he said to him.

"I'm Horace Pippin, and I'm wondering," he said as he kept drawing, "what's a young man like you doing in the army?"

"I don't know," Caesar answered. "I guess I'm trying to find my way."

Horace nodded in understanding, and they sat in silence, him drawing, and Caesar watching.

The 15th arrived at Camp Mills in Long Island, New Jersey, for more training and preparation before they would set sail for France. Everything seemed to be a major ordeal for the regiment.

"I'm tired of these stacks of paper we have to fill out," Stormy said.

"It's all the shots that we have to take that are killing me," Caesar added. "All this to-do, and we still don't have enough rifles to go around."

"If it only took marching in the street and looking good, we'd already won this war by ourselves," Stormy said chuckling.

The regiment had shifted around so much that they called themselves the Traveling Fifteenth. They were beginning to doubt if they would ever make it across the waters to fight when they received word that they had been assigned a ship.

"I can't believe we finally going to France to fight," Stormy said as the troops marched to the pier and boarded the *Grand Republic*. The ship that would transport them and their supplies and equipment to Hoboken, New Jersey. It was there they would board the S.S. *Pocahontas*.

It was becoming more real to Caesar, and the butterflies had returned to his stomach, except now they felt more like hummingbirds. The fluttering upset his insides, causing his bowels to empty, and for several hours, he couldn't move more than five steps away from the toilet.

It took two days to get everything loaded onto the *S.S. Pocahontas*. All of the muscles in Caesar's body were tight with apprehension; he forced his body to move with each trip back and forth as they carried the baggage.

"I thought I wanted to do this; now I'm not so sure," he said to Stormy as they walked back for another load. "I'm thinking about walking away."

"Well, if you gonna do it, you better hurry up 'cause we are on our way," Stormy replied.

When they finished, Stormy put his arm around Caesar's shoulder and said, "Don't worry, C. When we come back, we'll be heroes, and we can do whatever we want. Besides, what are we leaving that's so wonderful?"

Late into the night on November 11, 1917, Caesar stood against the railing on the side of the ship as the *Pocahontas* was ushered out into the Hudson River to join the convoy of ships. He watched the space between the ship and the pier widen, and he knew that the time for him to change his mind had passed. He stood there in the crowd of men as the city lights and shadows along the shoreline faded from his view. Caesar felt his stomach calm as his nerves resigned themselves to the unknown waiting for him on the other side of the Atlantic.

Few of the men had been aboard a boat, much less a ship of that size. Caesar had grown up near the sea, but he had never been on water where you couldn't see the shore. The ocean seemed to have no limits in its width or depth, and he felt lost. The comfort was in the number of ships that sailed around them.

"Bad news, soldiers," Colonel Marshall said, addressing the group a few hours into the voyage. "We're going to reverse course and head back to the pier in Hoboken. One of our steam engines has broken down, and we're losing speed. The convoy has gotten away from us, and we're vulnerable to enemy attacks sailing solo. We've been assigned to Camp Merritt in New Jersey for more labor duty, building on the camp while we wait for the repairs to the engine."

The excitement of the journey overseas dissipated like the air out of a popped balloon. The infantry's opportunity to fight was again put on hold.

Back at the pier, Caesar rushed off the ship with Stormy and Needham, wondering if this misfortune was a blessing in disguise. By the time the train got to Camp Merritt, they knew it wasn't. It was bitter cold and miserable there, and quite a few of the men with wives and children went AWOL.

"This war has me all mixed up," Stormy said. "I can't decide what's worse: taking my chances on crossing that ocean or staying here breaking my back with my toes freezing off."

"If I had known this is what it's like to be a soldier in the black man's army, I wouldna signed up," Caesar said.

"Well, if you want to go, you still got a chance, C. I ain't got nothing to go back to," Stormy said as he hammered two boards together.

Caesar gave it a second thought, but he had come so far, and he was determined to do what he came to do. After all, his grandy wouldn't have gone back. Then he remembered that he hadn't written his dad.

Dear Dad, It seems like it won't be long before my regiment sails out for France, and I've been thinking about you. You're the only family I have left, and I feel sorry for the way I left without talking about things. I want you to know that I never blamed you, and I didn't mean to make you suffer. Now that I am older, I can see that I didn't have to runaway. But I don't have any regrets for coming here. It was good for me to come. I figured out what I want to do with my life, even though I feel like I'm putting my plans at risk by going to fight. I don't have my grammy to pray for me, so I hope you will. I don't know what's ahead for me in France, but I'll be coming back home when it's all over. Love,C

For the next three weeks, the infantry battled against low morale and frostbite, while they worked in the freezing wet conditions of the camp.After a pitiful Thanksgiving, when they all had found little to be thankful about, Stormy woke up Caesar and said, "We're going back on the ship."

Caesar didn't know if he was happy or sad about the news. Back on the *Pocahontas* after a day of reloading the ship, he had barely laid his head down in his berth when the fire bell sounded.

"There's a fire in the coal bunker!" Corporal Pippin informed them. "Our sailing will be delayed yet again."

Caesar threw back his head exasperated. The ship was cursed. And when they got word that they would be confined on the ship while the bunker was cleaned out and reloaded, he was fit to be tied.

"We need to get this show on the road, or either shut it down," he complained to his buddies down below.

"Yeah, I'd rather pull my teeth out than sit here waiting like a mouse in a trap," Stormy added.

Once the *Pocahontas* was repaired again, it was tugged out into the Hudson River away from the pier to wait for the next convoy. However, the cloud of misfortune that surrounded them refused to lift, and they were engulfed in a powerful snowstorm through the night. The blizzard dropped blankets of snowfall on the river, and the strong gusts of winds felt like sheets of ice railing against the ship, and the white-out created zero visibility. They were already unnerved when they felt a big jolt and then a crash. Alarm shot through the ship when they realized that a British ship had collided into theirs.

"What was that?" Caesar asked, jumping out of his bunk.

"We got to see what's going on," Stormy said, rushing out of the door.

A large group of men had already gathered on the deck in the winter cold air to see the damage. Caesar stood with them until the frost accumulated around his eyes and in his nose, his skin tightened, and his lips were dry and cracked.

"I promise you that if we go back to the shore again, I'm not getting back on this God-forsaken ship, Stormy." He wouldn't get the chance. The machine shop unit repaired the hole in the bow on the spot. Two days later, on December 14, 1917, the *Pocahontas* set sail for France again, and the third time was a charm. Once the ship got out on the ocean, it was smooth sailing for the rest of the voyage.

***

"I want to volunteer for kitchen patrol," he said to Colonel Marshall.

He missed cooking and he hoped it would free him up from all the manual duties on the *Pocahontas.*

"Nobody on this ship is going to fight you for that privilege, Private Portunus, your request is granted."

For the rest of the kitchen crew, it was just a chore, but Caesar was back in his element preparing the meals on the ship. Like any man, he loved a challenge, and from breakfast through dinner, he was a formidable participant. He made the morning grits sing, and the afternoon stews kept many of the men from pining away for the food they ate at home. He remembered the lessons from Adam that half the battle was in the presentation and the aroma. Conversations strayed from the usual quick money, fast women, and how many Germans they would kill to what Caesar had for the next meal.

The Christmas dinner was his greatest triumph. He spent the whole day roasting the turkeys, fussing over them like a mother hen, until their skins were crisp and golden brown, having trapped all the delicious juices inside. The smells wafted through the ship and it actually felt like the holiday.

"Gon' and give the prayer, Needham," Jones said at mealtime. "A preacher's kid ought to know how to bless the food."

Needham said a short blessing, and they all started to eat. Caesar had seasoned the potatoes and the canned vegetables to perfection, and they tasted like he picked them from his grammy's Southern garden. He had also prepared dessert, a bread pudding shaped like a cake.

At the table, Horace said, "C, you didn't tell me you were an artist yourself."

Caesar smiled and said, "I have been told that I work a little magic."

"Making this mess taste good is not small-time magic," Horace said. "You, my friend, are a master magician."

After the feast, the band played Christmas songs, and the men danced and sang.

Two days later, land was sighted, and the ship arrived safely in the port of Brest on January 1, 1918. It was Caesar's eighteenth birthday when his feet finally touched French soil. Lt. Europe and the regimental band assembled and began to play the French National anthem in solidarity with the French soldiers, but it was premature. The 15th National Guard combat soldiers were loaded onto boxcars and transported to St. Nazaire.

"Looks like Jim Crow beat us over here," Stormy said when they saw the segregated toilets. "The black man's work is never done."

"Yeah, they shipped us over here to dig some more ditches," Caesar said.

"Stop your complaining," Colonel Marshall said. "What doesn't kill you makes you stronger." That was the truth, and the men got stronger unloading ships, hauling lumber, digging ditches, building roads, and making bomb shelters.

Chapter Ten

The YMCA set up sheds for the soldiers at Brest, where they could come and relax and read books and magazines when they couldn't get passes to leave camp. Caesar and his crew liked to go there and watch the entertainment from singers and musicians, to the picture shows in the evening. From time to time, the Y would sneak in lectures on health and moral behavior that the soldiers usually ignored.

The women of the Y planned a welcoming party to lift the morale of the men; they decorated the shed with lights and changed into evening dresses to add to the festivities. It was unfortunate that too few women were assigned duty around the black troops with the rationale that the black soldiers were too rough to be around. When the two lone women returned to the shed to host, it was filled with over a thousand soldiers, and the women were so overwhelmed by the sight of them that they canceled the event.

There was also a canteen run by a young black woman from the American Expeditionary Force. She sold donuts, pie, ice cream and hot chocolate to the soldiers.

"That's the one I want over there," Stormy said as he pointed to her and walked over to the canteen.

Caesar followed and she smiled and greeted them as she did all the soldiers. She knocked them over with dimples that accented a smile that lit up her whole face.

"Hello, ma'am, my name is Stormy Robinson, and I would like to make your acquaintance," he said as he held out his hand.

She laughed and put her hand in his and said, "Pleased to meet you, Mr. Robinson. I'm Sarah Thompson."

Stormy continued with his Southern gentleman routine. "May I ask if you are a married woman, Miss Sarah?"

"I am single, Mr. Robinson," she answered with a gleaming smile.

"Very good, ma'am, because I intend to make you my wife," he added.

They all laughed, and she poured them two cups of hot chocolate with donuts. After that, every chance he got, Stormy was at the canteen trying to sell Sarah on a life with him after the war.

Back at their barracks, they stretched out on their bunks, and Caesar drifted into thought. So many of the men in the regiment were anxious to fight, but that didn't make any difference to him. He was already looking past combat, wondering what he was going to do when he got back to the States.

He rolled over on his side and asked Stormy, "What are you gonna do when we get back home?"

"I don't have no home to go to," Stormy answered. "I'm going wherever you go when this is over."

"I want to open my own restaurant. I want it to be nice, with a classy band to play in it," Caesar said.

"That sounds good, man. I'll get a piece of land to grow you some corn, potatoes, and some greens," he said with a smile. "Shoot, I might even raise up some chickens for you to fry. Yeah," he said as he leaned back into a daydream. "Me and Miss Sarah. If I can get that sweetie to marry me and have some wild kids to run around the place, my life might work out after all."

Europe and his band had been transferred and reassigned for six weeks to entertain and raise the morale of the British and French soldiers all over France who were on leave. Some of the troops were assigned to guard the German prisoners; the rest of the 15th regiment were issued picks and shovels and served as manual labor for whatever backbreaking work that needed to be done. With no hopes of seeing combat, regiment morale was low within the unit; it went lower to nonexistent when they were assigned to lay railroad tracks down on the frozen ground.

"I guess every black man looks like John Henry to these white folks," Pippin said with a smirk while they worked.

"My grandy was a slave, and this don't seem much different than that to me," Caesar added as he hammered the huge nails down.

"Yeah, we thought we signed up to fight in the war, but we just sold ourselves back to the master," Stormy laughed.

They spent the rest of the brutal winter lifting and toting, but the seasons were about to change in more than one aspect.

Things shifted in mid-March when the battle-weary French army needed reinforcements. The 15th regiment was assigned to the French Fourth Army and renamed the 369th US Infantry Regiment of the 93rd Combat Division.

"My daddy said be careful what you ask for, and he was right on that. I can even hear the artillery firing and air raids from way out here," Needham said to Caesar when they got to the small village where they stationed.

It was about fifteen miles front the front lines.

"I never thought I would end up a soldier in the French Army," Caesar said, standing in the line where they were issued French equipment: brown helmets, brown belts and pouches, rifles and ammunition, bayonets, gas masks, knapsacks, and food. "I doubt they'll let me get on kitchen patrol. These French don't have no problem with us fighting."

"At least they showing us some respect. That's more than I can say for my comrades in the US Army," Stormy said.

"It won't matter when we crouching out in the trenches facing them German bullets aimed at us," Caesar said back in the barracks.

Lying in his bunk, he turned over on his stomach and did what his grammy always told him to do when he felt alone. He prayed.

Training with the French troops was like entering another world for Caesar. Away from any other American troops, they learned French combat tactics and trained in hand-to-hand bayonet combat. All the sparring boxing matches and roughhousing that Caesar and his buddies had used to fight off boredom in the camps had served to sharpen their defensive skills. And when they practiced throwing the dummy hand grenades, it was as simple as throwing a baseball at one of their games.

He and the men of the 369th learned enough of the French language to follow orders, and they did everything that the French soldiers did. They had red wine at 10:00 in midmorning and they had dinner at a much later hour. They ate together, did drills together, and they attended the entertainment shows together without any separation.

"Our time is coming, men," Colonel Marshall said to the trips on All Fool's Day after the morning meal, "The 369th regiment has been ordered to move closer to the front. You all will receive your assignments before we proceed. The leadership of the band will be passed over to Sergeant Sissle, and Lt. Europe will be the head of the machine gun unit. Lieutenant, come forward, and call off the names of your unit."

Lt. Europe began calling his list, and Caesar heard his name and then Stormy's.

"Attention, soldiers, we will be training to use the French machine guns," Lt. Europe said as the men gathered around him.

Caesar wouldn't dare admit it to anyone, but he was starting to feel afraid. He could feel the power of the gun vibrate as the rounds of ammunition shot out of its nose, but it was no comfort to him. He realized that as much as he wanted to live through this war, he didn't have a desire to kill anyone else.

After the evening meal, Caesar and Stormy stood side by side looking out toward the front lines in the darkness of night.

"It reminds me of the fireworks celebrations at Greenwood Park back home on New Year's Day and the Fourth of July," Caesar mused as he stared at the explosions and flashes of light from the gunfire and the rockets.

One week later, the band played as Europe and the 369th marched out of the small town with one French soldier for every soldier from the 369th, or as they were now known, the Black Rattlers. They were off to a ten-day tour of duty in the trenches on French night patrol. Horses pulled the wagons that carried the artillery guns, and the infantry men were weighed down with equipment, food, and canteens filled with everything from water to coffee, and even wine.

"Take your positions, men," Lt. Europe commanded as they dropped down into the trenches dug deep to their shoulders just before sunset.

There was a lull in the fire, but it didn't last long once darkness fell.

"Damn!" Caesar hollered when the adrenalin shot through his heart as he ducked the rounds of enemy fire aimed in their direction.

The shells blew away the fear that had taken residence there. In the midst of the onslaught, he glanced at the men around him in the trench-- Stormy, Horace, Jones, and three other French soldiers--as they huddled below the surface of the ground to reload their three-shot rifles.

"This is it, C. We gonna get our chance to fight!" Stormy said as they hunched low in the earth. Beneath the sound of Stormy's voice, Caesar suddenly heard rustling coming toward him and poised his rifle for attack.

"Oh, shit!" he shrieked when an army of fearless rats ran across their boots and through their supplies.

If Caesar didn't know it before, he knew it then; he had signed up for a stint in hell. The shots of enemy fire became the background noise to his battle in the muddied trenches. Late hours into the night and in the early morning were the toughest. It was then that he fought the Fritzies, the cramps in his legs from crouching, and the rats for his food. The daylight hours were easier; the artillery slowed, and the vermin ran for cover.

It was also in the light of day that Horace drew pictures of what he saw around them while Jones favored them with more stories of his exploits with beautiful women. Caesar did a lot of listening. He wasn't comfortable talking about himself; it only led to more questions that he didn't want to answer.

"You're a helluva shot, Stormy," Caesar said. "Where'd you learn to shoot like that?"

"Man, my daddy used to take me and by brothers hunting in Mississippi around the land we farmed all the time. Lots of days, that was the only way we ate. When we came home empty-handed from the hunt, our bellies stayed empty, too. That's how I got to be such a good shot. I got so I could hit a hopping bullfrog in the air, and its feet would never touch the ground."

"A man does what he gotta do to live and feed his family," Henry added.

When the relief came at the end of the tour of duty, they were more like brothers than when they first came out to the front. They had depended on each other and they had survived the tour. The first order of business was to get out of the filthy and muddy uniforms they had worn for the last ten days. The second was to sit down and have a good meal.

"I say we head over to one of the cafes in town," Pippin suggested after they were cleaned up. "I hear they treat us as well as anybody else here."

"Let's go," Stormy said, leading the way.

"That'll give me chance to get a taste of more French food," Caesar said in agreement.

"I hear that the wine flows in them places like water," Jones said, trailing behind them.

They found a nice cafe just outside of their base that was full of soldiers on leave. The French waitress made no difference between them and the other American soldiers who were seated on the other side of the room. The four of them--Stormy, Caesar, Pippin, and Jones--ate and drank in peace until they were all satisfied.

They sat there enjoying the mood and killing time, when Jones said, "I'm gonna get to know our pretty waitress a little better."

When she came over to the table, Jones stood up and leaned in close to her and whispered something in her ear.

"You are very funny," she said to him in English, but when she laughed, it caught the attention of a white American soldier.

He jumped to his feet and rushed over to the table and said, "What's wrong, nigger? That uniform got you thinking you somebody, that you can speak to a white woman? You don't need to fight, nigger. I'll kill you right here."

Before any of them could react, two French soldiers came over and got between them and the white American soldier. Their fellow American backed down, and they were all relieved.

"I didn't make it off that battlefield to die in a tavern over a woman," Caesar said to Stormy. "I don't need to come off the base."

"No, man, we just need to leave Jones behind," Stormy replied.

***

It was the second week of May, Caesar was on his third rotation and he had become more comfortable and confident with all the chaos that swirled around him. He was assigned to night watch and listening post duty with Privates Stormy Robinson, Henry Johnson, Needham Roberts, and Corporal Allen London. It was the most dangerous of positions on the field. They watched from a hole that was over one hundred yards ahead of the trench line to warn of possible attacks from the Fritzies.

Most nights, Caesar looked out into the black night so long that there were some moments in the darkness when he wasn't sure if his eyes were still open. But on this night, the moon was almost full. Henry Johnson and Needham Roberts were on dog watch, a two-man watch on the observation post several yards further out in no-man's-land.

"It seems like it might be quiet tonight," Corporal London said to Caesar and Stormy. "I'm gonna get some shut-eye."

"I could use some sleep, too," Stormy said, stretching out sideways in the trench.

It was in the early morning hours that they heard explosions close to their position. Caesar wasn't sure if he was still dreaming or if his nightmare was a reality. He listened in horror to the gunfire and whistles of flares fast approaching the observation post.

Henry Johnson had gone out to investigate a noise that he suspected was a rat, only to find German soldiers had cut through the barbed wire around the post in a raid.

"Here they come!" he yelled to Needham as he ran back into the hole.

The force from the grenade blast threw Henry and Needham against the back of the hole and showered them both with shrapnel, hitting Needham in his arms and legs and Henry in the head and back.

"Take this, Fritzie!" Henry shouted as he opened fire on the Germans.

Still in a daze and his ears ringing from the explosion, Henry shot one in the chest as they rushed into the post, but he was shot three times.

"Needham, I'm out of ammunition," he said to Roberts as he used the butt of the rifle to hit a homerun on the head of a German soldier who'd come into the post.

"Throw the grenades, Henry, maybe we can hold the rest back!"

Johnson and Roberts were still lobbying grenades from their cache when Johnson saw Roberts being overtaken by three German soldiers. Wounded and struggling to stay conscious and on his feet, Johnson took out his bolo knife and put the last of his strength in a blow that split one soldier's head open and nearly cut another in half at his belly. The German platoon had not expected this fierce fight and began to retreat before reinforcements came. Johnson threw more hand grenades behind them as they ran. It seemed as if he had fought them for an eternity, but it had happened in a matter of minutes.

"Something's going wrong in the observation post," Corporal London said, awakened by the commotion.

He got his bearings and eased out to investigate. He signaled for Caesar and Stormy to follow. With rifles in their hands, they hustled low to the ground up to the observation post.

"They're both hurt bad, but they're still alive," London said when they reached the hole.

They saw Henry had multiple wounds from knives and bayonets, and when he saw them, he mumbled some words before he lost consciousness.

"We're gonna have to carry them back. Neither of them can walk," Corporal London said.

Corporal London and Caesar carried Johnson and Stormy carried Roberts back to the station, where they were both rushed to a French hospital.

"Man, they saved us fighting off those Germans," Caesar said, impressed by Henry's courage and determination.

Inspired by the two young men, Caesar swore that he would never lay down and die. He had seen the blood of the Germans, and it had flowed red just like his own; they weren't much different than him. They were all just young men sent out there to fight for something they barely understood. One thing was true: they could die as easily as anyone else.

Chapter Eleven

The 369th continued to fight on the Champagne front in eastern France and gained the name Hellfighters by the Germans for their unyielding tenacity in battle. They were even responsible for the Germans shifting from offensive attacks to defensive tactics. In the battle of Belleau Wood, the French commander ordered them to retreat, but they refused when they received the order. They moved forward relentlessly, stepping over bodies and taking down all that stood in front of them. They had so much to prove.

The 369th Infantry raged on in the trenches of the front line until July 3rd. In mid-July, they were shipped to Marne, eighteen miles outside of Paris, where they held the line in the trenches. Caesar loaded his gun, shot, reloaded it, and shot again for hours. His arms ached from the continuous motion, but he dared not stop while his platoon fired rockets out into no-man's-land. The smoke from the guns blurred the vision on both sides, with neither wanting to look into the eyes of the enemy. Flashes of light lit up the sky and erased the darkness with explosions, as the 369th were bombarded with German artillery for over five hours without a single casualty in Caesar's company.

At the end of July, they marched for three days to the rear, only to be sent back to the front to continue their stalwart advance into enemy territory. On August 12, 1918, Caesar and his company had just rotated to relief when they heard about another comrade, Sergeant William Butler. He had single-handedly blasted a German raiding party that had captured six American prisoners, including a lieutenant, from the frontline trenches while on duty in a forward post. He took down ten German soldiers, and captured their lieutenant, and rescued the American prisoners. The 369th were proud of the heroics that they continued to demonstrate. They had fought valiantly and had nothing else to prove.

"There's going to be a major offensive where we will fight alongside the American army," Colonel Marshall informed the 369th Infantry. "The plan is to attack the German army from three sides with the French and American troops in Meuse-Argonne."

"Are they sure they want fight with niggas?" Stormy asked under his breath just so Caesar could hear.

"We've already shown we can stand up to anybody. They need all the bodies they can get," Colonel Marshall told them.

"Now they want to put us out there to die for them," Jones uttered in a low voice.

Jammed in 150 trucks rolling single file, the Harlem Hellfighters rode for hours in the night, unaware of their destination. When the trucks stopped, they were led on a march on dirt roads for nearly twenty miles. The 369th soldiers went into the frontline trenches armed with rifles, ammunition, grenades, wire cutters, and their gas masks at their necks. They had filled canteens, canned rations, sardines, bread, and chocolate. Hearing of the approaching onslaught, a German airplane dropped pamphlets where they were stationed that stated:

To the Colored Soldiers of the United States Army,
Hello, boys, what are you doing Fighting the Germans?

Have they ever done you any harm? Some white folks told you that the Germans ought to be wiped out for the sake of humanity and Democracy. Do you enjoy the same rights as the white people do in America, the land of freedom and Democracy, or are you not rather treated over there as second-class citizens? Can you get into a restaurant where white people dine, get a seat in a theatre where white people sit, get a seat or a berth in a railroad car? Can you even ride in the South in the same streetcar with the white people?

"That's the way it is now, but after this war is over, things are gonna change," Stormy said after Caesar read the paper. "They got to be fair with us after we done bled for this democracy."

"From your mouth to God's ears, Storm."

The seasons were in transition, and the men of the 369th didn't have overcoats. Deep in the trenches, the nights were cold and damp; and they used their blankets to keep warm, even though they couldn't sleep. Caesar watched as Corporal Pippin lit his last cigarette. He could see the smoke mix with all the haze and fumes that filled the air.

"Anybody want a drag?" Pippin asked, holding it out to offer after taking another long drag.

"I'll take one," Jones said, reaching for it.

The small light shone around his face, and his eyes were full of fear. The noise of the constant rockets and bombs reverberated in Caesar's ears, and moved down to chest, and made his heart beat as if he were running. In the morning, Matt Bullock, from the YMCA, brought out more cigarettes and cigars for the men. After two weeks of fielding attacks and counterattacks it was time for the troops to move forward.

"Here we go back into 'no-man's-land,'" Caesar said as he and Stormy gathered their gear and left the trench that had been their home into the light of day.

The morning was heavy with a misty fog that was more thick and ominous than the dark of night. You couldn't see a man in front of year until you bumped into him. Advancing forward from trench to trench, Caesar was enveloped in the chaos of gunfire and was confounded by the sight of the once solid strong soldiers of the 369th Infantry and the French army falling at his feet. Seeking cover in the next trench, he could see the injured men suffering from shock and hear grown men cry, some with their bodies intact but their minds blown to bits.

The one they called Preach leaned down deep and prayed for the dead, while others haphazardly wrapped the wounds. In the evening lull of battle, Caesar looked on the horizon above the trenches, and the light from the fires of rockets showed the dead bodies amid the dense brush of the field. He and Stormy took turns on alert, and Caesar slept as he always did, with his rifle in his hands.

The great assault began on September 25. The problem was that as the troops advanced, they moved faster than their artillery support, and they were caught in the open with no cover. The French, who rode the horses pulling the big guns, were slowed by rough ground and barbed wire. It was then that they truly crossed over into hell.

When darkness crept back over the battlefield it was as if a vicious thunderstorm had covered them. The sky cracked, and it looked like lightning, sounds of booms and crashing seemed to rock the earth beneath them, and the shells flying created a wind. But it wasn't drops of water coming down on them; it was raining bullets and shrapnel from guns, grenades, and heavy artillery. If you had the misfortune to be soaked by that torrential downpour, it would be from the flow of your own blood.

The casualties were of a magnitude that they had never seen before. They stood on the hill as targets for the German machine guns and rockets and suffered huge losses, yet they moved forward and took the hill. The 369th stormed into German trenches, where it was hand-to-hand combat. At this point, Caesar wasn't sure what the war was about; he was fighting for his life. He used his knife as Adam had showed him, and he sliced one of the Fritzies like he was a hog. In his peripheral vision, he saw Stormy wrestling with the last German who had tried to escape the trenches, and he jabbed him in the back with his bayonet. Caesar and Stormy gave each other a look of victory as they moved forward in the rush of soldiers, and in that instant, Caesar felt an ill wind just before Stormy's chest burst open.

The two of them fell to the ground, and Caesar could feel the motion of men from the regiment stepping over them and moving on.

"Stormy, talk to me! Say something!" Caesar pleaded as he leaned over him and tried to shake the life back into his body. But it was no use. Stormy's eyes were blank, as if he'd never known what happened.

"Noooo!" Caesar screamed in agony from the pain of helplessness that ran throughout his being, unable to change the course of events.

This wasn't supposed to happen, they had made plans, and now what was the point of it all? His screams had no sound in all the mayhem that surrounded them. He sat there for a moment not knowing how to leave his friend. It didn't seem right, but he couldn't stay there. He searched Stormy's pockets for anything of value to take back. He found a few dollars, some chocolate, and a letter that he had written that morning to his twin sister in Mississippi. Caesar took them and stuffed them in his own pockets.

Flashes of his own life appeared in his mind's eye, and he began to panic. It dawned on him that in a minute, in an hour, or in a day from now, he too could be a dead man. It was in that realization that he decided to survive this hell and live. Their motto was to move forward or die.

Caesar stood up with a pat to Stormy's shoulder in a goodbye to his fallen friend and raced forward like a bat out of hell. He roared like a wild beast as he threw his grenades and the 369th gained more ground. He felt the terrain trembling from the sound and impact of the mortars and their rockets beneath his feet, and the deathly beat vibrated all the way up to his throat, feeding his anger. When they took charge of the German trench, Caesar's heart was absent, and he stepped on the dead as if they were mounds of dirt. The machine gun unit set up, and he shot out into the battlefield at everything that moved until the lull of daylight gave him pause.

Four days later, after fierce fighting, thousands of bullets shot, hundreds of grenades and bombs thrown, they had backed the Germans out of the Sechault village; but it wasn't without great losses. More than a thousand of the regiment had been wounded; more than one hundred had been killed; and Caesar's best friend, Stormy Robinson, was one of them. He kept seeing the vision of him lying there on the ground and the battle moving on.

No one cared who died or when, and he hated it. Stormy wasn't just a casualty; he was his friend. All the lifeless bodies on the field meant something to someone. Dying was just too easy, it should be harder. He couldn't understand how the life or essence of a person could be separated from their body so quickly. So many soldiers around him had been shot, gassed, or killed, Caesar wondered if he had been specially blessed by not having suffered an injury, or was it as the French said, Bonne chance, a matter of luck.

It was less than a week later when Caesar became alarmed that Pippin hadn't come back from his observation post. He sunk down into the back relief trench, praying that he was alive, but it seemed like every person close to him had been taken away. He looked at the picture that Pippin had drawn of him and Stormy. He kept it folded in his pocket and hoped that God would protect him and his gift. Two days later, Caesar's prayer was answered when Pippin was brought in by ambulance. He heard that he had been shot three times. He begged for a pass to the hospital, wanting to see for himself that Pippin was all right.

"It's good to see you alive, man," Caesar said when he walked over to Pippin's bed.

"It's good to be alive my friend, Pippin answered.

"What happened to you out there?" Caesar asked.

"I was advancing out on the field, moving from shell hole to shell hole, when I was hit by a sniper in the neck, shoulder, and my arm. I had been lying in a hole, hungry and bleeding for a whole day before one of the French soldiers saw me there. On his way into the hole, he had the misfortune of being shot by the same sniper."

"Tough luck for him," Caesar said, shaking his head.

"He dropped down on me, dead as a doornail, and I didn't have the strength to push him off. I was so hungry; I reached around him to see if he had any food on him. I drank his water and ate his bread. He had coffee in his canteen, and I drank it, too, and it gave me enough power to push him off. I sat there with his body there in the hole for another night, with him bleeding onto my drawing book. I saw his blood mix with the ink and change colors, then it dripped off the pages as they stuck together. That's how we were until they found us. It was hell for sure."

"Yeah, but you lived to tell about it," Caesar reminded him.

Halfway through October, the 369th, was relieved. The regiment left the front lines and moved to the Vosges Mountains.

The Harlem Hellfighters were cited for their bravery and heroism in newspapers all over the world. "The Regiment never had a man taken prisoner, gave up a trench or a foot of ground. One hundred and seventy-one members, including Henry Johnson, Needham Roberts, and Horace Pippin, were decorated with the Croix de Guerre, or

Cross of War, for their brave and victorious battles in Champagne.

On the eleventh day of the eleventh month on the eleventh hour, the Armistice was signed, ending the war. Within a week, the 369th Regiment made its last advance and was honored by the French to be the first of the Allied units to reach the Rhine River on November 26, after having served in combat for 191 days. Germany had been defeated.

It was a time of celebration. The French were thankful for the supreme sacrifices made by the soldiers and invited them into their homes. They were all given a three-day leave so they could do some sight-seeing around the country. The wine and champagne flowed like a river in Paris, the parties were endless, and the women were generous. But Caesar had been raised not to give the white women a second look, and he didn't.

"I'm not going back, C," Jones said, packing up his duffle bag. "They've treated me well here. Why I need to go back to being a nigger again?"

"I hear quite a few plan to hang around," Caesar said. "Paris is a beautiful city, but it ain't my home."

"Well, for me, it's about to be," Jones replied.

"Take care of yourself, Jones. I'm going to see the black Madonnas I had heard about in Myans and Puy on my leave, and then I'm heading back to the States," Caesar said as they parted company.

"I ain't ever heard of Jesus' mother being a black woman," Jones shouted after him.

"They say seeing is believing," Caesar yelled back.

On December 12, the regiment was no longer assigned to the French army. The war was over. The YMCA held their final party at the Brest Camp while the soldiers waited for embarkation. This time, there were about 300 men and nine women to dance with all of them. They divided the time of the dances, with each soldier getting three minutes before the women had to change partners. Sarah was there, too, with her smile, even though some of the sparkle was missing.

When Caesar got to dance with her, she said, "I'm sorry about Stormy. I really like him."

"I'm sorry too," Caesar said.

"Are you going to see his family when you get back?" Sarah asked.

"I hadn't thought about it, but I think I will," he told her as the timer buzzed to change partners. So much had been lost in the fight, but the men were hopeful that their sacrifice had made a difference. Time would tell.

Chapter
Twelve

Caesar stayed to himself on the voyage home letting, the waves that swayed the ship comfort him as a mother rocks her baby. He didn't feel like he had a lot to celebrate. Stormy was dead, Pippin's right arm was practically useless, and Henry would never be the same. The price was too high as far as he was concerned. As they approached New York Harbor on the 12th of February the band played at the helm of the ship. As the ship glided into the pier, Caesar saw the Welcome Home sign and he felt glad to be home and alive. He walked up the ramp with flashes of the war running through his mind. He had only been gone a year, but it felt like a lifetime ago. He decided to send a cable home.

Dear Dad,
Our ship has arrived in New York safe and sound and I will
be coming home soon. Love Caesar

At Camp Upton, the men were ordered to wait at the only Hostess House where black women worked for demobilization, and Caesar knew nothing had changed.

Once David got the letter from Caesar about his enlistment and his impending shipment overseas, he had waited on edge for a letter saying that he was safe and sound. Once he heard that Caesar's regiment was participating in actual combat, David became afraid of getting any telegrams. No news was now good news. When the cable arrived at the store, he was afraid to read it. But when he saw that it was good news, that his son was alive and coming home, he packed his bags for New York. He couldn't stand to wait until Caesar got back to Nashville. For over a year, he didn't know if his son was alive or dead. There was nothing that would keep him from getting there to bring his son home. He would have another chance to make up for the past. He closed the store, grabbed his bags, and headed for the train station.

David hadn't been able to find out where the 369th were stationed, so he stood in the crowd of over two 200,000 people waiting for the grand ticker tape victory parade on February 19, 1919, that would welcome the hometown heroes back to Harlem. The infantry began their march on Fifth Avenue before noon in French formation.

Caesar looked to his left, where Stormy had always marched, but there was someone else marching there. He was about to sink into his blues when the cheers of the crowd, black and white alike, shocked him out of his melancholy. They waved flags, and signs that said "Welcome, Fighting 15th" and cheered with a volume that nearly drowned out the band. Caesar looked into their faces as they chanted for the men, and some even cried, and the spirit of pride and celebration was contagious. His spirit was lifted, and with it his head and his feet, he stepped higher and absorbed all the adoration of the families represented there.

When they got to 110th Street, they turned onto Lenox Avenue, up into Harlem. The band, led by Lt. Europe played "Here Comes My Daddy," while Bill "Bojangles" Robinson danced in front as the drum major. Caesar could feel his chest swell against the rifle he held firmly on his shoulder, and then he saw his dad standing on the street in front of the crowd.

"Caesar!" David yelled loudly above the noise of the crowd, and he rushed towards him and wrapped his arms around him, gun and all. They both held onto each other, needing the strength of the other to stand. Each of them had been through an ordeal.

"Dad, I can't believe you came all the way to New York! Did you get my telegram?"

"Yeah, I did, but I had to come up here and bring you home," David said, leaning back to look into his face. It was then he saw that his son had left a boy, and now he was a man.

"I missed you, Dad, and I'm so glad to see you!" Caesar said overwhelmed.

Seeing his dad there on the street, Caesar stood there and cried like a baby. He had seen too much and had felt too much, and he had to let it go. It was pure pandemonium on the streets as the spectators were now participants and flowers and confetti rained down on them.

"Meet me at the Marshall Hotel," Caesar said as the crowded receded.

When the parade got to 145th Street, the Fighting 15th was hustled down into the subway, where they were taken to 71st Regiment Armory for a congratulatory banquet. The next day, they returned to Camp Upton, and within a week, Caesar was honorable discharged.

Caesar was torn, happy, and sad at the same time. It was hard to think about not seeing these men again, men he had seen sweat, fight, and bleed, men he had seen laugh and cry. They had been like brothers and uncles; but at the same time, he couldn't wait to put the horror of it all behind him. One thing was for sure: he felt proud of the job they had done.

He rode the subway train over to Midtown to the Marshall Hotel. On his way there, strangers shook his hand, patted him on the back, and gave him nods of approval. It made him feel like hero, and he wished that Stormy and several other guys could be with him to share it. It was a payday for all the times it felt like nobody gave a damn. He got to the Marshall around the lunch hour. When he walked into the lobby, Jimmie saw him and laughed out loud.

"Welcome back, son! I'm glad you made it! I saw you in the parade. You done us proud," Jimmie said as he ushered Caesar to the restaurant."

"Hey everybody!" Jimmie cheered at the entrance, "Our magic man got out alive!"

They all clapped and Caesar saw David sitting at a far table. He took four long strides to cross the room, David met him, and they both hugged while David patted his shoulders without words to express his joy.

"I'm sorry for leaving like that, Dad," Caesar said.

"No, son, I'm the one who's sorry. I'm so sorry that I didn't see what was happening under my own roof," David protested. "You're the most important person to me in this whole world, and I would kill anybody who tried to hurt you."

"That's what I was afraid of, Dad," Caesar said with a smile, and they hugged each other again.

"Come on in the kitchen, soldier boy," Jimmie said. "They really missed you back here."

Caesar motioned for David to follow them, and they went through the rear door. It was if he had never left. Adam was talking, Ruth was humming, and Johnny was complaining.

"What's the problem in here?" Jimmie said with his arm around Caesar. "Look who is back in one piece."

Ruth quickly wiped her hands and took Caesar close to her chest, letting her tears soak into his uniform.

"God is good, chile! I been praying for you," she cried.

"Thanks, I needed every one," Caesar said.

He moved to the side near the sinks and held out his hand to Johnny.

"I been missing you round here, C," Johnny said, shaking his hand. "I shoulda gone with you. These folks around here been trying to work me to death."

Caesar looked over at Adam. There was so much he wanted to say to him, he had treated him like family, and he didn't know how to let him know how much that meant to him.

"Sir," was all he could say without choking up and embarrassing himself.

"How are you, Red?" Adam asked. "You didn't get hit over there did you, son?"

"No, sir, but believe it when they say war is hell," Caesar answered. "This is my father, sir, David Mallory," Caesar said, turning around to introduce them. "Dad, this is Adam; he's the one who taught me how to cook."

"You have a fine young man there. I was glad to help him in any way I could. You should be very proud," Adam said.

"Believe me, I am," David replied as he put his arm around Caesar's shoulder.

"Go on out there, and sit down, soldier. We gonna feed you today," Adam said to ease the emotions that had gripped the room.

Caesar sat down at the table with David and smiled to himself as he ate the pot roast. It was the same meal he had at the Marshall when he first came to New York. When he had eaten his full, they went up to his dad's room.

"Dad, I got a little business to tend to before we leave town."

He still had the habit of keeping his money in three places. He had left one third in Jimmie's safe, a third in a savings and loan, and the last third he had kept sewn into his knapsack. The next evening, after he collected his money and said his goodbyes, he told David he was ready to go home. Early in the morning before breakfast,

David watched him get dressed meticulously in his uniform, and he regretted the words that he was about to say.

"Son, I don't think it's a good idea to wear your uniform while we're traveling home. It's not worth the risk."

"Dad, I been at risk every day and night for a year. I ain't scared of nobody," Caesar told him defiantly.

"I know that, son, but they're lynching black soldiers back in the South for no other reason than for wearing their uniforms. You have just come out of a war with folks trying to kill you every day, and I don't want to take a chance on some crazy white sonofabitch shooting at you before we get there. I just want to get you home in one piece," David replied.

"If they want me to fight them, I will," Caesar said. "Besides, none of my old clothes fit me anymore."

"I bought you a new suit, C, when I got here, and I'd be grateful if you would wear for me," David said.

"For all the worry I put you through, I'll wear it. Not for them, but for you," Caesar said.

Caesar changed into the dark blue suit and looked at himself in the mirror. It had been a long time since he had worn any civilian clothing. He felt good and fresh. It was a new beginning in his life. The uniform was a part of the past, and it was still painful. He put on the grey overcoat, and they walked down the stairs.

"Be safe young man," Jimmie said, giving him a salute.

David and Caesar stepped out into the cool morning air, walking side by side, an older and younger version of each other. When they got to Grand Central terminal, David bought their tickets, and in less than an hour, they had boarded a train headed south. David looked across the seat at his son, sorry that he had left one war only to come home and have to fight another one. At least over there, the enemy had the courage to fight an armed adversary, not like these cowards who ran in packs, attacking one man at a time.

It took two days to get to Nashville, and Caesar was looking forward to staying put for a while. He had been traveling for two years, looking for his purpose or reason for being, and now he thought he knew where to begin. He was happy when the taxi pulled up to a different house, he really didn't want to go back to where all the fuss had started.

"It's just the two of us now," David said when they got to the front door. Caesar nodded his head relieved.

The next morning, David made some breakfast, and the smell of food woke Caesar up. He followed it down the steps.

"Good morning, son," David said, and the words felt good rolling out of his mouth.

"Good morning, Dad," Caesar replied.

"I was thinking that you probably might need some time to adjust to being out of the army and finding what you want to do for the rest of your life," David said as he put two plates of food on the table.

"No, Dad, I don't need to," Caesar said. "I'm already sure of what I want to do. I've got some money saved, and I want to open up my own restaurant."

David took the seat across from Caesar and tried to choose his words carefully. "That sounds good, but do you think you have enough money and experience to get your plans going?"

"Like I said, I have some money saved, and I know what supplies I need, and besides all that I am a good cook," Caesar said.

"First off, there is some business that we haven't discussed that you need to know about. When your mama died, she had a nice sum of money, and it was placed into a trust for you that you will receive on your twenty-first birthday. Your grammy also left you provided for and her property will be turned over to you on your twenty-fifth birthday. C, you are a fortunate young man. You will have seed money to grow any kind of business that you want. I just want you to take some time, learn as much as you can, and be prepared to do your restaurant right."

Caesar ate his breakfast in silence; his dad had given him a lot to think about. He remembered when Mr. B told him to take his time and that a young man needs time to play.

After thinking about it, he said, "You're right, Dad. I think I will look for a job where I can learn everything I need to know. By the way, do you know what Ed is doing?"

"Yeah, he works with me down at the store," David answered. "Come on down when you get ready. He'll be glad to see you."

Caesar smiled as he watched his dad clear the table and go into the kitchen.

***

Caesar took his time putting his things away; each thing that he touched brought back a memory of his time with the 15th. He saw the letter for Storm's sister that he had folded with the picture that Pippin had drawn of him and Stormy, and he read the letter again. In it, Stormy told her how much he missed and loved everybody, and he promised that he was going to send for her, and they were going to start a new life in another city. Caesar thought about mailing it, but he thought it might upset them more. He decided that he would take the letter to her one weekend after he got settled.

Chapter Thirteen

Caesar got dressed in a clean, pressed shirt and slacks; put on his overcoat, and went out to look for a job. To him, it felt odd to be back in Nashville after living in New York and spending a year in France. The city was a lot smaller than he remembered, and it seemed to be moving in slow motion as he took the streetcar downtown. I've already worked in a hotel and restaurant; and if I could do that here, it would get me ready to run my own, he thought. He got off the streetcar and walked the block over to the Hermitage Hotel.

"Can you tell me where the employment office is?" Caesar asked the white man at the desk inside the lobby.

The balding man looked at him over his glasses and told him, "Down the hall to your left, and make two right turns. There's a sign on the door."

Caesar walked into the door and there was another man there at another desk.

"What you looking for, boy?" the man asked.

"I'm looking for a job," Caesar replied.

"Sorry, we don't have any more cleaning jobs right now," he answered back.

Caesar took a deep breath and said, "I worked in the kitchen at a hotel in New York, sir, and I can cook."

"New York, huh?" he said. "What are you doing here?"

"My dad lives here, and he is the only family I got. I came back to be near him."

Unbeknownst to Caesar, he had touched a nerve in the man with his words.

"Wait here," the man said, and he walked back through another door in the rear. When he came back a few minutes later, he said, "We need some extra help washing dishes. You can wash dishes, can't you?"

"Yes, sir, I can," Caesar answered.

"Come back tomorrow morning at 10:00 sharp, and we'll give you a trial run," the man said.

"Thank you, sir," Caesar said and walked out satisfied. He had what he had come for: a chance.

He headed back out to South Nashville to his dad's store to tell him his good news and to see Ed. When he got off the streetcar and saw the store, it reminded him of the nightmare of living with Grace; but now it really did feel like a dream. He hoped that they both would be spared the awkwardness of seeing each other. He guessed that Grace must still live at the house and work with her groups at the church. She was probably sitting in the first row of the pews every Sunday, he mused.

The store hadn't changed much from the outside, but when he walked in, it had a lot more things stocked in it. He saw Ed standing behind the counter, and they both smiled. Caesar walked over to his friend, and they traded an affectionate punch to the shoulder.

"Hey, C, good to see you back home, man," Ed said.

"Yeah, my friend, I'm glad to be back."

"That's good, but I need to talk to you for a minute," Ed said with a worried look on his face.

Caesar walked behind the counter and they both sat down on the short utility bench they used to reach the high shelves.

"I don't want you to feel like I stabbed you in the back when you left, C, but there are some things that you need to know," Ed said, looking at the ground.

"I know you wouldn't do me wrong, Ed," Caesar said, hitting him on the shoulder again.

"Look, C, first I told your pops what happened with your stepmom and everything," he said before Caesar interrupted him.

"I know that, Ed, and I'm glad you did."

"The other thing is Rose and I kept hanging out after you were gone, and over time we got close. She's my girl now, and I hope it won't cause us no problems."

Caesar was relieved that it wasn't any more serious that and said, "No, man, it's no problem. I don't blame you. Somebody else was going to move in anyway. I didn't think she'd be sitting around here waiting on me. I didn't even know if I was ever coming back here anyway. Ain't no hard feelings, Ed. Y'all both are friends of mine for life. Now that just frees me up to play the field," Caesar said, standing up.

"Okay, good-time Charlie, you musta been running around with all them French girls over there."

"Naw, Ed, I played it safe. I had enough going wrong without my johnson burning."

David had heard Caesar come in, but he waited until the friends finished talking.

"You look like you got somewhere to be, C," David said.

"I been downtown this morning, and I got me a job," Caesar said.

"Man, you ain't been here for a day yet. How you gonna have job?" Ed asked him with a chuckle.

"For real, y'all, I got a job."

"Well, where you working?" David asked with his arms folded.

"I'm gonna be working at the Hermitage Hotel in the restaurant kitchen, starting tomorrow," Caesar said, pleased with himself.

"I got to hang with you, C. The good Lord got to be sitting on your shoulder 'cause that's a miracle."

"I done had my share of the blues, man. I got to get some blessings sometime," Caesar said.

"Since you hot, we going down to the Bottom this evening. Let's see if your card game is working any better," Ed added.

"No way, man," Caesar laughed. "Unlucky at cards; lucky in love."

"We'll see," David said, and they all laughed.

***

When Caesar arrived on the job the next day, he knew he was in for a challenge. He didn't mind, though. He was there to learn as much as he could, and one day he would have a restaurant that would put theirs to shame.

"Go on around to the back, there's an entrance out there that leads to the kitchen," the man in the front told him.

Caesar knocked on the door, and a fat white man with bright red hair swung open the door.

"Whatya want, boy?" he asked with a heavy Southern twang.

"I'm here to work, sir. My name is C," he said, careful not to appear too high-minded.

"Oh, yeah, they told us we had some more help coming in today. Stop standing there like you don't know which end is up."

The man turned around and let the door swing in Caesar's face, but Caesar grabbed it before it shut and walked in behind the big man.

"Pat, this is-what you say your name is, boy?"

"C," he replied.

"Yeah, C, this here is Mr. Farrell, and I'm Mr. Bullock. Mr. Farrell is the main chef around here, and I'm the baker. On that front counter, that's where the orders are received. The tables are bussed, and the dishes are taken to the washroom that is through that side door. What you gonna do is keep the cooking pots and utensils clean and bring us the clean plates from the kitchen. You got that?"

"Yessir, I got it," Caesar said.

"I hear you got some experience cooking?" Farrell asked.

"Yessir, I worked as an assistant cook at a restaurant in New York and then the mess halls in the service," Caesar replied.

"Where you from, boy?" Bullock asked.

"I'm from here, sir," Caesar answered.

"Long as you ain't got no funny ideas, boy, you won't have no trouble," Bullock added.

Caesar kept a low profile and didn't say much on the job, he was just there to learn. He liked the efficiency of the kitchen and the dishwashing being away from the food preparation area. There were also a lot of things that he didn't like. They skimped on quality, something that Adam told him never to do, and they treated their paying customers with disdain. He had seen many times when food was dropped on the floor, and they picked it up and threw it in the pan without washing it. Bullock was a slob, and he smelled bad. Caesar knew enough to know that you don't let a filthy man cook in your kitchen. It was a miracle that people didn't get sick from eating out of there.

Farrell was the one who kept the place in business. Caesar had to admit that he could cook. Beef was his meat of choice; he roasted huge hunks of meat and sliced them at different ends, according to how the customer liked it. He made a thick beef stew that was very popular served with bread and butter.

Caesar got there early in the mornings and laid things out to make the cooks' jobs easier, and they liked that. He looked over their shoulders and took in everything. He learned where to order supplies and food, where to buy illegal liquor since prohibition started, the price for a prime meal, and how much to pay the workers.

***

Life was beginning to settle down a bit, but it was just the calm before another storm. When the heat of the summer months began to rise all hell broke loose across the country. Jobs were hard to find, and the frustrations from empty pockets and bellies had tempers flaring.

"Dad, it says here that Lt. James Europe was stabbed by member of his band," Caesar said while they were reading *The Nashville Globe* over breakfast.

"That's too bad, son. I know you had a lot of respect for the man."

"He's probably one the reasons I'm still alive," he said with his good mood turning sour.

"These white people are going crazy. They're attacking black soldiers in uniform and lynching blacks like it's going out of style" David said, reading another article. "The newsflash is that black folks are fighting back with a vengeance, and white folks can't believe it."

"What else we gonna do, Dad? We got to defend ourselves."

What would have been small skirmishes between a few people grew to wild mobs and then morphed in to full-blown riots from the South to the North and even moving out West. Caesar fought an urge to get back in the fight, but he knew all too well that a life was easily lost, and he had a lot of things he wanted to get done before he gave up his ghost. Fortunately, there hadn't been any major blow-ups in Nashville, but blood was spilled in riots in thirty-three other cities from May until October.

Chapter Fourteen

Caesar had laid low for most of the summer, he and Ed didn't hang out like they used to. Ed spent most of his time with Rose and was even talking about jumping the broom. Caesar had met a few girls since he had been back, but none of them were that special.

There was Jean, who was too quiet, and he tired of making conversation with her and trying to figure out what she was thinking. Deborah played games with him, kissing him and touching him and then stopping, telling him that after they were married he could have it all. The problem was he didn't want to marry her. Linda was always trying to make him jealous with other guys at parties, and he thought she needed too much attention.

Caesar could get any of the girls in town that he wanted, but he didn't want to play games. He needed to know what was on their minds and that he could trust them. He didn't want to make a mistake and end up with a fool or be one himself.

David and Caesar had started taking turns making their meals, and now David was a believer, the boy could cook. Caesar now did most of the food shopping and prepared most of their dinners, unless he had to work late. The travel season at the hotel was slowing and so was the violence that had spread across the South.

"The holiday season will be starting soon. This might be a good time for me to take a few days off from work and go see Stormy's family in Tunica," Caesar mentioned over dinner.

David felt overly protective of Caesar. He knew his son was a man and could take care of himself, but he wanted to go with him on the trip.

"I haven't been there in years. I'd like to get over on Beale Street. I hear they play a lot of that blues music. I've had my share, and I bet I could out sing some of them," David laughed.

"You want to come with me, Dad?" Caesar asked, catching the hint.

"It'll be fun, if you don't mind," David said. "We haven't gone out on the town in a long time, and the drive won't take all day.

Caesar was just glad he didn't have to take the train. The plan was to drive to Tunica, give the letter to the Robinson family and then drive back to Memphis, check into Church's Hotel, and then head to Beale Street. Except, things don't always go according to plan. It turned out to be a strange trip.

"Blacks folks are getting out of the South in droves," David said, watching the steady stream of cars filled with black people traveling in the opposite direction.

"I know a bunch of families that have left Nashville heading North, Dad. They say they're sick of Jim Crow and scratching in the dirt for a living."

Caesar had always lived in the city, but he knew he was blessed to have never had to plow a field in his life. When they got to the other side of Memphis and they crossed the border of Mississippi, it looked like the days of slavery had never ended. Caesar could see the remnants of cotton growing and the acres of red mud stretched out as far as his eyes could see. They stopped at grocery store filling station just in case it was the last one left before they got to the

Robinson's house. There was young boy, around ten, dressed in too-small clothes, sweeping outside.

"Do you know where the Robinson family lives?" Caesar asked the boy while he poured the gasoline in the car.

Caesar couldn't believe their luck when the boy told them the Robinsons lived just three miles down the road and to the right. He paid for the gas, bought a candy bar, and he and David were back on their way. There on the dirt road, Caesar saw the humble shack that the Robinsons called home, and all the stories that Stormy had told him began to take shape in his mind. Before now, he hadn't thought about what he was going to say, so he was a bundle of nerves as he struggled to find the right words. Mostly, he wanted them to know that their son was a hero.

David stood behind him while he knocked on the door. When the door opened, Caesar was stunned. The pretty young woman who stood there had to be the twin sister that Stormy had always talked about. She looked like Stormy; and standing there in front of her, Caesar felt a connection and an attraction that he had never felt before.

"Hello," he said with a slight stutter, "My name is Caesar Portunus. Are you family of Stormy Robinson?"

"Yeah," she said with a mellow voice that seemed to sing her words. "He was my brother."

"He and I were in the New York National Guard together, the 15th Infantry," Caesar explained, "He was my best friend; we served in the 369th in France together. I have a letter for your family."

She looked down at the floor in contemplation for a moment and then opened the door wider and said, "Please come in."

She was tall, lean, and strong like Stormy, but he couldn't help but notice she was shaped up nice.

"My name is Rainbow. My daddy died about a year ago. My mama is up the road right now and should be back soon. Can you wait until she gets back?"

"Sure we can," David said after Caesar hadn't responded, he was still mesmerized.

Rainbow walked over to the couch and extended her arm in an offer for them to sit down.

The silence felt awkward after a few minutes, and she said, "Would you like me to show you around some, see Stormy's room?"

"I'd like to see it," Caesar said. He stood up and followed her to the back room on the left.

"This was his room that he shared with my other brothers," she said as she stepped to the side so he could look in.

The room was plain, with a set of bunk beds and a cot in the corner. There wasn't much in it besides a lamp and a shelf, but everything was neat and in its place. What drew his eyes was the window, you could see far out onto the land until it blended with a forest of trees. It reminded him of some of the fields that they had run across and fought on in France.

"Do you want to go outside?" she asked with a smile.

Caesar was overwhelmed for a minute and just nodded yes. He followed her looking at the back of her hair that puffed out of the scarf that she had tied around the front. He looked at the smooth skin on her arms as she grabbed a sweater on the way out.

"We don't own this land," Rainbow said. "Without the money Stormy sent us, we will have to be moving soon. One of my other brothers ran off when he heard about Stormy. He said if he was going to die young, he wanted to have a good time first. My baby brother still goes to school."

Caesar listened to her voice, but his attention was only on her. She was the color of maple syrup, and Caesar could tell by her smile that she was just as sweet. When he saw her mama coming down the road with her arms full of laundry, it reminded him of why they were there. When Mrs. Robinson got close and saw him standing outside, questions were written all over her face.

"Mama, this is one of Stormy's friends from the service. He's got a letter for us from Stormy."

She seemed a little confused at first as she handed the basket to Rainbow and said, "Come on in the house." She was even more surprised when she saw David sitting inside on the couch.

"That's my dad, Mrs. Robinson; he drove me down to see y'all."

"Hello, nice to meet you both," she said as she sat down in a chair opposite the couch.

Caesar reached down in his pocket, pulled out the letter, and handed it to her. She handed the letter to Rainbow, who took it, knelt down beside her, and began to read.

"Dear Mama and Daddy, I think about y'all every day and I hope y'all are doing fine. Things are getting tough here, the weather is so cold, and the fighting never ends."

She had barely finished one sentence before the tears began to roll down her mama's cheeks. Rainbow reached out and grabbed her hand and continued to read.

"When I get home I'm gonna get y'all outta that jail of a house and land and go somewhere we can really live. I'm gonna make you proud. My good friend Caesar and me, we got big plans. Hold on, this war has got to end sometime. I love all y'all, Stormy"

The room was thick with her grief, and Caesar covered his face with his hands. It was an emotional scene. It seemed as if Stormy's voice had taken the place of Rainbow's, and Caesar could hear him saying the words to them for himself. When Rainbow finished reading, she handed the letter back to her mama and she sat there in silence for a while before she stood up and extended her arms for a hug from Caesar.

"Thank you so much for bringing that to me. It's the most precious thing I got left," she said. "Will y'all please stay for dinner?"

"Yes, ma'am!" Caesar said with enthusiasm.

David could see that Caesar was obviously taken with Rainbow, so he took off his coat, realizing that they weren't going to see Beale Avenue that evening. They listened to the women's voices in the kitchen as they prepared the meal. Later, they heard the sound of the back door opening. Caesar guessed that it was the younger brother who had come home from school. He heard them say a few words, and then Rainbow laughed. It sounded a lot like Stormy's laugh, and it made him smile down in his insides.

After a while they came into the parlor, and Rainbow said, "This is my baby brother, Winston. Winston, this is Stormy's army buddy, Caesar, and his daddy," giving a glance to David.

"My name's Mallory," David said to them both.

Dinner was a relaxed time between them, as if old friends who hadn't seen each other in a long time had been reunited. They talked about the war, how the cotton fields had died, and the black folks who couldn't get out of Mississippi fast enough.

"Thank you for inviting us to eat with you, Mrs. Robinson," David said when they had finished eating. "It's getting late, and we plan to spend tomorrow on Beale Street before we head back home."

"Call me, Dottie," Mrs. Robinson said.

Then Caesar chimed in, "Would y'all like to go with us to Memphis?"

Now it was David's turn to be stunned, but all of them were surprised by the invitation.

"Thank you, young man, but it's a little fast for us, and we've got a lot of work to do around here," Mrs. Robinson said with a chuckle.

"Is it all right if I write to you Rainbow?" Caesar asked her, but looked at her mama with a pleading look.

"I don't see why not," Mrs. Robinson said, looking at her daughter.

"Thank you again for the delicious meal, Dottie, and we'll keep in touch," David said as they put on their overcoats and walked out the door.

Caesar stood outside wanting to say something else, but he dared not say what was in his mind or heart. He reached in his pocket and gave Rainbow the chocolate bar he had bought at the filling station and got in the car. He looked back and waved goodbye as his father car drove away while Rainbow and her mother stood inside the doorway.

"What's on your mind, C?" David asked after driving in the quiet for a few minutes.

"I can't explain it, Dad. When I saw her, it was like I already knew her. I felt like I had done all of this before. I couldn't just get up and leave. I wanted to spend some more time with her," Caesar said, sounding perplexed.

David shook his head and laughed, saying, "Like father, like son. I was a fool over your mother at about your age. Now I guess it's your turn to lose your head."

David couldn't stop shaking his head on the drive back to Memphis, why couldn't things have happened at a more opportune place and time. Caesar was young and had just come back home. David had wanted to convince him to put his dreams of a restaurant on hold and go to college, but Caesar had gotten a job so quickly. Now his son was ready to put a lock on his heart and throw away the key. One thing that David had learned was that Caesar was going to do what he wanted, and there was nothing he could do about it. He decided to keep his mouth shut and let it be. He had made a mess of his life as far as women were concerned. Maybe Caesar would have better luck than he did.

The next morning, Caesar wasn't in the mood to go up and down Beale Street. He was lovesick, and there was nothing that could be done about it.

"We'll come back again, C, when the weather breaks. In the meantime you can do what you said and write her a letter," David said.

When they got back home, Caesar went straight to his room and picked up a pencil and paper.

Dear Rainbow, I know this is going to sound silly, but when you opened that door a rainbow appeared in my life. All of sudden the clouds were gone, and I could see the sun and brighter days ahead. I don't know how you felt, but I didn't want to leave, and when I had to go, I wanted to take you with me. I know I probably sound like a fool because I just met you, but now when I think of my plans and what I want to do they include you. First, I want to know if you are sweet on another guy around there or if you've made any promises that stand between me getting to know you better. Please write me as fast as you can so I'll know if I can hold onto this new hope I feel. Sincerely, Caesar Portunus

Caesar was as impatient as he was when he was a little boy waiting for a letter from his mama when she was away on the road. He wished he wasn't so far away so he could say things in person and see Rainbow's face. He prayed that she didn't have a fella and wanted to see him again. This was the first time that he had been nervous about a girl. They usually were already interested, and it was he who didn't care that much. When the letter from her finally came, he was almost afraid to read it.

Dear Caesar, It was nice to finally meet the young man that my brother was always writing about in his letters. He thought a lot of you, and I'm grateful that he had a good friend like you in that war. He said that I would like you and he was right. It made me happy to read your letter; I've never had a boy send me a letter before, and I felt very special. I wished you could have stayed longer and we could have had more time to talk. I'm not sweet on anyone around here, most the young guys can't stand it around here and leave. I like the idea of me in your plans and hope to get to know you much better. Yours truly, Rainbow Robinson

Caesar was busy over the next weeks of the holiday season, but his mind was on Rainbow, how he could see her again, and how he could bring her to Nashville. He felt like he had learned enough at the Marshall and Hermitage hotels to open his own restaurant, but he didn't have enough money to start the type of place he wanted. He knew he was going to ask Rainbow to marry him, and he wanted to give her all the things that she deserved. He just needed time to move faster and get him to the day when he would see Rainbow.

On his twentieth birthday, Caesar wished he could shorten the year before it was his twenty-first. He and Rainbow continued to exchange letters, and with each one the bond between them grew stronger. The qualities that he admired in her were the same that had drawn him and Stormy together as friends: sincerity, kindheartedness, and a sense of humor. Rainbow saw the same in him and remembered her twin.

In February, she wrote,

Dear Caesar, Sadness and grief stay as close as my shadow. My mama fell ill over the winter holiday and the doctor's thought it was TB. They weren't able to get her the expensive medicine, and with the chill in the house, she couldn't get any stronger, and she has passed away. I am relieved in a way to see her out of her misery; it had gotten too hard to watch and hear her cry in the night. I figure she's happy now, reunited with the ones she missed so much. My little brother was sent to live with an aunt in Tupelo, and I'm staying with a family from our church so I can keep working. Yours truly, Rainbow Robinson

Caesar felt her pain. She had lost everybody who was close to her; her whole family was gone and she was alone. She's just like a soldier he thought to himself, she just keeps pushing, even with all the casualties at her feet. He promised himself that he would protect her and make her happy for the rest of their lives.

When the dormant season drew to a close, Caesar was anxious to bring his plans to fruition. He bided his time and hung out with Ed whenever Ed wasn't with Rose.

Walking in the Bottom after work with Ed, Caesar said, "Ed, I'm gonna ask Rainbow to marry me. I want her to be my wife."

"C, you still got the war blues. You need to slow down your locomotion," Ed said with concern. "You only saw her one time, and it was under sad circumstances. Wait until you spend some more time together before you fall all over yourself. You can have any girl you want in town."

"I don't need to spend any more time with her to know she's the one I want. I never felt like this about any girl before, and I never even had the thought of getting married until I met her. I thought I was going to be by myself for the rest of my life," Caesar replied.

"Well, what you gonna do?" Ed asked.

"Her birthday is May 22, and I'm going to Tunica to celebrate with her and when I come back, she's going to be with me, or I'm not coming back," he said with a surety that Ed knew better than to doubt.

David was afraid to let Caesar drive his car alone down in Mississippi.

"These po' white folks are still acting a fool, C. Take the train, and then hire a ride when you get there," he said.

"Dad, I want to take her around in Memphis," Caesar said exasperated. He was tired of changing and doing things to make the white man happy.

"Send her a cable, son. Ask her to meet you at the train station in Memphis," David said. "I just got a feeling and it ain't worth taking chances when you don't have to."

That made Caesar think. He didn't want anything to jeopardize his life with Rainbow. He sent the cable, and she sent one back that said she would meet him at the train station on Friday.

Early Friday morning, Caesar had in his mind to make this the best birthday she had ever had. He got a fresh haircut and bought new shoes. He even bought Rainbow some Baby Ruth candy bars to give her at the station. He packed the new suit his Dad had bought him after the war and put it with a white shirt he carefully pressed himself. The day before he left, he went to the One Cent Bank to get some money for his trip. He took out ninety dollars of his savings. He put thirty safely hidden in his small suitcase, thirty in the bottom of his left shoe, and the last thirty in a wallet in his right pants pocket.

David drove him to the train station. When he got out of the vehicle he leaned into the window and asked him, "Dad, can I bring my wife back here to stay with us?"

David felt a rush of heat circle his head. "Sure you can, son, but I want to stand up for you when you get married," he said, not showing his shock at the question.

"We'll see, Dad," Caesar said as he waved and stepped back from the curb.

David watched him as he walked inside the station and wondered if this man he loved so much, and was so proud of, had ever been a little boy in his life.

Chapter Fifteen

C aesar was thankful that the train ride wasn't a long one; he had waited long enough. It had been six months since he had seen his Rainbow. When he met her at the train station, she was even prettier than when he first saw her. She had on a cute yellow dress and a hat to match. She had let her hair hang natural to her shoulders and he liked it. It was thick and wavy, but on the ends it fluffed like cotton. They greeted each other with a smile and then a quick hug.

"Let's go get settled before we find some food," Caesar said as he offered Rainbow his free arm and lifted his bag with the other. It felt good to both of them to have someone to hold on to as they walked. Caesar hired a cab to drive them to Church's Hotel. He got two rooms next to each other so she could have her privacy.

On the steps, Rainbow said, "I didn't bring anything with me."

"That's no problem," he said. "I'll buy you whatever you need."

Rainbow held onto his arm tighter, she never dared to dream that anyone would ever treat her like this.

At the table in the hotel, before they ordered their meal, Rainbow said, "Thank you for coming back and bringing me here. This is the most special birthday that I've ever had. I've never eaten in a restaurant before."

Caesar smiled and said, "I don't want any to be as special as the one that I will make for you."

He loved the way Rainbow was open and honest. She didn't say things that she didn't mean, and she wasn't afraid to say what she liked and what she didn't like. When he asked her what she wanted to eat, she didn't hesitate and told him. If she liked it she said so and if she didn't she said that also.

When they finished the meal and Caesar had paid the bill, he asked, "Now that we've eaten, what else would you like to do?".

"I'd really like to go the picture show," she answered with a sweet smile.

"Is there a picture show around here that we can go to?" Caesar asked the waiter.

"*The Homesteader* is playing at the Metropolis Theater not far from here," the waiter said.

He told them how to get there, and they started out walking. Caesar reached for her hand, she closed her fingers around his, and that's where he wanted them to stay.

In the movie, Caesar saw Jean Baptiste, the leading character, find the woman he wanted by chance and lose her by fate and then marry someone else he didn't want. He thought about it and realized that's what happened to his dad and mama and he promised himself that he wouldn't let that happen to him.

He turned to Rainbow on his right in the darkness of the theater and said, "I've lost a lot of time with the people I've loved in my life, and I don't want that to keep happening to me. I know that I love you, and I don't want to spend another day without you. I want you to be my wife, and I want to take you home with me."

Rainbow smiled and said, "When you came to our door, all my prayers were answered. I just wanted somebody I could love who would love me back. I'd marry you right now if I could."

Caesar put his arm around Rainbow's shoulders and pulled her close. He just wanted to hear her words roll around in his head until the movie was over.

They were quiet after the movie was over and the lights were turned up. Both of them felt a little awkward and embarrassed that maybe they had said too much.

"You know, we always gonna be together," he said as they walked out.

"Yeah, I know," said.

"Well, let's get married tomorrow," he said, looking straight ahead not wanting to see if she thought he was crazy.

"That won't give you enough time to change your mind," she said with a laugh.

Caesar loved her laugh. It wasn't loud or screeching; it was a deep gurgle that bounced around in her belly and then rose to her chest. When she laughed, it moved him, and he felt it down deep inside himself.

"I'm gonna buy you a ring in the morning, and then we're gonna get married."

"Okay," she said and laughed some more.

Caesar laid awake in his room next to Rainbow's that night, content that this would be the last time he would sleep without her next to him. He wondered if she was still awake and if she was thinking about him, too. He thought about her lying there next to him, and he began to sweat. She was so pretty, and he ached to touch her all over, but she wasn't just some girl he wanted to have some fun with, he loved her.

He had fooled around with other girls some, even with a few while he was in the army, but Johnny had told him not to go all the way with them, or they'd try to saddle him with a baby. He wanted to do everything right with Rainbow because she would be his wife.

He reflected back on his encounters and realized that he had never shared a bed with a woman. Then he shuddered when he thought about that night when Grace had climbed into his bed, and his sweat turned cold. He turned over and forced his mind to go to sleep, and his body soon followed.

***

In the morning after breakfast, they went down to Lowenstein's Department Store to buy Rainbow a dress. They got many a dirty look, but Caesar didn't care; he had money to spend.

He looked at the blue-haired white woman working there and said, "Rainbow, get anything you want."

She looked at several dresses on the racks, with the disgruntled saleswoman close on her heels, until she found her wedding dress.

"This is it, Caesar, this is the one I want," Rainbow said, holding it up.

It was white, with thin straps and soft flowing fabric and had a sheer covering that looked like it was painted with pastel-colored flowers.

"You can't try it on," the saleswoman said with a nasty tone in her voice.

"We'll take it," Caesar said without hesitation.

"It's ten dollars," the old woman said with the satisfaction that he couldn't afford it.

Caesar reached into his pocket and counted off ten dollars and placed the money on the counter. Rainbow grinned and held back her snicker. The saleswoman's faced twisted as if she had suddenly tasted something sour. She put the dress into a bag without another word, her lips tightened with the flavor of contempt, and the unfazed happy couple left the store and headed to Beale Street to buy rings.

They walked until they saw a pawn shop, and Caesar asked, "Is this okay with you?"

"Why wouldn't it be?" Rainbow asked.

"Can I choose it, or would you like to choose the one you want?" Caesar asked, looking into the glass case.

"You choose mine, and I'll choose yours," she answered.

"That sounds fair," Caesar said.

For her he chose a gold band with diamond chips set in it because he thought she was so precious. She chose the widest gold band she could find so every girl could see he was spoken for. Caesar dug deep into his left shoe and paid the man for the rings. They only had one hour to get married before the Shelby County Courthouse closed; it was only open till noon on Saturdays. On the corner, he bought her some flowers, and they hurried down to Third Avenue.

When they arrived at the courthouse, Rainbow went inside the colored restroom to change into her dress. After she combed her hair and colored her lips, she looked at her reflection and let out the laugh she had held inside.

"I'm about to get married, and I'm happy," she said to herself. "Two things I had my doubts would happen for me, and he's so fine in more ways than one."

When she came out of the restroom Caesar couldn't believe his eyes. She looked like a queen to him. Her standing there in that dress reminded him of the women he had seen on the stage in the show that he had seen with his dad so many years ago. Fantasy women that you could see but never touch. He never dreamed he would have one of them, so beautiful of a lady to be his own wife. He finally felt he was blessed, just like his grammy said he was. He was thankful for all the things that had led him to that day: running away to New York, joining the guard, meeting his best friend Stormy, and going to Mississippi to deliver the letter. It was meant to be.

Caesar and Rainbow stood in front of the judge and made their vow to each other, some the judge heard and others that were spoken simply through their eyes. They exchanged the rings, and when they kissed as man and wife, it was the first time that Caesar had held Rainbow that close and kissed her for more than a moment. They both forgot where they were. The judge cleared his throat and motioned for them to leave.

"Here's your marriage certificate," the clerk at the desk said to them on their way out.

Caesar carefully folded it into the envelope and put it in his suit coat pocket next to his heart.

"Do you want something to eat?" he asked, smiling. "I don't want my wife to be walking around hungry."

"Yeah, I do," she said as she laughed. "I surely don't want my husband going around town on an empty stomach."

They laughed some more, grabbed hands, and headed out to Beale Street to find something to eat.

Caesar saw a barbeque joint and said, "The food here looks and smells real good, and it probably tastes even better."

Rainbow hesitated at the door and said, "C, I don't want to get barbecue sauce all over my new wedding dress."

"Don't' worry about it," he said. "If you do, I'll just buy you another one."

She shook her head and followed him to a table where they sat down.

"My wife and I will have the pork ribs and some potato salad," Caesar said when the waitress came over to get their order.

Then Rainbow understood things were that simple to Caesar. He lived within the present moment. She looked at him and wondered if that was the way soldiers lived in the war or if had he always been like that. For her, she had always lived in the future; her past and present were things she never dwelled on. She had known her parents' blues all her life, and then she had her own. The good times were what she had to look forward to. Looking at Caesar, she became conscious that her future sat across from her, here and now.

They took their time eating. Rainbow had wrapped the hand cloth around the collar of her dress and pulled her chair close to the table to be sure no food would fall in her lap. They talked and filled in the blanks that were left in the letters they had written to each other. She told him about growing up dirt-poor and never having enough of anything but love in their house, about living without her brothers, and how it felt to watch her mama and daddy die of broken hearts.

Caesar told her about his mama, how she was a well-known singer who had traveled around the world, how she couldn't leave her career to raise him, and how she died in an automobile wreck. He told her about his grammy and grandy who raised him in Savannah, Georgia, and how he came to live with his dad and his stepmother in Nashville.

"I always dreamed of coming to Memphis," Rainbow told him. I thought I could come here and learn to sew or do hair or something; but when Stormy had to leave town, I dropped out of school and went to work. After that, I never thought I would get out of Tunica."

"It's good you didn't leave," he said. "I wouldn't have known where to find you."

They went over to the park to relax and digest their meal. They sat for a few hours watching the busy birds and squirrels scurrying around for their evening meal.

"Let's go listen to some music before it gets late," Caesar said.

He grabbed the bag with her things in it with one hand and pulled Rainbow up with the other. Then they walked back to Beale Street. They stopped when they saw a crowd had gathered around a young brown-skinned woman who was sitting on a stool playing a guitar. Rainbow noticed the woman's teeth were brown from chewing tobacco but that her face was smooth and attractive.

"Who's that?" Caesar whispered to someone in the crowd.

"Memphis Minnie; she's always out here," the stranger said.

They listened for a while, taken by her musical talent, and then she started singing the blues. Her voice was deep and rich with life experiences that held them captivated. Hearing her song of blues and hard times, Caesar and Rainbow prayed individually that theirs had ended. Then some of the crowd dispersed because they were ashamed to hear her scandalous words, but Memphis Minnie sang louder with no shame in telling her story. She paused to spit it her cup, and Caesar dropped a dollar in a jar at her feet before they continued down the street.

He then heard some upbeat band playing in another joint.

"Let's go in here," he said as he led Rainbow in by the hand.

He found a table against the side wall where they sat down side by side. They listened to the music for a while, and when folks started to get on the dance floor, Caesar extended his elbow.

"Rainbow, you wanna dance?" he asked.

"No, I want to watch for a while," she answered.

Caesar wondered if she had been dancing before. Listening to her talk, it seemed like all they did was work all the time.

After a half hour, she said, "I'm ready to dance now."

He was pleasantly surprised that Rainbow could not only dance, but she was the best one out there. The music was fast like ragtime at first, and they did the shimmie. When the music changed tempo, they did the foxtrot. And when it slowed even more, Rainbow moved close to him and he tightened his arms around her. He could feel his blood rush through his veins, and he was flushed. He was excited by her and wondered if he should pull away, but she just laid her head on his shoulders, and they swayed to the music.

"I think we've danced enough," she told him after a while, and he got their things from the table, and they got a cab to take them to the hotel.

At the top of the steps, Caesar opened his door, but Rainbow just stood on the outside with a questioning look. Caesar stopped, worried that she wanted to stay in her own room.

"Aren't you supposed to carry me over the threshold?" she asked with one hand on her slim hip.

"Yes, ma'am, I am," Caesar said, much relieved.

He put down her bag and lifted her high in his arms and carried her into their room and kicked the door shut with his foot.

"Thank you, kind sir," she said as they laughed together again.

He put her down on the chaise in the sitting area. Then he took off his jacket and sat down beside her.

"Thank you so much for this day, C. I have got to be the happiest black woman in Tennessee," Rainbow said as he hung on her every word.

She touched him on his arm as she talked, and each of the hairs on it stood at attention. He looked deep into her eyes, touched the side of her face, and he knew she understood all the unspoken words that he wanted to say. She had taken full possession of his heart, and it would never be his again. He kissed her full on the lips in a way he had never kissed anybody before, and she returned it as the kiss she had been waiting all her life to receive.

Caesar turned off the light, but the room was still dimly lit from the city lights that shone through the window. Rainbow moved to the window to see the view. Caesar joined her and put his arms around her waist. They stood there for a minute and then he reached down and pulled her dress up and then she raised her arms so he could pull it over her head. Caesar just wanted to explore and touch every inch of her body. He brushed her hair to the side so he could see her neck, and then he kissed it.

"I'm feeling shaky," Rainbow said. "Can we sit on the bed?"

"Sure, do you want me to carry you?" he asked with a smile.

"No, I can make it over there," she said smiling back.

She undressed him and fulfilled her own curiosity and took off her under clothing. They spent the rest of the night kissing, touching, and making love. It was an experience that neither had ever known. It was new, and the more they tried to satisfy their passion for each other, it only seemed to grow stronger. Sheer exhaustion gave them the respite they couldn't find between themselves.

"Good morning," Rainbow said from the window when she heard Caesar stirring.

"It is a good morning," he said to her and threw back the covers, inviting her to join him.

She walked over and got back into the bed, and he hugged her tight glad to have someone to love who wouldn't leave him.

"There's no reason for us to stay here," he whispered behind her ear.

"I know you have a life to get back to," she said.

"No, we have a life to get back to. Besides, we're nearly out of money. If we don't leave today, we won't have enough for train fare, and then I'll have to walk my wife all the way back to Nashville," he said with a chuckle.

"Well, then we had better get dressed and catch the next train outta here, 'cause I'm not about to wear out my best shoes."

Caesar was happy and proud as they sat together at the rear of the train; he had succeeded in doing everything he had come to do that weekend. Riding the streetcar to the house, Rainbow took in all the sights of the city that would be her new home.

David was sitting out on the porch and watched them as they approached the house. They looked good together he thought and he silently wished them all the happiness in love that he had never found for himself.

"It's good to see you again, Rainbow, and I'm proud of you, son," David said as he welcomed them home with a hug. "As usual, you're just in time for dinner."

"I want to cook for Rainbow, Dad," Caesar said.

"I want to cook dinner for you," Rainbow added, not used to anyone waiting on her hand and foot.

"Well, I'm the best cook in the house," Caesar protested.

"Who told you that?" Rainbow asked, faking insult.

"You two can fuss about that one tomorrow because this day's dinner is already done," David said, and they all laughed.

He had never seen his son so happy. That was all he had ever wanted, and that made him happy, too.

Chapter Sixteen

The summer went by fast. Caesar and Rainbow stayed busy going to the movies and picnics, or strolling down Jefferson Street with Ed and Rose. On Sundays, they went to church, but their favorite pastime was watching the Nashville Elite Giants play baseball.

Caesar kept working in the kitchen at the Hermitage Hotel, and he had even begun to make a few dishes. Bullock was lazy and gave Caesar more leeway on cooking since it gave him more time to sit back on his laurels. Rainbow helped David and Ed out at the grocery store. She had wanted to find a job on her own because she she was used to working and didn't want to sit around the house all day, but Caesar didn't want to hear about it.

"You said you been working for as long as you can remember. Rest for a while. I don't want you washing no other folk's clothes or scrubbing their floors. We'll get a chance to work together soon when we open our restaurant."

"All right, Caesar," Rainbow said, compromising. "I'll just help your dad at the store."

"That's a good idea; he can always use the help."

Rainbow was headstrong and independent, but she didn't push. So far, Caesar hadn't given her any reason to complain. Anyway, she liked working at the store. She used the leftover produce to make wine like her father her taught her years before he died. Besides that, she got to meet more people and she could see that they all cared for David and Caesar. But she could sense there was some deep secret that no one dared speak about.

When the fall season took over and the temperatures moved lower, Caesar's anticipation of his twenty-first birthday and what it would mean to him increased to a fever pitch. He dreamed of getting a house for him and Rainbow and finally opening up his own restaurant. He already had the name for it. He planned to call it The Storm's End.

It was two days before Thanksgiving, and Caesar had already begun cooking.

"I thought I could at least make the first Thanksgiving dinner for my husband," Rainbow commented when Caesar began his preparation.

"If you let me do this one, then you can have all the others," Caesar told her.

"Can't I even help you?" she asked, anxious to do something.

"You can come carry the bags at the market," he answered, teasing her.

At the Farmer's Market, Caesar did as Adam taught him and picked the freshest peppers, onions, and celery for his meal. He boiled his cranberries slow until they burst on their own, he sweetened them and then he peeled oranges, removed the skin, and added them to the sauce. He shelled walnuts and pecans and chopped them into small pieces and added them, then he put the dish in the ice box to gel. He and Rainbow picked the winter greens that she had planted behind the house, and he sorted through them, choosing only the best leaves to be cooked. For him, each dish was a masterpiece that he gave his undivided attention.

He invited Ed and Rose to come and share in the feast to celebrate with them. He had so much to be thankful for and wanted to share his good fortune with them.

Caesar sat at the right of David who was seated at the head of the table and started the circle of thanks. "I want to thank the Lord for covering me in the war and making a path for me to find Rainbow. And I want to thank my family, especially my mama, for making it possible for me to have my dream come true."

Rainbow stood up next. "I want to thank the Lord for sending me a man who I can love and who loves me."

Ed stood up next, even though it was Rose's turn. "I want to thank the Lord for good friends who are like family and for Mr. Mallory for trusting me to run his store in the new year. I would also like to ask Rose if she would do me the honor of becoming my wife."

Rose stood up beside him and said, "Now I really have something to be thankful for. I was wondering if you were ever going to ask me. You will have a wife before Christmas."

They all laughed and clapped happy for Ed and Rose.

David stood up and added, "Last but not least, I want to thank the Lord for keeping C safe and bringing him back home. Son, I love you, and I want to help you get your restaurant going after your birthday. As Ed mentioned, he will be running the store from now on, and after you get going, I'm going to retire and wait for my grandbabies."

They made a toast with some of Rainbow's peach wine and began to eat.

It was an unforgettable meal that fed their minds, bodies, and souls. There are few opportunities where you can rejoice without a cloud in the sky, and this was one of them. They were content to enjoy the company of each other, but they had the added blessing that each one sitting around the table had so much to look forward to.

The celebration didn't end that night. It steadily gained momentum, with Ed and Rose getting married in a small service at the church on Christmas Eve, and then a big New Year's party at Greenwood Park. The fireworks that exploded at the moment when Caesar turned twenty-one were a sight that Rainbow had never seen before.

She grabbed him around the waist for a kiss and said, "Now you don't have to live with an older woman."

Caesar felt his body tense for a minute, then shudder, and then relax. Rainbow was just about to ask him what was wrong when a smile spread across his lips, and he gave her a sweet kiss that she wished would last all year long.

Caesar learned that his mother had left him a little more than $18,000, and he received the check on the 5th of January. He deposited it into his account at the Citizens Savings Bank. He decided to keep working at the Hermitage for a while. He made good money there, and it would add to what he needed for his own place. Caesar was raised comfortable and had never done without, but he wasn't a fool about money. He never saw his grandy or His grammy waste what they had. His mama had worked her whole life for what she left him, and he was determined to make it into something she would be proud of.

"I found the perfect spot for the restaurant," Caesar said to David after he got home from work on the weekend. "I saw it a week ago when we were hanging out with Ed and Rose after their wedding."

"That was pretty fast. I'd like to take a look at it," David said with some apprehension.

"Let's go now. I'll drive. I'm ready to get things moving."

Caesar drove a straight line from South Nashville, just past the black business district on Charlotte, to an empty lot on Jefferson Street on the corner of 12th Avenue North.

"This is it. What do you think?" Caesar asked, parking the car.

"I think it's a great location," David said, surprised that Caesar had chosen so well. "I think we should make an offer."

Caesar bought the lot for five hundred dollars before the month was over. He and Rainbow stared at the deed; it was the first thing of real value that either of them had ever owned. Caesar placed the paper in the envelope with their marriage license and put it under the mattress where they slept.

A few days later, David arranged a meeting for Caesar with architect Moses McKissack III and his brother, Calvin, to talk about a design for the building.

"I'd like to be able to sit one hundred and fifty comfortable and have a stage for live entertainment," Caesar told them. "I want a large kitchen with the food preparation area and cleaning area separated. I'll need to have an office for myself and a room for Rainbow to do whatever she wants. I want it to be high-class, but I also want the costs to stay within a budget of $20,000."

Caesar planned to put up half in cash and borrow the other half from his Dad's proceeds from the sale of his furniture store.

"I think we a clear idea of what you want, Mr. Portunus. We'll draw up some plans for you to take a look at within ten days," Moses said.

It didn't take Moses McKissack long to come up with a vision for the restaurant, and he came by the house to show them the plans.

"The entrance is primary," Moses explained. "It gives a preview of what your customers can look forward to in the inside. So to give that majestic feel, we've drawn a façade of the building that is two stories high, with four columns supporting the overhang and framing a large arched double door. There is a lobby, or waiting area, with bathrooms before a grand entrance into the dining room. Inside the dining room, there is a domed ceiling, and the tables will be in the center. There will be a winding staircase that leads upstairs to more tables arranged in a semi-circle."

"I love it," Caesar said. "I can see that I have space at the front of the restaurant for a stage that would accommodate a large band and a singer or dancers."

"That's right. And on the left side, there's a small dance floor, and the right side leads into the kitchen," Moses McKissack showed him. "The kitchen will be spacious, with two ovens, a grill, and multiple stovetops. There's ample storage area for supplies, and the clean-up area has two separate stations."

"There's a back entrance for deliveries and another door for refuse," Calvin added.

"I can't believe it," Caesar said. "It's everything that I dreamed off drawn out down to the last detail on a roll of paper in front of me."

"We aim to please," Calvin McKissack said.

"This is it, Mr. McKissack, this is exactly what I want. This is The Storm's End. How soon before we can get started?"

"We can get it going as soon as the paperwork is done," Moses McKissack said.

Once the construction of the building started, Caesar was glad he had second thoughts about quitting his job. It would have been hard watching and waiting without having something to occupy his time and keep him busy. The seasons changed, and he relaxed more now that his dream was coming to fruition. He enjoyed having someone to come home to and plan with. In their bedroom, Caesar and Rainbow would talk about restaurant and her ideas of color schemes that she wanted to have in the dining room.

"What job am I going to have in the restaurant?" she asked him.

"Your job will be to look pretty and to say hello to all our guests."

"How much does that pay?" she asked with a laugh.

"It's all for you anyway. You're the one who's going to have to pay me," he said and then she really laughed and he loved it.

"Let's see if I can get some work out of you tonight," she said as they tussled around on the bed.

"Now how much can you pay?" he asked and kissed her on the mouth before she could answer.

David would hear them carrying on, and it made him lonely for someone of his own to grow old with. He didn't think that he would ever have wanted another woman in his life after the mess with Grace, but he could see that Caesar was making a life for himself and that he should do the same before he was an old man. Most of the women from the church had given up on him, thinking that he had decided to stay alone, and they had been right. He thought of Rev. Taylor, who had remarried after his wife's death, and he seemed to be happy. Maybe he would try again to love somebody.

***

"David Mallory, it's been a long time. How have you been?" J. Finey Wilson asked when they bumped into each other at the bank.

J. Finley Wilson was the exalted leader at the bank and a member of The Improved Benevolent Order of the Elks of the World.

"I'm doing well. How are you?"

"Good, good. We've missed you down at the Elks."

"I've been busy, but things are easing up some," David said. He hadn't been an active member for years.

"Perfect timing. We're having our April social at the Baron Club tomorrow night with The Phyllis Wheatley Women's Club. You should join us."

"I think I'll do just that," David said.

It might be the perfect opportunity for him to get his feet wet again. The next day, he pulled out his best suit and got a fresh haircut at his barber's on Cedar Street and headed up Jefferson Street to see what he could find.

The minute David walked into the club, heard the music, and felt the energy that circulated in the room, his heartbeat quickened, and he was more alive than he had been in years. Regrets over the last five years that he had spent brooding rose to the surface, and he smiled to himself at the thought of a sixty-year-old man coming back to life. His eyes perused the room and zeroed in on the table that was front and center. There were three women and two gentlemen sitting there. He recognized the men as James Napier and his pastor, Preston Taylor, as he approached the table. In his distinguished manner, J. C., as he was better known, stood up to greet David.

"It's good to see you out and about my friend," J. C. said as they shook hands. "David, I don't know if you have met my wife, Nettie. I'm sure you know Preston and Ida. And Addie Russell, meet David Mallory."

"I know who he is," Addie said. "I lived next door to your Aunt Lilly on Scovel Street. I also went to Pearl High School, and I heard you sing at Fisk with the Jubilee Singers, and I've even shopped in your stores. You never noticed me, but I know all about you."

"Well, you have my attention now," David said as he sat down in the seat next to her. "Is your husband here with you tonight?"

"No, I'm a widow," she answered, and David scooted his chair over a little closer.

Throughout the evening, David tried to learn as much about Addie, as she seemed to already know about him.

"What years did you attend Pearl?" he asked.

She answered him, "I'm as old as you want me to be and as young as you need me to be."

They looked at each other with a smile that soon broke into laughter. David liked Addie. She was not only pretty and elegant, but she was fun, but not in a silly way. She was an intelligent conversationalist with witty repartee. He even thought she was sexy, with her exaggerated movements that made her seem as if she were dancing.

"I'd like to see you again," David told Addie at the end of the evening.

"I've always been here, and I'm not going anywhere. You can call on me," she responded.

David didn't waste any time. He moved fast to catch back up to the life he had let pass him by, and Addie was his central motivation. He accompanied her to church on Sunday morning; they ate dinner together most evenings; and on Saturdays, he took her out on the town. As the summer months heated up, he discovered that passion is not only reserved for the young and that love and lovemaking were for whosoever was inclined to partake. Addie had come into his world at the most opportune time, granting him a relationship free from complications, and it was only a matter of time before she would be his wife.

By the time the cold season had taken hold the outer frame of the restaurant had been closed in and promises of the opening of The Storm's End were made for the upcoming New Year. David and Caesar made plans as they looked over the new construction.

"Addie and I are getting married in the spring," David told Caesar as they stood outside.

"I'm happy for you, Dad; you deserve to have somebody to love."

"She's a good woman, and besides, who wants to grow old all by themselves. We only have one disagreement: She doesn't want to sell her house."

"Why does she have to, Dad?"

"Son, I have made many mistakes pertaining to the women in my life, but I know better than to take up residence with the ghost of my future wife's first husband."

"I hadn't thought about that," Caesar said, shaking his head with a chuckle.

"I also know from nature that there can only be one queen bee in a honey bee hive, we all need our privacy and space. I think it'll be best if you and Rainbow move over to her house until you get a place of your own, then y'all two can get to work on my grandbabies."

***

Blessings poured down like rain in the spring. David and Addie were married in a small, private ceremony in her living room. It was David's compromise after his insistence that they live in his home. Caesar and Rainbow planned a big dinner for David and Addie on Easter Sunday to celebrate their good fortune. They also invited Ed and Rose.

"Come on to the table, everybody. My hubby has prepared a beautiful feast for y'all," Rainbow said as she finished setting the table.

"I'll bless the food," Addie said as they joined hands at the table and she began to pray.

"Amen," Ed said, but before they had taken one morsel, he made an announcement. "Rose and I are having a baby."

"That's good news," David said, reaching for the mashed potatoes.

For him it was a mixed blessing. He loved Ed and was happy for him, but in his heart he wished it was Caesar instead. He prayed silently that Rainbow wouldn't be childless like Grace and avoid all the problems that they had endured.

"Congratulations!" Caesar said as he slapped Ed on the back. "That's an unexpected surprise for today.

"Let's make a toast to Rose's health and the new baby," Rainbow added as she poured her pear wine into the glasses.

Caesar hadn't given babies much thought, even though he and Rainbow went through the motions of making one nearly every night. His main focus was the impending birth of his restaurant.

"I couldn't help but feel a tinge of jealousy at dinner," Rainbow said to Caesar that night when they went to bed. "Rose is my friend, and I'm happy for them, but I want us to have a baby, too."

"We will, sweetie. We aren't doing anything to prevent it," he said with a squeeze to her behind.

"I guess I'll just have to wait until it's my time. We'll probably be too busy to take care of a baby for while anyway."

The time had come for Caesar and Rainbow to focus their energies on the opening of The Storm's End.

In the morning, he told Rainbow, "Today is gonna be my last day at the Hermitage."

"It's time to let it go," she agreed. "Don't ruffle any feathers on your way out."

Caesar went to the Hermitage as usual and did everything that he normally did, but at the end of the day, just as he Farrell and Bullock were leaving, he stopped them.

"I want to thank you two gentlemen for the opportunity to work with you, but I'm going to have to quit to because of some family business that needs me right now."

"I'm sorry to hear that," Farrell said, stunned at Caesar's news. "We both have come to depend on you in the kitchen. You know, you can get things worked out and then come on back to work."

"I couldn't ask y'all to hold that spot open, and I've got to hurry on home," he said, rushing away before they asked a lot of questions.

He'd learned at a young age not to create a problem where there wasn't one.

The McKissack brothers had worked their crews at an accelerated pace to have the restaurant ready by the date Caesar had given them, Sunday, May 21, the day before Rainbow's twenty-third birthday. Moses and Carl had brought his dream to life, and everything he had envisioned and described to them was there in brick and mortar, wood and glass, cast iron and stainless steel, fine fabrics, porcelain, and crystal. He had less than ten days to get the necessary supplies in place before he could cook the first meal.

Rainbow had stocked quite a collection of fruit wines that included blackberry, plum, watermelon, and peach at the house. She planned to serve them discreetly since prohibition was still the law to special customers to compliment C's varied seasonings. She had also spent some time experimenting with combinations of teas and coffees and adding ginger and cinnamon to create different flavors to add to their beverage offerings. She decided to take charge of the drinks since C was possessive about the food preparation for the restaurant.

"I still need to hire waiters, assistants in the kitchen, and clean-up crew; and I need to print up the menu," Caesar ranted to David as they took in the grandeur of the finished project. "And I still don't have any musical entertainment to bring this place to life for the opening."

Caesar had moments when he was overwhelmed by the enormity of the whole thing and doubted he was ready to manage it all himself.

"It's a lot to organize in a short time, but we're gonna get it done, son. Don't worry," David said in an effort to appease his anxiousness. "That's why I turned over the store to Ed, so I can be here to help get this running."

David had no trouble ordering all the restaurant furniture, kitchen supplies, and staple foods from vendors he had known over the years. They worked side by side organizing account books to keep track of spending and supplies.

"I really want to make the opening special for Caesar and Rainbow," David said to Addie when he got home. "I've got some old friends still in the music business I can get in touch with for the entertainment."

"That would put the icing on the cake if you could work something out," Addie said, massaging his shoulders.

"I only need to know who might be coming through town or close enough to it where they will stop by the restaurant for a short set."

Good fortune smiled on them when he found out that Ma Rainey was leaving a show in Memphis and traveling to St. Louis for another booking during the third week in May and she always passed through Nashville.

David sent her a telegram saying, "There's a WWI hero of the 369th who's opening a restaurant in town and needs some entertainment. Name your price for you and your jazz band for one night."

She replied, "A Harlem Hellfighter is the only man I can't say no to. The expenses for my band are the only fee I'll require."

David breathed a sigh of relief that every base had now been covered. Now the only worry was filling up the restaurant with paying customers.

Chapter Seventeen

Any worries that David or Caesar had turned out to be wasted. A line had gathered at the front of The Storm's End by five o' clock. Jefferson Street was the place to be for black folks in Nashville, and many had watched the restaurant be built from the ground up and wanted to be the first to get in. Caesar's cooking wasn't a secret to most in town, and some had heard rumors that Ma Rainey was going to be singing there for the opening, so it looked like it would be filled to capacity. A flat fee of one dollar would be charged for each person for the dinner and the show.

"I decided to serve traditional fare that I know they'll like, with a dash of my own flair for tonight," Caesar said to Rainbow when walked into the kitchen of the restaurant. "I'll wait a while before I add the dishes I learned in Paris."

"That's right, honey, don't give them all you got on the first night," she said, giving him a quick kiss on the cheek.

"You look like a pretty picture," he said to Rainbow, who was dressed in a brand new yellow gown similar to color she had worn when Caesar had asked her to be his wife.

"I'm glad you noticed," she said twirling in a circle. "I brought your finest suit for you to change into if the food is all prepared.

Addie and Dad are out front dressed to the nines. He's got on his black formal suit, and she's wearing a powder blue gown."

"I saw them; they're all set to open the doors as hosts at 6:00. Ed is going to stand in as head waiter. The band is here already, and when they finish setting up, I'll feed them something light that'll hold them through the set."

"You've got it all under control. Enjoy your night," Rainbow said, taking his suit into his office.

It was a night that no one who attended would forget if they lived two lifetimes. When the double doors finally opened at the top of the hour, the dinner guests were transported into another atmosphere. The décor was regal and they were all seated like royalty. A smooth orchestra flowed out of a phonograph and the service was first class.

There was no menu for the evening; Caesar had prepared a three-course meal that started with a salad of romaine lettuce, chopped ham, boiled eggs, parmesan cheese, and topped it with bread crumbs. He made a special dressing of olive oil, vinegar, lemon juice, pepper, and Italian spices. The main entrée was a choice of roasted pig, New York steaks, or fried chicken, with grilled whole potatoes and green beans in a mushroom sauce. Dessert was peach cobbler or coconut marble cake. Rainbow's strawberry and watermelon wines, mixed teas and coffees flowed throughout the meal.

At the end of dessert, the lights were dimmed, and the band began to play, first a slow jazz, then a more upbeat New Orleans Style, and then it turned bluesy. The lights blinked off and then the spotlight came on, and there was Ma Rainey. She gave the audience a devilish smile, and her gold teeth reflected the light back toward them. She began to sway to the music, and her sequined dress flashed and moved to the beat. But the shine of the necklace of twenty-dollar gold pieces drew the audience's attention back to her face. She started to sing her song, "Wild Women Don't Have No Blues," and the room was electrified. She made them laugh, blush, shake their heads, and want to cry; and they clapped their hands until they were red. They listened to her troubles and forgot about their own. When she finished her set and left the stage after little more than an hour, they all knew what it was to have the blues.

The lights went up, and Caesar came out on stage, tall, handsome, and looking very debonair in his dinner suit.

"I want to thank you all for coming out to the opening of 'The Storm's End,'" he said. "I hope you enjoyed the meal, the music, and the service. I would like to thank my father, David Mallory, for all of his help and support in making this night possible; my best friend, Ed, the McKissack Brothers; and my hard workers who gave above and beyond whatever I asked of them to make this dream a reality for me. Most important, I have to thank my partner and real dream come true, my wife who is truly my rainbow at the end of the storm."

The room broke into applause, not only for the glorious meal he served them, but for his graciousness in doing so. The opening had been a triumphant success.

***

Running a flourishing business was time consuming and energy draining, but it was a labor of love for Caesar and Rainbow that kept them close. In the fall, Ed and Rose had a baby girl they named Violet. With all the things that Rainbow juggled through each day, she felt empty-handed. The seasons changed and changed again and again.

Time rushed on, and then it was the new year in 1925, and Caesar's twenty-fifth birthday. The family gathered at The Storm's End.

"Caesar, I'm so proud of you, and I'm sure your grammy is, too. She chose this day and made arrangements for you to receive the inheritance from her estate," David said, handing him an envelope.

Inside the envelope was a check for $40,000, more than double the one he had received from his mother.

"Thank you, Dad. Without your help, I don't think I could have pulled everything off. The restaurant is turning a nice profit, and now I can pay you back for the loan you gave me."

"You don't owe me anything, C. I'm glad to be able to share in your success," David said.

"My greatest success is yet to come," Caesar exclaimed. "I'm happy to announce that Rainbow is pregnant, and our baby will be born in July."

"Now, that's what I wanted more than anything!" David cheered, even happier than the expectant couple.

"Since we're all making announcements, how about one more?" Ed said. "Rose and I are having another baby."

"This is going to be a great year," Caesar said, raising a glass of champagne in a toast.

A week into the new year, Caesar rewarded himself with a new automobile, a blue 1925 Buick. He pulled up in front of the restaurant and beeped the horn until his dad came out.

"This is a beauty, C," David said, sliding into the passenger side.

"I've got something to show you," Caesar said, driving off. "I talked to the McKissack brothers about building a new house for Rainbow and the baby; they're drawing up some designs for us."

He stopped the car in front of a lot at the upper end of Jefferson Street near Fisk University.

"This is the spot; I bought it so we can still be close to the restaurant."

"You've been a busy man, C. Don't tell me anything else for a month," David said, grabbing his chest feigning a heart attack. "I need some time to catch my breath."

Caesar always kept his money in three places, and he did the same with the remainder of his inheritance. One third was placed in Citizen Savings Bank, another third in the People's Bank, and the last third in a safe only he knew existed. There were times when Rainbow could scarcely believe she was living her own life; it was so different from the life she had known in Mississippi. There wasn't much she wanted that she couldn't have.

The season changed for them on March 15, just as the last chills of winter faded. It was a Sunday afternoon at the Lea Christian Church.

"I'm going to church with Rose this morning," Rainbow said to Caesar.

She was restless and he was usually busy on Sunday mornings at the restaurant.

"That was a good service. Rev. Taylor sure can preach," Rose said after the service.

"The choir was on fire, Rose. I thought I was going to shout," Rainbow added.

"I would've put another dollar in the offering plate to see that," Rose said laughing.

They were casually talking and walking out of the sanctuary when it seemed as if the members following them suddenly bunched up at the door and lurched forward behind them. Rainbow stumbled and fell forward, the heel of her left shoe caught on the steps, and her hand was just an inch short from reaching the banister than ran along the steps.

Shocked from the fall and the pain that shot up her back, Rainbow looked up in agony at Rose and saw her glaring at an older dark-skinned woman still on the steps above them. In moments a couple near them tried to help Rose lift Rainbow to her feet, but she couldn't stand.

They carried her back inside the church. "Somebody get us a doctor!" Rose shouted, staying close behind Rainbow.

"Nooo, help my baby," Rainbow screamed, she began to cry with terror when she felt the warm liquid flow down the inside of her leg and onto the pew.

"Stay still, Rain," Rose said, grabbing her hands and trying to calm her, but she was inconsolable.

Dr. Beckman, who ran a clinic on Cedar Street, had attended the service and rushed in to help.

He examined her quickly and said, "Let's get her home."

True to form, bad news travels fast, and Caesar burst in the door just minutes after the doctor was done attending to Rainbow.

"What happened?" he asked with his arms open, pleading for an explanation.

Rose stood up to speak, "We were walking out after church service, talking and I think she missed a step and fell. There were so many folks on the steps, and she couldn't catch herself."

Caesar shook his head in disbelief. It didn't make sense. He turned to the doctor for an encouraging report, but he shook his head, saying, "It was nothing I could do."

Caesar moved swiftly past him and went into the bedroom he and Rainbow shared, and the tears on her face broke his heart.

"I'm sorry, C," she said. "I should have stayed home today or gone to the restaurant with you, and this never would have happened. I wish I could turn everything back."

"Quiet, pretty girl," he said. "It's not your fault; bad things happen that we don't understand. The most important thing is that you are all right. We'll have another baby, I promise."

Ed went over to David and Addie's to give them the news.

"Something terrible has happened," Ed said when Addie opened the door.

"What is it?" David said, coming up behind her.

"There was an accident at the church after the service. Rainbow fell down the stairs, and she lost the baby.

David felt his body weaken, and he reached in the air around him for a place to sit. Addie guided him to the couch in the living room.

"How could this happened?" he asked, just as upset as Rainbow was about the baby.

"I don't know," Ed said. "But Grace was at church today, and Rose suspects that she might have pushed Rainbow on the steps."

David's blood pressure flew to dangerous heights at the mere thought that Grace could again be the cause of their misfortune. For a moment, he even regretted that he'd had the restraint to let her live years ago after what she had done.

"I'm calling a doctor for you," Addie said, rushing out of the room.

David was ordered to bed rest, and Addie made sure that he followed doctor's orders. Caesar had to hire replacements for both of them at the restaurant.

A week later, Rose came by to visit Rainbow.

"Rose, who was the woman you she gave the hard look to at the church?" Rainbow asked, referring back to that fateful day.

"I don't want to cause any trouble, but I feel that you have a right to know," Rose answered. "That woman was David's first wife, Grace. She couldn't have any kids of her own. When Caesar first came to stay with them, she hated him. She would hit and scratch him every time David's head was turned. When he got older, she still couldn't keep her hands off him, but it was in a different way," she said with a sideways look that let Rainbow know which way. "That's the reason he ran off to New York and went in the service, to get away from her. David left her faster than she could blink to keep from killing her. I don't know if she had anything to do with you falling, but when I looked up, she was standing there. I didn't say nothing because I didn't want Caesar or Mr. Mallory to go after her. She's evil, and nothing good could've come from it."

Chapter Eighteen

B lack performers traveling through Nashville all stopped at The Storm's End. It was the place to be on Jefferson Street. Bessie Smith had sung a song before her late meal after her show at the Bijou. W. C. Handy, Louis Armstrong, and Mamie Smith had even stopped by when they were in town. The restaurant was flying high, but the Portunus house couldn't shake the blues. Rainbow rarely came out of the house, and some days she never made it out of bed struggling with the pain of her loss and her anger toward Grace. Caesar tried everything to raise her spirits.

"I got a present for you," Caesar said excited, coming home to check on her in the afternoon before her birthday."

"I don't want anything," she said sullenly, turning over in the bed.

Caesar's heart sank lower. He sat down on the bed and turned on the radio he had bought for her. Music flowed out behind the sound of a fierce trumpet playing. The sounds touched something deep inside near Rainbow's grief. She sat straight up in the bed and let the sounds capture her.

"Thank you, C, I love it!" she said with her eyes focused on something he couldn't see.

Rainbow spent hours listening to the radio and not much else. It seemed to take her further away from Caesar, and he worried that he would never hear her sweet laugh again.

Then one morning in August, Ed came into the restaurant and said, "Rose had the baby last night; it's a girl."

Caesar rushed home to tell Rainbow before someone else did. He thought she might go over the edge when she heard the news.

"Rain, Rose had a baby girl last night," he said with some hesitation.

"She did. That's wonderful," she answered with a smile. Then, surprisingly, she got dressed up and insisted on going with him to Ed and Rose's house to see the new baby.

Caesar was relieved and nervous at the same time.

"Come on in here," Ed said, opening the door, "Rose will be happy to see y'all."

"I'll wait out here for minute and talk to Ed. You go on back, honey," Caesar said.

Rainbow took tiny tentative steps to the bedroom, not wanting to disturb the quiet.

"I'm so glad you're here," Rose said when Rainbow appeared in the doorway. "I've been missing my friend. Come over here. I'd like you to pick out a name for her?"

"Can we call her Hope?" Rainbow asked thoughtfully looking at the newborn. "Because that's what I see when I look at this baby."

"That sounds perfect," Rose said, reaching up and handing the baby girl to her. "Hold Hope for a while. I'm tired."

Rainbow took the baby and sat down on the bed beside Rose, rocking the new life in her arms.

Nature's season of hibernation may have been upon them again, but Rainbow was coming back to her life. She started going back to the restaurant and coming up with new combinations of beverages to compliment Caesar's new recipes.

"Here, try this," she said to Caesar one day. "It's my new creation."

"Ooo, that is bitter," Caesar said, making a face and twisting his lips.

"It can't be that bad," Rainbow laughed, and with that sound, his own heart began to heal.

He kept teasing her, joking and doing things just to hear her laugh because it was then he knew that his world was all right after all. Slowly, they recovered from their tragedy, and joy filled their lives again.

"The house is finished," Caesar told Rainbow a few weeks after the anniversary of that critical day.

"I guess I should start packing our things," she said unenthusiastically.

It was torture for them to move in and see the empty room they had planned for the baby, but Dr. Beckman said that there wasn't any health problem that would keep her from getting pregnant again, so they kept trying.

Rainbow and Caesar pulled themselves back together, but David never fully recovered. Over the next few years, his high blood pressure damaged his kidneys and sapped his energy, and he wasn't able to work at the restaurant. He and Addie sold the Mallory grocery store, and Ed went to work fulltime with Caesar.

***

"You know we haven't had any time off since we got married eight years ago," Caesar said to Rainbow at a picnic in Hadley Park, where they were celebrating Hope's third birthday. "I think it's time for us to have a holiday."

"Do you really mean it?" Rainbow asked, getting excited. "I'd love to go somewhere I've never been before and breathe some different air for a change."

"I mean it," he said. "We've been through a lot together, and some days I feel so much older than 28 years old. I heard from some of the guests that Paradise Garden, this resort in Idlewild, Michigan, is a beautiful place to relax and have fun."

"I'm ready to go today," Rainbow said, wrapping her arms around his waist.

The following Monday, Caesar called the resort and made reservations for him and Rainbow to go there for a week. Rainbow was overjoyed about taking a trip; she hadn't traveled three hundred miles from the place where she was born. Caesar had been halfway around the world, but he had never gone anywhere to relax and enjoy himself.

"Do you think we need to close the restaurant until we get back?" he asked Ed.

"No, man, the assistant cooks can hold things together until you get back," he assured Caesar. "I've got the rest covered."

On the first weekend in August, Caesar and Rainbow took the train to Detroit; and from there, they rode the Pere Marquette Railroad to Idlewild. When they arrived, the resort was in the middle of its Third Annual Carnival and Chautauqua, and that would make their vacation even more special and eventful. Caesar had to spend extra on a larger cottage because the resort was tightly booked.

While they were unpacking their clothes in their cottage Rainbow grabbed Caesar's hand and said, "I just want to thank you for being so good to me."

"Baby, there's nothing I wouldn't do for you. Before I came to give y'all that letter, I didn't know I could be this happy."

"Me too, C, but sometimes I feel bad because we lost the baby, and maybe I can't have another one," Rainbow said, working hard to hold back her emotions.

"The only thing that matters to me is that you're my wife," Caesar said as he pulled her close. "I'm satisfied with just you. Now, let's get this honeymoon going."

They found that Idlewild was the "Black Eden," having everything anyone would need to have a good time. The cottage was comfortable, but at times they felt like they were camping out. They saw deer, red foxes, bears, and a host of different birds. Rainbow loved the water, and they spent most of their time on the beach by the lake, swimming or in a boat, where they never caught a single fish. There were lectures, dramatic oratories, and concerts by famous black people and parties scheduled for the annual celebration, where they danced into the early hours.

"I can't believe we're going to get to hear W.E.B. DuBois speak at the Paradise Clubhouse after lunch today," Caesar said to Rainbow, marveling at their good fortune.

"That's nice, but it's Bessie Smith who's gonna steal the show this evening in the Paradise Lounge after dinner," Rainbow replied.

"She can't hold a candle to you; you'll be the star tonight when we get back to the cottage."

Caesar and Rainbow spent every night wrapped in each other's arms, adding to the heat of the August nights and enjoying the sex and passion they had for each other. It was the most romantic time that they had ever had together.

"Promise me we'll take a time off for a vacation every year," Rainbow whispered.

"Whatever you want, baby," Caesar answered.

It had been good to get away and feel young and carefree for a while. The week went by in a blur, and they had so much fun that Caesar wished that they could have stayed for another week.

"We're packing our bags, and I can't wait to come back," Caesar said.

"Maybe we should stop packing," Rainbow said seductively.

"I wish we could, but we've got a business to run."

The couple headed back on the train to Nashville looking good with their skin gently toasted and feeling refreshed and energized. They had been entertained and informed; some of the lectures they heard had Rainbow thinking about taking some college classes.

"We should go by the restaurant before we go home and make sure it's okay," Caesar said as soon as the train pulled into the station. But when he got there, he saw that everything had run smoothly in their absence.

Their next stop was to check on David.

"Hey, Dad, we're back home. How are you feeling?" Caesar asked, coming into the living room when they stopped by the house.

"Much better now," David answered from the sofa, and their glow seemed to brighten him some when he saw they had returned safely.

***

Business was back to the usual in a few weeks, and Rainbow registered for two morning classes at Tennessee Agricultural and Industrial State College. She was thinking she might like to become a social worker and help orphan children find homes. She was so excited about going to college and doing something on her own that her nerves unsettled her stomach every morning as soon as she sat down in the classroom.

Rainbow hated the feeling, and it ruined her concentration, so she delayed eating breakfast until after the lecture and walked down to the restaurant after class. She loved sitting there among the other students, listening and taking notes from Professor Haynes. Her skipping breakfast didn't turn out to be such a good idea when on the morning after her mid-term examination, she fainted in front of Smith's Funeral Home.

"I haven't had anything to eat today," Rainbow said after Mr. and Mrs. Smith revived her.

"Let's get you inside," Mr. Smith said, bringing her in their waiting area.

"Here's some coffee and sweet bread while I call for Caesar to come and pick you up," Mrs. Smith said kindly.

"Thank you, ma'am," Rainbow said, biting into the bread.

"There's no need to get upset," Mrs. Smith said, giving Caesar the news on the phone. "She just fainted in front of our storefront."

"I'm on my way up there," he said, hanging up the telephone, nearly scared out of his mind, and talking to himself. "What in the hell was Rainbow doing at the funeral home."

"I'm fine, I'm fine," Rainbow said to calm Caesar when he rushed in, but he drove her home and sent for Dr. Beckman to come by and give her a check-up.

Caesar couldn't explain, it but he had a fear of losing her, and he wanted to make sure she was all right. It was probably because it seemed as if everyone he ever really cared about either died, or he was separated from them for one reason or another.

"You can stop your worrying, Caesar; there's nothing wrong. Your wife is pregnant again."

"Thank you so much, Dr. Beckman," Caesar told him, feeling relieved and cheerfully surprised. "I was just about to get used to the idea that maybe we weren't going to have kids of our own."

The news was like a miracle cure to David. Within weeks, he was on his feet, and he and Addie were hosting at The Storm's End again.

"I'm not going to let you out of my sight this time," Caesar said, taking extra precautions to protect Rainbow. "There won't be another unfortunate accident. I promise you that."

"You don't have to do that, C. I'm going to drop my class and be very careful this time."

Rainbow was very cautious and spent most of her time at the restaurant or at home.

"Let's go shopping for the baby furniture and things," Rose said when she dropped by one morning. "My mama has the girls, and you need to get some exercise."

"I can't Rose. I promised C I wouldn't go anywhere without him," Rainbow said. "I don't like it, but I understand his worry. I do my best to stay occupied around here."

"I guess I can't blame him," Rose said, feeling partly responsible for the accident at church.

"Pray for my patience, girl," Rainbow said as Rose was leaving.

It was fall, also the season for those things which grow beneath the surface to be hidden from sight through the winter for spring blossoms. Rainbow eased out by herself and went to the Farmers' Market and bought tulip and daffodil bulbs to plant in a garden on the side of the house.

"When they bloom, it'll be time for my baby to be born," she said to herself.

At their traditional Thanksgiving feast, Rainbow's tummy was beginning to round and they truly had much to celebrate and to be thankful for. Their anticipation continued to grow with the swell of Rainbow's belly over each passing month; and by the time the rainy season began, carrying the extra weight of the baby was becoming a strain. She was encouraged when the daffodils and tulips she'd planted bloomed in a kaleidoscope of color in the yard, letting her know that it wouldn't be long before the life she carried would come into the world.

"Have you thought about names?" Caesar asked her in the darkness of the bedroom.

"If the baby is a boy, we'll name him Caesar after his daddy. And if it's a girl, we'll name her Helena."

"Those sound good to me," he said, feeling the baby move under his hand on her belly.

***

"I can't take it much longer," Rainbow said to Rose when she brought the girls over on Mother's Day for a visit. "I pray this baby will be born soon. The pain in my back is nearly unbearable," she said, feeling impatient and irritable. "Dr. Beckman has me confined to this bed all day."

"I know it's hard, but you don't have much longer," Addie said to comfort her. She and David had come to stay and calm her agitation, while Caesar did his best to stay at work.

Rainbow felt the first pain of labor on the afternoon of her birthday, but after a few hours, they subsided and she felt well enough to come down and eat the special dinner Caesar had cooked for her.

"I made all of your favorites, sweetie: barbecue chicken, potato salad, green beans, and chocolate cake."

"I'm ready for all of it," Rainbow said, fixing herself a plate.

"You're mighty hungry, aren't you, Mrs. Portunus?" he said, teasing her about her appetite as she ate heartily.

"Don't forget, I'm eating for two," she laughed.

They spent a relaxed evening on the front porch under a soothing breeze to digest their meal. They went to bed early, and Rainbow got a much-needed restful night's sleep. She awoke late in the morning with her back stiff again, and Caesar had already gone to the restaurant.

When Addie heard her stirring, she knocked on the door and asked, "How you feeling today? You want something to eat?"

Rainbow opened her mouth to say something sarcastic, but a sharp pain mixed with pressure that radiated from the small of her back in all directions caught the words and for almost half a minute, she couldn't speak and then she looked at Addie wide-eyed and said, "I think the baby is coming. Go get C!"

They didn't have a telephone at the house, so David drove to Dr. Beckman's office to let him know that Rainbow's pains had started.

"How long has she been having pains?" Dr. Beckman asked.

"She just had one around eleven o' clock," David answered.

"All right, I've got a few more patients to see, and then I'll be there," Dr. Beckman said, "Doesn't sound like the baby's in an awful hurry just yet."

David was hesitant and unsure about leaving without him, but he needed to get the restaurant to bring Caesar home. When he walked into the restaurant kitchen, he didn't have to say a word. Caesar dropped whatever was in his hands, pulled off his apron, and followed him out to the car. Caesar jumped into the driver's seat, and David got in quickly, lest he find himself standing on the curb and having to walk back to the house. The car sped through the few blocks, and Caesar was up the steps in three long strides.

"I'm here, Rain," he said, sitting on the bed beside her.

He did his best to distract Rainbow in between the birthing pains. He rubbed her back and talked about what was going on at the restaurant.

"Finally, he's here," Caesar said, and they all breathed a sigh of relief when they heard Dr. Beckman's knock on the door a couple of hours later.

Dr. Beckman had his nurse, Brenda, with him. Addie led them up the stairs where he examined Rainbow while everyone waited outside.

When he came to the door, he asked, "What's for dinner? We got time to eat."

This was probably the first time that Caesar wasn't in the mood to prepare some food or eat.

"Come on down, Doc. Addie can warm something up for you and Brenda," David said nervously.

The doctor seemed to enjoy the leftover meal from Rainbow's birthday celebration, and he went on and on about the money he was making on his investments in the stock market. For a while, they wondered if he remembered that there was a baby about to be born upstairs and when he was going to get back to the business at hand.

"Her water's broken!" Caesar yelled down to them, and finally Dr. Beckman and his nurse went back up the steps.

It was around eight o'clock, and Rainbow's labor intensified as the evening went into the night. Her painful screams unnerved Caesar and he began to breathe like he had been running a mile at top speed. Dr. Beckman gave a warning look to David and then a nod to Caesar.

"Why don't you take a short walk with me. It'll calm you down," David said, getting the message that Caesar needed some air.

"You're about to be a father, C, and I want you to know how proud I am of you and what you have done with your life," David told him. "I know you'll all be fine."

It was after midnight when Dr. Beckman saw the crown of the head. Rainbow's piercing cry as she pushed out the baby drew Caesar back into the room.

"You got yourself a boy child," Dr. Beckman said to them as the baby cried out.

He wiped the baby's face, tied the cord, and handed the baby to Miss Brenda. Rainbow fell back on the bed exhausted, and Caesar grinned with pride. Dr. Beckman exhaled loudly as the nurse cleaned up the new baby. But then Rainbow's body heaved forward, twisting with an agonizing thrust of pain. Dr. Beckman put his hand on her shoulder and leaned down to check for the afterbirth, and he wasn't sure if he could trust his own eyes.

"She's got another one!" he said, seeing the small feet of another baby, a twin in the breech position.

The tension that had flowed out of the room surged back.

"I need you to push again," he said to Rainbow. "There's another baby coming."

Confused, Rainbow grabbed the bed sheets and balled them up in her fists and screamed as she drew her energy from somewhere and pushed.

"It's another boy child," Dr Beckman said with less enthusiasm than the first.

This baby wasn't breathing, and his skin was an off shade color of gray and blue. The doctor cut the cord, and Nurse Brenda took the baby.

While he searches for the words to say to them, Rainbow yelled to the nurse frantically, "Give me my babies!"

The nurse laid them on either side of her. Rainbow looked at them, and her eyes filled with tears, happy and sad. Caesar, who had stood frozen, kneeled beside the bed to hold his sons. One baby looked lifeless, and the other was strong and healthy. Rainbow pulled them close in her arms to her chest to hold them close. The babies touched as they were in her womb, and the life force of the healthy baby surged across through the flesh of the other, and he began to breathe. His color changed and then he cried. Rainbow threw her head back and laughed in relief. Caesar watched the whole scene in amazement and the rest of the room was silent, unable to believe what their eyes had witnessed.

David came in the room with Addie and shouted, "Thank you, Jesus!" and his shout brought them out of the daze, and they exchanged grateful hugs. It was the greatest blessing that they could have hoped for, twin boys born in the early hours of May 24, 1929.

"I'm going to name both of them Caesar--Caesar Blue and Caesar Bless Portunus--for the one who was born blue, and his brother, who blessed him," Rainbow said joyously.

Chapter Nineteen

Rainbow marveled at her baby sons, the bond between them, and how they cared for each other. If this was the payment for all the grief she had suffered, she had struck a solid bargain.

They kept her busy day and night, and nursing them presented a challenge.

"Caesar, these babies are something else, neither of them will nurse unless the other is being fed at the same time. And while I hold them at my breast, they stretch their bodies discontent until their little feet touch."

"I don't even know why I bought that extra bed either because they refuse to sleep unless they're both in the same one," Caesar added.

"I'm glad they love each other. You need somebody with you in this life you can depend on," Rainbow said. "I just wish my mama could have seen them. They would have made all the difference, and I sure could use her help. I miss her so much now."

"I guess nobody can take the place of your mama," Caesar said thoughtfully. "Addie will help out as much as she can, but she's got her hands full with Dad."

"I'm not complaining, C. We're fine."

The first three months around the Portunus house were hectic, but none of them would have had it any other way. One morning, Caesar walked into their room and saw that Blue had climbed out of the crib and was hanging over the side.

"Oh my God!" Caesar hollered, horrified as he rushed over to the baby bed to catch him and found that Bless was holding onto Blue's hand through the railing. "You should have seen them," Caesar explained to Rainbow once he had them back in the bed. "The sight touched my heart. It reminded me of the many nights I spent on the battlefield with Stormy, where we had to depend on each other for safety. I thank God for the chance to raise these boys."

"Me, too, C," she replied. "We've been blessed."

Caesar couldn't be happier. His life was truly complete with a family of his own.

There are never highs without lows. Business at the restaurant had begun to slow down for the first time since it opened. Factories were laying off employees, and construction had slowed to a crawl. The atmosphere in the city was filled with talk about the party that was the 1920s was about to come to an end. The bottom was about to drop from under the dance floor.

"Things are getting real tough, C. We might have to make some changes around here," Ed said to him one morning. "Folks don't have the money to eat at home, much less in a restaurant."

Caesar leaned back in his chair and thought about the decade, and he had no complaints. He had been through ups and downs, but all in all it had been a season of life and love for him. He had found his soulmate and married her; he had built the restaurant that he wanted, and it had been a successful and profitable venture; he had built a home for his wife and family; and he had two sons he cherished. He was content.

"I think we need to reduce the staff until things pick up," Ed said, waiting for Caesar's response.

"I don't want to make things harder on anybody; but we do have families to provide for now, and I want to leave my boys with something to help make their dreams come true, just as my mama and grammy did for me. Make whatever changes you feel are necessary, Ed."

The boys were five months old on October 24, Black Thursday, the day the lights began to dim. Four days later, on October 29, the lights went out, and the stock market crashed. Panic spread around the country, and the prominent black folks of Nashville who had invested in stocks felt the pain. The restaurant was practically empty for weeks at a time. David came by on a particularly slow night to talk.

"I'm going through hell, son," David told Caesar. "I took most of the profits from the sale of the grocery store and invested them in stocks."

"Damn, Dad, you didn't need to take that chance," Caesar said to him in frustration.

"I was making huge gains for a while, and then I invested more of my savings on the advice of Dr. Beckman when he was at the house when the boys were born. It's all gone except pennies on the dollar."

"Well, don't let it run your pressure up and kill you. We all gonna be fine. I can pay you back the money you loaned me for the restaurant."

"I know. I'm fortunate enough to have some savings left and the house.Still, I'm so mad I could spit. I wish I could kick my own ass. It was my own bad decisions that caused me to lose so much, and I did it willingly with only the promise that the good times would never end."

Addie did what she could to ease his frustration, but David was disappointed in himself for being reckless with the money from his life's work. Caesar and Rainbow brought the boys over to play to take his mind off of things, but it only lasted during the time they were there. David's anger swelled from his gut as the weeks passed until it reached his right temple, and then he had a massive stroke just before the fall holiday season began.

David lay in his bed, unable to move his left side with his speech impaired and watched his family fuss over him. He reflected back over his life. He was seventy years old; he had a good run, and knew he wouldn't make into the new decade. He praised God for giving him a son like Caesar and allowing him time to know him. He was thankful for meeting Addie and for the chance to be loved again. He was grateful for the opportunity to see his grandsons and feel the immortality that his legacy would live on.

David was satisfied that after all the misfortunes and blues that had come down on him in his life that he could leave this world with a sweet taste in his mouth. He had been blessed. He smiled as he closed his eyes thinking, they were right when they said, "You can't take it with you."

***

"This was the happiest year of my life until a few days ago," Caesar said to himself as he watched his two sons asleep on the bed in their Sunday outfits after the funeral services. He mulled over the mystery of life and its sense of balance, why our joys and sorrows come together, and how we can be happy and sad at the same time.

"I had everything that I wanted, and now my father is dead. If it wasn't for Rainbow and these boys, I would be all alone. I don't have any more family."

Caesar was almost thirty years old, without a mother or father, aunt or uncle, sister or brother. He realized how much living from day to day was like the life of a soldier in a brutal war. You have to live in the moment, tomorrow isn't guaranteed, because something or someone is always out to get you.

Late in January, the boys were eight months old. They would play and entertain each other all through the day and race across the kitchen floor on their knees while Rainbow cooked.

"You sure have you hands full," Rose said when she stopped by after she got the girls off to school.

"Yes, I do. When I feed the boys in their high chairs, I have to alternate a spoon for each, or they get upset. When they drink from their baby cups, if Blue finishes his first, Bless will give him whatever he has left," Rainbow told her.

"I guess these two are gonna be as inseparable as the day they were born," Rose said.

The boys looked very much alike, although they weren't identical. They were both caramel-colored, with soft black hair and bright brown eyes, yet Blue and Bless were as different as the way they entered the world. Bless used his head and was cautious, but Blue jumped into everything feet first. They were the two sides of the same coin. Blue was the first to stand up on his feet, and when he did, he reached his hand down to pull Bless up. It took them longer to walk because they were both trying to hold the hand of the other before they had their own balance.

The restaurant barely made enough to stay open, with Caesar and Ed running it pretty much by themselves, but their children were thriving. Blue and Bless grew teeth and charmed everybody with their smiles while they ran Rainbow ragged from the time they started walking. Violet and Hope were both in school, and Rose took in washing to help make ends meet.

Before 1930 was over, misfortune fell around them like the leaves off the trees. Most of the businesses on Cedar Street closed down; and in the fall, the panic spread to the banks. There was a run at the Peoples Saving and Trust, and Caesar lost most of the money he had deposited there, but he was better off than most. The third of his money that he kept at Citizens Savings Bank was safe and sound. Keeping his money in three separate places proved to be a blessing.

"The best part of my day is when these boys wake me up early in the morning," Caesar said, crawling out of bed to check on the ruckus.

Blue and Bless were mischievous toddlers and were always up to something.

"You've spoiled them with loads of toy trucks, boats, teddy bears, and all kinds of things they can wind up, except they prefer to tear up the house instead of playing with their toys," Rainbow remarked as she slid her feet into her slippers.

Making a mess with whatever was in their reach was what the twins loved best. They would pull clothes out of the drawers they could reach in their bedroom, books off of the shelves in the parlor, and pots and pans out of the cabinets in the kitchen.

As the years went on, Rainbow learned to take the boys outside to make it easier on herself. She would dress them in cotton shirts and shorts in the summer and in short coats, high-top shoes, and caps when the weather turned cold. They would have fun just running together and then falling over each other. They would wrestle and play catch, anything that would burn the endless energy that flowed between them.

Chapter Twenty

The slowdown in jobs and the circulation of money turned out to be the Great Depression, which is how most folks felt about the whole situation. The season of deficiency lasted for a decade, similar to the season of excess before it. Times were hard, and Caesar used a good amount of the cash in his secret safe to carry his family and the restaurant through the lean years. Black folks eventually got tired of wanting and sitting home with the blues; and as the years moved forward, they came out swinging.

Caesar hired a small jazz trio called the Merry Men to play the new sounds. The customers who came in may not have had much money to spend, but they could do the jitterbug. Prohibition was over, and Rainbow had gone back to work making her cocktails with an extra zing. In 1937, when Joe Louis was scheduled to fight James Braddock, Caesar threw a party at the restaurant so patrons could listen to the radio broadcast. He brought the boys along so Rainbow could enjoy the night.

"Look at Blue and Bless acting like they're the ones boxing," Ed said as they listened to the fight and watched the eight-year-olds.

"Those boys don't ever stop clowning," Caesar said, smiling at them with pride.

When Joe Louis landed the knockout punch and became the Heavyweight Champion of World that night, all the folks in the restaurant probably raised the roof an inch with their cheers and celebration.

Caesar tucked the boys in after the late evening. He always tried to be at home to help put the boys to bed, even when he had to go back to the restaurant after they were sleep.

"Tell us about your horse in Savannah again, Daddy," Bless would urge.

"I want to hear about when you were in the war again, Daddy," Blue insisted.

"I'll tell you two short ones, so we can do both," Caesar said, refusing to disappoint either of them.

They loved to hear his stories, and he loved to tell them about growing up in Savannah, coming to Nashville, his antics with Ed, going off to New York, joining the army, going overseas, the war, and meeting their mama. It was even more special when they would wrestle around on the floor, and they would share with him what happened in school and what trouble they got into. The twins never argued or fought, and Caesar guessed that neither knew what a blessing it was for them to have a lifelong friend from birth.

**

Jefferson Street started booming as the Depression lifted. Initially, it was a boon to business at the restaurant, and then it brought more competition from supper clubs like the Del Morocco, the Club Baron, and after the war, Greenwood Park expanded with Club Forrest, but Caesar prepared a meal that was superior to them all. All the clubs had fine chefs, but the magic was in his hands. Social clubs and other black organizations mushroomed in Nashville and kept them busy during 'club season,' which started in the spring and ran through the holidays.

Things got hectic for Rainbow managing the twins and working at the restaurant, and at the annual homecoming parade of Tennessee A & I on Thanksgiving morning standing with the family in front of the Storm's End, she fainted again. Caesar got her inside the restaurant and called Dr. Walker, their family physician.

When Rainbow came to, Caesar asked her, "Rain, I know you didn't wait this late to have us another baby."

She gave him a weak laugh and said, "I don't know, but the way I've been feeling, you'll have to carry it this time."

"Dr. Walker says to bring you over to the clinic," Caesar said, lifting her to her feet.

Dr. Walker met them at his clinic and asked Rainbow several questions and ran some tests. When he was done he talked to them about the results in his office.

"Rainbow, you have diabetes. Your blood sugar levels got too low, and that's why you fainted. There are other times that it may go too high. You'll have to take insulin everyday and cut out the sweets."

"Are you sure, Dr. Walker. Maybe you can run some more tests," Caesar said worriedly.

He and Rainbow were shocked. They didn't think it was a baby that caused her to faint, but this wasn't the news they expected. Dr. Walker gave her some glass syringes and showed them how to use them, and he gave her a prescription to take to the pharmacy for insulin. It took some time and effort, but they made the adjustment to Rainbow's condition. The hardest thing for her was not the daily shots; it was giving up the candy bars that she loved.

***

When the 1940s began, business was almost back to normal at The Storm's End, even though the country and the rest of the world were at war. The twins were eleven years old, still different as night and day, despite their nearly identical outward appearance, yet they were as close as two people could be. Caesar and Rainbow loved Blue's spirit of adventure and Bless's easygoing manner and thoughtfulness. The boys were fifth-graders at Cameron Junior High School, and Blue kept Principal Johnson busy with his mischievous antics, while Bless supplied him with alibis and explanations.

"Blue, I don't know why you can't behave," Mrs. Starks said for the second time that morning.

"I'm sorry, Mrs. Starks, I don't mean no harm. But it's hot in here today, and I think I need some air," he said, wiping his brow with a sly smile.

"Hush your mouth, boy, and stop interrupting me while I'm teaching."

"Yes, ma'am," he said. "I'm going to be so quiet you won't even know I'm here."

"You're trying my patience, Blue. Keep it up, and it's going to be hot on your behind," Mrs. Starks warned.

"Stop it, Blue, before you get your butt paddled," Bless whispered to him.

"I'm not worried," Blue said. "Mrs. Starks knows better than to lay a hand on me."

"Now, if we can get back to the lesson," Mrs. Starks commanded as she tapped on the blackboard. "Bless, can you tell me where we left off?"

Bless was Mrs. Starks favorite student. He was smart, but he didn't show off by raising his hand all the time. If no one else knew the answer, then he would then volunteer.

"We were reading on page 56," Bless answered.

They had barely begun when the lunch bell rang. On the way out, while Mrs. Starks held the door for her students, Blue slipped behind her desk, reached into her top drawer, and grabbed her keys. When they were all out and she closed the door, he used her key to lock her inside the classroom."

"What are you doing?" Bless asked when he saw Blue lingering at the door.

"Run!" Blue said as he darted in front of him. "I just taught Mrs. Starks a lesson about being stuck in her classroom.

They were down the hall and halfway out the door when they heard the banging and the screaming start. When they got home, Rainbow stood at the door with her switch, ready to pop Blue's behind for another one of his pranks.

***

The twins were tall for their age, just like their parents, both intelligent and strong, natural athletes, and both played on the basketball team. Blue played center, and Bless, shooting guard.

"Those two are a team within themselves," Principal Johnson would remark to Caesar when he came to their games. "The other three might as well be spectators."

"They're used to playing together," Caesar told him proudly.

The twins anticipated each other's passes and always knew where the other one was on the floor without looking.

"Blue gave us some trouble over the years, Mr. and Mrs. Portunus, but your boys have been a joy to watch," Principal Johnson told them at the end of the year.

It was a happy and sad day at Cameron when the boys graduated and were headed off to Pearl High School in 1944.

As teenagers, the Portunus boys, Blue and Bless, were beyond handsome, with carved bodies that could have been replicas of the Greek gods. They were a sight to see when they walked around Nashville. They were the princes of Jefferson Street, the sons of the successful and well-liked Caesar and Rainbow. The twins loved each other with all that was within them, but their paths were splitting off in different directions.

"I'm going to try out for the varsity football team. It's a more aggressive sport than running up and down the court all day," Blue announced at dinner one nigh. "Would you care to join me, my man?"

"No, man, I prefer a game of finesse versus getting my head knocked in," Bless answered.

"Don't forget, I'm going to be one knocking heads," Blue said, throwing his right fist into his left hand.

"You're right on that, brother," Bless said, nodding in agreement.

"Those boys are like night and day," Rainbow said to Caesar after the twins had left the table. "Bless spends his spare time reading books and going to the movies, while Blue hangs around the Bottom drinking beer and shooting dice. I'm getting worried about Blue's rambunctious behavior."

"He's all right, sweetie. Ed and I ran the streets down in the Bottom doing the same thing," Caesar said to soothe her mind. "The one thing they do have in common is that they can both spot the good-looking girls from a block away."

"Yeah, but the difference is Bless wants that special one, and Blue wants as many 'fast floosies' as he can juggle," Rainbow added.

All through high school, the characters of Blue and Bless continued to develop, and their individualities were even more pronounced. Still, the supernatural bond between them since birth remained steadfast. Honor students at Pearl, they were both ambitious and analytical in their thinking; but they still loved a good time and spent their weekends and free time enjoying themselves at the restaurant or The Silver Streak Ballroom.

"You slowing me down," Blue said to Bless as he tied his tie in the mirror.

"What's the rush? They'll be some girls left waiting there for you when we get there," Bless said.

"You're right about that," Blue said. "I am the life of the party."

Having a cultivated taste for the finer things in life from their privileged upbringing, each boy had his own personal sense of style. Bless would dress conservatively in tailored suits or tweed jackets, while Blue would sport flashy zoot suits and they would paint the town red on Friday and Saturday nights. At the Silver Streak, got to see Duke Ellington, Ella Fitzgerald, Cab Calloway, and Count Basie. They listened to the bands play swing while they danced the jitterbug.

It was not Caesar's or Rainbow's intention to spoil them; they just couldn't deny them anything, and they had the money to lavish on them. Bless was humbled by their generosity and his good fortune from God. He was a kind soul and never hesitated to share with anyone. Blue was conceited and arrogant, he's angry and cruel at times, unbefitting of someone whom good fortune had smiled on.

"This is a special moment for the Portunus Family," Caesar said as he squeezed Rainbow's hand at the twins' graduation from high school.

"I had my doubts on many days," Rainbow said as she and Caesar beamed with pride as the brothers walked across the stage and received their diplomas in the order they were born--Bless first and then Blue.

"I thank God for allowing me to see my sons grow and witness this day," Rainbow said as her eyes strained to see them with the diabetes taking a toll on her vision. She hadn't mentioned it, but on many days she felt as if she was seeing the world through a fog.

"I want to thank you all for coming to share the accomplishments of my sons. It's cause for a big celebration," Caesar said to their guests.

He carved a side of beef and made a cornucopia of side dishes for them all to enjoy, and baked them a cake that was two feet tall. He booked a group called the Maxim Trio that had a young blind singer named Ray Charles, who played the devil out of the piano. His voice sounded like Nat King Cole, and the guests went wild over him.

At the end of the night, Caesar had another announcement. "For your eighteenth birthday, I have planned a trip for the whole family to go to Idlewild for two weeks."

Caesar's hands had been aching for a while, and sometimes his fingers hesitated to move when he wanted them to. He thought the rest would be good for him and Rainbow, and he wanted to treat the boys to a vacation before they went to college in the fall.

***

"You boys can drive as well as I can, so we're going to take turns at the wheel," Caesar instructed as they piled into the car. "I want you two to see some of the country since neither of you have been outside of Nashville."

They drove north through Kentucky and into Indiana.

"This is what I remember growing up," Rainbow said, looking out on the fields and mountains of the open road.

"Look at all the cows and horses," Bless hollered, getting a kick out of them as they watched the cars as they passed by.

"I forgot I'm the only country bumpkin in this car," Rainbow said, amazed at their excitement over a cow in a field.

"These boys may have been raised in the South but they didn't know any more about farming or raising animals than kids in New York City," Caesar said.

"How much longer before we get there?" Blue griped. "We've been driving all day."

"We should be there in about an hour," Caesar yelled back. "We're passing through Grand Rapids now.

"Thank goodness," Rainbow said. "Somebody is getting cranky."

"This place is a lot larger than it was when we were here before," Caesar said as they pulled up. "It really has expanded."

"Don't forget that was almost twenty years ago," Rainbow chuckled. "Even though you promised to bring me back every year."

"I don't know where the years went," he replied, shaking his head.

"Just look behind you," she said. "They're right there."

"Who knew you were going to come up here and get pregnant."

"I don't recall doing it by myself."

"Good thing we rented a large cottage. Trying to make another one with them here, we'll need ample space," he said after they checked in.

"You must think I'm crazy. That's all you're getting out of me. What we really need to do is stock up on food for the hungry mouths we already have."

"I have to agree on that," Caesar laughed.

After they unpacked, they went to Harry's Grocery and the Log Cabin Store, where they bought lots of food and supplies to have a good time.

"We got enough stuff for you boys to camp out if you want to," Caesar said.

"You've got to be kidding, Dad. Who wants to go camping," Blue said, "Where's the club?"

Caesar and Rainbow soon realized that they had raised city boys who preferred to eat in the restaurants and hang out in the clubs rather than hunting, fishing, and camping in tents near the lake.

"Maybe I spent too much time working. I should have spent more time doing things with Bless and Blue," Caesar said to Rainbow when they got to the cottage, questioning how he had raised his sons for the first time.

"Don't even think that," Rainbow said to him. "You worked hard and long hours to give them the best of everything."

"The war took the desire to hunt out of me, but maybe I should have taken them fishing or doing other guy things," he said, wondering if it was too late.

"They're practically men now. There's no way we can reverse it and do it differently," Rainbow said. "They'll be fine."

"I don't worry about my boys making a life for themselves in the world. I imagine that Bless will be given his wants and desires on a silver platter, and Blue will take whatever he wants and desires from the world with no apologies offered," Caesar muttered.

"From now on, they will be living their own lives, just like you've done," she said, taking his hand and walking into their bedroom.

He looked at Rainbow as she finished dressing for dinner; the next phase of his life would be centered on her.

The entertainment at Idlewild was outstanding; Louis Armstrong and Sarah Vaughn were performing every other night in the Flamingo Club.

"Armstrong is a master on the trumpet," Bless said after the show. "He made it sing, made it laugh, he even made it scream. When you hear him blow, he tells the audience those familiar stories they never get tired of hearing. I can't wait to hear Sarah Vaughn tomorrow."

The next night, Sarah Vaughn serenaded them with her soft as silk voice, which was rich and full-bodied as fine red wine and made them feel just as mellow.

"Dad, you should have brought us here a long time ago," Bless said, enjoying the show.

"I meant to son. Believe me I did," Caesar said, meaning every word as he looked at the young man across from him.

"Now, we've both died and gone to heaven," Blue said when the twins set eyes on the showgirls in the Paradise Club.

They were all dressed in sexy costumes that revealed the most exquisite women for miles around. If one of them couldn't dance, the audience didn't even notice.

"This is living," Bless said, taking in the beauty of the show.

"Yeah, we finally got to the good part," Blue said with a grin.

Over the next two weeks they rested, they relaxed, they rode horses, they were entertained, and they made precious memories.

They talked and laughed and learned about each other on other levels. Caesar and Rainbow got a chance to see their children as adults; and Blue and Bless got to see their parents as a couple, a man and a woman who loved each other.

"My only regret is that we didn't come back when Bless and Blue were younger," Caesar said. "They would have had a lot more fun."

"I don't think they have any complaints," Rainbow assured him.

They drove back to Nashville, with Blue and Bless in the front seat taking turns driving and singing along with the songs on the radio.

"I guess it's their time to get in the front seat now," Caesar said to Rainbow as he looked at the back of their heads.

"Now they have to make their own dreams come true, just like you did," Rainbow said, closing her eyes and lying down on Caesar's lap.

"I know. In my mind I feel as young as they do sitting up there, but my body is starting to feel the accumulation of the years."

Caesar looked down at his hands and wondered why the body surrendered when there was so much more fight in him. He looked down at Rainbow resting her head on his lap with her eyes closed. He watched the breeze coming through the window play with the loose hairs around her face, and he wished he could make things all right for her. He knew her eyes were weakening; he had seen her stumble and noticed her reluctance to read him stories out of the newspaper like she used to.

Chapter Twenty-One

Rainbow and Caesar dealt with their personal struggles silently. Her vision was clouding and clearing without warning. Some days she could see like she always had; and on others, the features in the mirror were less defined, and the words on the morning newspaper blended together in an ugly shade of gray.

"It's the sugar that's clouding your eyesight," Dr. Walker told her. "You have to keep a check on it better, Rainbow, or you could end up blind."

Rainbow cried on the way home and when she tasted the salty tears on her lips, she almost laughed, thinking they should have tasted sweet.

Caesar took his turn at the doctor's office.

"My hands are numb more often and when they do have feeling, its pain that burns like a stove on low heat," he complained to Dr. Walker. "Some days my fingers and wrist lock in mid-motion, frozen in animation when I'm cooking."

His grip even loosened around the most important tool of his craft: his knife.

"It's rheumatism," Dr. Walker explained to him. "There's not much you can do to relieve it except for moving to a warm and dry climate."

Caesar nor Rainbow wanted to worry the other as time passed and their limitations increased. The summer season drew to a close, and the time for the twins to decide where they were going to school wouldn't be put off. They had applied to the same schools, and both of them were accepted to the same schools.

"Have you guys decided what school you're going to, and what you're going to study?" Caesar asked them one evening.

"I'm going to enroll at Fisk and major in business," Blue said without hesitation.

"I'm already registered at Tennessee A & I to study English and journalism," Bless added just as quickly.

"I guess we're the last ones to hear the news," Caesar said to Rainbow.

"As usual," she replied, nodding her head.

Rainbow had some reservations about her sons leaving home and living on campus, but Caesar knew that they would be fine. Both of them needed to be independent and become his own man. Exceptional students, neither Blue nor Bless had trouble with college classes. Blue practically had a photographic memory, and Bless only had to hear something once and it was committed for recall.

***

"I've thought about this while you guys were on campus, and we've decided that we'll be cutting off your weekly allotments of cash," Caesar explained to Blue and Bless when they came home for Christmas break. "You two gentlemen will have to find jobs for your spending money. Also, I'll take this time to inform you both that upon your graduation, each of you will receive $10,000 to get you started in whatever career venture you choose."

"That sounds like an offer I can't refuse, Pops," Blue said.

"You don't have to give us anything; Dad, me and Blue can make our own way."

"It's what was done for me, and I want to do the same for my sons. Your mama and I love you guys so much, we'd give you the world if we could."

Blue and Bless were never lazy, just complacent, both of them quickly found jobs. Bless started working at *The Nashville Globe* newspaper, and Blue got a job on a construction crew with McKissack & McKissack.

Bless was anxious to learn as much as he could in his classes and on the job at the newspaper. He'd always had a thirst for knowledge, and he was one of those people who cared, not only for his family, but for people in general, especially his own. He saw where the paper could be used to spread information that could help black people better themselves. Blue loved working with the McKissacks. He thrived on the physical work of construction and the feeling that he was a part of creating something from the ground up. It made him feel powerful. He already knew that he wanted to start a construction company of his own. Graduating from Fisk was just the means to getting him closer to his own business. He went to all his classes and made good grades, but he was only still there for one reason: Blue was going to find the mother of his children.

"I know the kind of woman I'm looking for," Blue said to Bless when they were hanging out on the weekend.

"Really? What kind is that?" Bless asked. "I didn't know you had any restrictions."

"When it comes to my future Mrs. Portunus, I have a few," he smirked. "First, she's got to be the opposite of me: a lady, refined, who would never go into a club, one who belongs to the proper organizations, and one who smiles more than she laughs. That would be the fine woman who will be my queen."

"Okay, Blue, but are you prepared to play the role of her king?"

"Don't worry, I got that covered, Bless."

Blue found her in Carol Jefferson in the spring of their freshman year.

"Excuse me, I don't think I've made your acquaintance," Blue said when he saw her walking across campus in a pale pink dress. "I'm Caesar Blue Portunus, this is my first year here."

"Carol Jefferson," she said. "I'm a sophomore. Maybe that's why."

"I like your accent. Where are you from, Carol?"

"I'm from New Orleans, Louisiana."

"Interesting city I've heard, I've never been there," Blue said, staring down at her.

"Maybe you need to broaden your horizons a bit more," she said, with an air of superiority.

Carol was a true Southern belle from a prominent family that ran the largest funeral parlor in New Orleans. She was pretty; light-skinned, but not too light, and kept her hair pressed and curled in a French roll. She was tall and slim and was always sharply dressed and camera-ready. She'd heard some talk about the free-spirited freshman who was turning all the girls' heads. Now that she had met him, she knew he would soon belong to her.

"Would you grant me the pleasure of taking you to dinner?" he asked with a smile.

"For a meal off campus, I think I'd be willing to take the chance," she answered, hiding her delight at being the one who snared the big catch on campus.

Blue strolled into The Storm's End that evening with Carol on his arm.

"Hello, Dad. I would like you to meet my future wife, Carol Jefferson," he said when Caesar came over to his table.

"Pleased to meet you," Caesar said, surprised at the introduction.

"My pleasure, Mr. Portunus," Carol said, seeing the resemblance between the two.

"What would you like to have for dinner? I'd love to make you something special," Caesar said.

"She'll have the same thing that I usually have, the steak," Blue said brashly, speaking for her.

"All right, Blue," Caesar said, tickled at his attitude. "A waiter will over in a minute."

Carol sat at the table pleased at her good fortune. Her father was a strong personality, and she had no problem yielding to Blue's dynamic and controlling disposition.

After that night, he brought her to the restaurant to eat at least twice a week. He was the perfect gentleman and took her wherever she wanted to go, the movies at the Ritz and went to church with her on most Sundays, but he reserved Saturdays for hanging out with Bless and his other friends.

The twins always made a grand entrance when they went out, and they loved the attention they got from the other loyal patrons. In the local clubs, they were envied and admired by other men and desired by most of the women.

"Let's go the New Era tonight," Bless suggested. "They have the best singers and musicians."

Bless liked to go to go the New Era; he loved the music. He focused on the tone of each instrument and how they changed the mood of the songs.

"We can start there and take it uptown; the music doesn't matter to me," Blue said, "It's simply the untamed atmosphere in the club that excites me, the freedom of it, the loss of inhibitions from the dim lights and the alcohol, the feeling that anything could happen at any time."

Blue even liked the danger and the challenge of coming out alive when fights broke out.

The next weekend, Blue went solo. He often frequented the Del Morocco near A & I campus by himself without the presence of his conscience in his brother, Bless. Blue put on his sharpest suit--black with satin trim and pocket square, white shirt with tie pin and cuff links--and he donned a hat that complimented the look. Cary Grant had nothing on him, and he knew it.

"Hey, Uncle Teddy," Blue said, walking in like he was half-owner of the place.

"What's shaking, Blue?" Uncle Teddy said, giving him a warm greeting. "I've been looking for you. Where you been?"

"I been trying to get here, that's all I know," Blue answered.

The Del Morocco was the only serious competition on Jefferson Street for The Storm's End; and the owner, Theodore "Uncle Teddy" Acklen, loved the fact that Blue favored his place. The Del Morocco catered to the clientele who had more of a taste for the risqué.

"I'm gonna have a drink in the music room and browse for a minute," Blue said, flashing him a knowing smile.

"Help yourself, son."

Blue ordered a drink and let his eyes wander in search of a woman who would usually be everything Carol wasn't: flashy, sexy, and uninhibited.

"Hello, doll face," he said when he saw tonight's selection. "What's your name?"

"Patti. Who's asking?" she answered.

"The name's Blue. Would you join me for dinner in the Blue Room upstairs?"

"I'd love to," she said playfully, admiring his style and good looks.

Blue let her take his arm, and he kept her next to him, even in the secluded room in the back where the dice rolled, cards played, and money was exchanged.

"I'm tired of winning. How about we get some rest at Brown's Hotel?" Blue proposed, feeling lucky.

"I could use some rest," Patti said without hesitation, still holding on to his arm.

***

Bless also had his pick of the women on campus, but he wanted a smart woman who could be his partner, just as his mama was to his daddy, someone he could talk to about anything in the world. Bless found her when he met Cassy, short for Cassandra in his junior year.

"I'm interested in joining the staff of the paper," Bless said, walking in the office of *The Meter*, the campus newspaper.

"I've seen you around campus. What's your name?" Cassy asked.

"My name's Bless Portunus. And you are...,?"

"I'm Cassy Philips, an art major and the resident photographer," she answered.

Cassy was a brown-skinned beauty from Baltimore. She wore her hair pulled back in a ponytail, leaving her prominent cheekbones in full view. She had a body like a Coca-Cola bottle, and she didn't try to hide her curves.

"I can hear in your voice that you're from up north," Bless remarked.

"Not too far north, Baltimore, Maryland."

Bless loved to hear her talk in that Northern accent, which was good because she talked a lot. She was adventurous and saw every experience as something she could capture in a photograph or draw on paper. They were practically inseparable by senior year; and eventually, he started bringing her along when he hung out with his brother, even though Blue never brought Carol.

Chapter
Twenty-Two

C aesar had a big New Year's celebration at the restaurant on January 1, 1951. Bless was there with Cassy, but Blue had gone home with Carol to New Orleans to meet her family. "Today is my 51st birthday, and I think it's time for me to make some changes. This will probably be a shock to all of you," Caesar said to his family and friends, "Rainbow and I have decided that when the twins graduate from college, we are going to sell The Storm's End, and we will be moving out west to Los Angeles, California."

It wasn't something they had dreamed about or planned for, they had a good life in Nashville, and wanted to be close their sons, except the health challenges that he and Rainbow faced everyday weren't getting any easier.

"The climate out west would be ideal for your rheumatism," Dr. Walker advised him. "It'll be a new place for you and Rainbow to explore and find a new dream."

"I hope we can work something out between us where I can keep the restaurant in the family," Ed said. "We are brothers, you know."

"I know that, Ed," Caesar said to him. "If that's what you want, that's what will happen."

"Mama, this is so sudden. I think we need to talk about this as a family," Bless whispered to Rainbow. "Blue isn't even here."

"It's all settled in our minds, Bless. Your father is tired, and his hands ache so badly. He's been working since he was a young boy without any time to just sit back and look up in the sky. The doctor says he'll feel much better out west where it's warm and dry most of the time."

"You two have always been here whenever we needed you, Mama. If you and Dad need us, we want to help. Going to California is way across the country."

"You both are grown men. We can take care of ourselves, and you and Blue can, too. Besides, we'll only be a phone call away," Rainbow said.

"What if you get lonely out there, Mama?" Bless asked.

"I know that you are only a phone call away, too, son."

Bless and Cassy had plans of their own after graduation. They had talked about using Bless's starter money and starting a magazine specifically for black readers. They loved each other and knew that they wanted to be together, but Cassy wasn't in a rush to get married.

***

"Mama, I'm ready for Blue and me to get engaged," Carol told her mother when she and Blue were in New Orleans. "I want to have a June wedding after graduation."

"I know you're ready, Carol," her mother responded between sips of her café au lait. "Your father and I were well aware that you didn't go to college to find yourself a career. When you brought your beau home, we figured you had made a choice. The question is, How ready is Blue?"

"He's ready when I say he is, Mama," Carol said confidently, "I'm nobody's fool. I know he ran the streets of Nashville hard and tough, but marriage will settle him down once we're living under one roof."

Mr. Jefferson took the opportunity to be alone with Blue while he gave him a tour of the family estate.

"I am very impressed with your home, Mr. Jefferson," Blue said, thinking that it looked like the mansion of any pre-Civil War plantation master. He was in agreement that any form of ostentation should be done in excess.

"A man's home is his castle," Mr. Jefferson said pompously.

Over dinner, Mr. and Mrs. Jefferson looked Blue over from head to toe and gave him an interview that would have made the FBI proud.

"I like you, Blue," Mr. Jefferson said, seeing a younger version of himself: handsome, bold, ambitious, and maybe even a little ruthless.

Mrs. Jefferson saw all the same things, and for that reason she had her reservations. She knew from experience, these men only loved themselves, and the wife was another accessory they wore to complete the image. She hadn't been raised with money, so she knew there was life without it, and other things were much more important. But Carol was her father's daughter, and she was going to marry Blue, whether her mama liked it or not.

Blue and Mr. Jefferson talked alone in his private office while he smoked a Cuban cigar and offered Blue some of his finest French brandy.

"Carol is my only child and I love her more than anything, and I would protect her with my own life. She has her heart on marrying you, and I want what she wants," Mr. Jefferson said as he blew a thick cloud of smoke. "What exactly do you want, Blue?"

"I only want to marry Carol and make her happy," Blue said to alleviate his fears. "I plan to start my own construction business after we graduate, and she will be provided for in the same way that you have provided for her."

"That gives me great comfort, son," Mr. Jefferson said, extending his hand in agreement.

"I hope you would allow me to give you the ring that my mother wore to present to Carol. It's been in our family for three generations," he said, holding Blue's hand tight in his firm grip.

"It would be an honor, sir," Blue answered as he flexed the muscles in his hand.

During the New Year's Day celebration at the Jefferson home, Blue and Carol's engagement was announced, and Blue slid the family diamond heirloom on her finger with a roguish smile, thinking about all the money he had saved by not having to buy an expensive ring.

"I'm so happy!" Carol said. She had gotten the prize again and felt she would be the envy of all her sorority sisters at Fisk.

The last semester of college was busy for them all. Carol was busy planning the wedding that would be the social event of the year. She mailed invitations, had dress fittings, interviewed caterers over the phone, while Blue partied like there was no tomorrow. Jefferson Street was hot with rhythm and blues singers, and Blue hopped from one club to another. He loved the wild crowd in Club Revillot, where a no-holds-barred singer named Little Richard was nearly tearing up the place. He would meet his best man, Bless, and Cassy at the New Era, where they would fight the crowd to get in to hear B. B. King play his guitar and sing the blues.

***

The end of the spring months ushered in the season of commencement, a period of new beginnings.

"Can you see Bless?" Rainbow asked, nudging Caesar when Caesar Bless Portunus was called to receive his college diploma and walked across the stage at Tennessee A & I.

Rainbow strained her eyes to see her son, but what she saw was just a silhouette of color.

"That's him on the steps," Caesar said as he let out a sharp whistle, his hands refusing to straighten or come together and clap.

All the same, it was a proud moment for the family as Blue stood up and cheered for his brother, with Carol sitting fashionably dressed and coiffed beside him. They all went for a special lunch at The Storm's End, with Ed and Rose and their daughters, Violet and Hope and their respective husbands.

"I want to thank everybody for their support in helping me get to this day," Bless said, with Cassy sitting beside him. "And I'm very grateful that Cassy and her family are here to share in the celebration for both of us."

"There are times when I can't believe how fortunate I am. I'm so thankful to see how our family has grown and will continue to grow," Caesar announced as they all sat at a table together. "Now, Bless, here's the check you were promised."

Bless graciously accepted it, and Caesar grabbed Rainbow's hand and kissed it in appreciation for how she had been a blessing in his life.

The following week, the celebration was repeated after Blue presented his college diploma to his mama after the graduation ceremony at Fisk.

"These are the most beautiful words I have ever seen," Rainbow said as she looked through her glasses and saw Caesar Blue Portunus written on the diploma. "Both my sons are officially college graduates."

"I can't say that my sons gave me much trouble once they got on their feet," Caesar said. "They are independent, and they rely on each other more than they do on their mama and me, but we are happy to get the chance to host the graduate luncheon in the couple's honor since their wedding will be in New Orleans. Here's your check that was promised, Blue."

"We are so pleased to meet the family that she will be marrying into," Mr. Jefferson said at the table. "We've found you all to be kind, sincere, and very successful people."

"Yes, and I've discovered that Mrs. Portunus and I have a lot in common," Mrs. Jefferson added. "We were both raised in small towns in West Mississippi."

The two mothers bonded quickly, and Mr. Jefferson was comforted that the marriage wasn't about a slick young man trying to marry his money and taking his daughter along for the ride.

***

The wedding of Caesar Blue Portunus and Carol Ann Jefferson was the event of a lifetime. Mr. and Mrs. Charles Jefferson spent a small fortune on the nuptials of their only daughter, and all of New Orleans' black high society was in attendance. The wedding ceremony took place at the St. Augustine Catholic Church. After the priest entered, the elegant wedding parties proceeded into the church as Blue and Bless took their place at the altar. When Carol came down the aisle, escorted by her father, she looked like she had stepped off a magazine cover. The dress was a cloud of white silk that floated around her. There was singing and prayers before the vows were taken.

"Lord, I hope Blue will honor her in the way he just pledged," Caesar said to Rainbow as he looked at his sons standing handsome and strong at the altar. "Pray Bless can do what he's always done and keep his brother out of trouble," he added as his eyes shifted to Bless.

"They look like royalty," Rainbow whispered as she watched the ceremony from the honored seat of the mother of the groom with clear eyes.

She shed a few tears, thankful for another precious vision she could place in her mind's eye. Seeing the couple receive Communion, she regretted not insisting that the boys attend church more regularly. Maybe Blue's heart would have been a bit softer.

The reception was at the Jeffersons' home, and Caesar thought he had died and gone to a food heaven. There were cold and hot hors d' oeuvres, shrimp salad on artichoke leaves, finger sandwiches from every kind of meat he could think of, crawfish pies, and mushrooms stuffed with seafood. There was a huge variety of cheeses and crackers, fruits, with varying berries and grapes. They feasted on French cuisine as well as gumbo and jambalaya. They toasted with the finest wines and champagne.

When they couldn't ingest another bite, the guests retired to the tent outside where a jazz band played and good liquor was liberally poured. It was party that appeared as if it would go on and on and on. On the first dance, Blue and Carol looked like a king and his queen, and Mr. Jefferson presented the newlywed couple with a generous check.

At a rare moment when they were alone together, Bless grabbed Blue and gave him a big hug and a kiss on the cheek. Bless was his brother's keeper and had spent a lot time worrying about Blue and his hot temper and impetuousness, but it seemed like he was making a step in the right direction of being responsible. He was officially a married man, and even if he thought he wasn't going to settle down, it came with the territory.

"Congratulations, my brother! I was first coming into the world, and you are the first going out," Bless teased. "I'm happy for you, man. You've got a lovely wife."

"You know me better than anybody on this earth, Bless, so you know not much is going to change. I wanted a wife and a family, and now I'll have one; but I'm still my own man."

"Give it a chance, Blue. Don't hurt her; she can make you happy."

"I'm not going to hurt her, Bless. I love her, but she's got to remember her place, and that's not getting in the way of what a man's got to do."

"Blue, you're crazy, what you got to do?"

"Brother, I got to do all the things that they tell me not to: drink, gamble, and run around with some wild women. But don't worry. I'm gonna take good care of Carol. She'll be the queen of my castle and the mother of my children."

"Okay, Blue, I know you got it all under control, but you know I'm here for you always."

"Same here, Bless," Blue said as Carol waved for him to come back inside to cut the cake.

The photographer from *Jet Magazine* was ready to get the picture of the happy couple that would appear in the next issue.

"I can't wait until we leave for Martha's Vineyard tomorrow and we get to spend the whole summer there," Carol said to Blue, excited as the guests started to leave.

"I can pay for my own honeymoon," Blue said, irritated when he thought about the gift, courtesy of Mr. and Mrs. Jefferson. Truth be told, he didn't even want to go to the bourgeoisie vineyard.

"They just want us to have a good time," Carol said, rubbing his back and trying to smooth things over.

Blue appreciated their generosity, but he didn't like to accept gifts, especially when he thought they came with attachments.

"As long as they remember the only man who's going to run my household is me," he added.

He had let them know early on that any ideas of him moving to New Orleans or being a part of their family business was pure fantasy, and they need not waste any efforts to convince him otherwise. The starter money from his dad and some ill-gotten gains he made at Club Morocco were all he needed to give his construction business a firm foundation, and he already had a name for it: Empire Construction Company.

The long drive back home after the wedding festivities gave Bless some much needed quiet time to listen to his inner voice speak. When Rainbow fell asleep, Caesar moved up to the front seat so they could talk.

"I've been thinking, Dad, and I've decided that Cassy and I should move slowly and methodically in starting our magazine.

I think we can benefit from a year or two of full-time work experience on *The Nashville Globe* before investing all of our resources," Bless said, knowing that they only had one shot to make it a success.

"That sounds a smart move son; I worked at a restaurant downtown for a while before I opened The Storm's End. Experience is not a bad thing."

"I want us to get married and settled first, too, because once we get started, the magazine is going to need our full attention."

"That's true, son. Take your time," Caesar said. "Speaking of time, Ed has asked me to hold off on the sale of the restaurant until he can try and raise enough capital to buy The Storm's End for himself."

"Can you hold off on your plans, Dad?"

"I want to give him that chance. He can't cook, but he has a head for business and already ran the place the place without a hitch whenever I was out. Ed has always been a loyal friend and a brother, and I will be glad if the restaurant can stay in the hands of family."

***

"I feel like a caged animal," Blue told Carol after the long train ride to Massachusetts, and the ferry ride to Martha's Vineyard didn't make him feel any better.

"You have to admit that it's beautiful here," Carol said, looking out at the view from their cottage.

"It is a peaceful place, but it ain't my scene," Blue said, thinking he would suffocate from the antiseptic air of the island before the summer was over.

"Once you get used to it, you'll love it. Besides, we're invited out for drinks with some old friends of mine," Carol said, going to change her clothes.

A month later, Blue was almost out of his mind with boredom. He was living without the elements that were as essential as oxygen for his survival. He just didn't have an appetite for good clean fun or for the daily cocktails with the well-to-do. He tried to alleviate his restlessness through sex, but Carol was a quiet lover, reserved when they came together. There was no heat or sweat, and their passion lacked the fire that Blue craved.

It wasn't that Carol was an apathetic woman or ineffectual, she was actually quite demanding and forceful; but she had been raised to be a proper lady of society, and in her mind there was acceptable behavior assigned to it, and everything else was beneath her. It was unfortunate, because had she loosed her contained emotions and allowed her conduct to venture, and explored her basest passion, she may have been the perfect match for Blue.

Chapter Twenty-Three

Crosswinds of change were blowing across the South, and Nashville was caught up in the gales. Bless could sense a season of violent storms brewing precipitated by the racial conflicts and discontent. Seeds of defiance were spreading, and grassroots movements were taking hold. More disturbances and turbulence developed with each passing day, as well as moments of victory. Bless and Cassy wanted to be front-row witnesses and tell the stories--Bless with his words and Cassy with her camera. The legal case challenging "separate but equal" was headed to the Supreme Court; and if it was successful, it would bring monumental changes in all of their lives.

The summer months came to a close, and Blue and Carol returned home after their extended honeymoon in the Vineyard.

"Home at last," Blue said, putting down their bags and feeling relaxed for the first time in months.

"Now we're in our own fabulous house," Carol said, reaching her arms up around his neck and looking him in his eyes.

"I guess you could say that," he said with sarcasm, "even though we paid for it with the money your daddy gave us as a wedding gift."

"I'm not going to let you ruin my mood. I've got work to do," Carol said as she occupied herself with setting up the house.

"Don't worry. I'll be out of your way. My next order of business is to put on a sharp suit and head out to the clubs with Bless," Blue hollered out as he skipped every other step on the stairs up to their bedroom.

"This is more like it," Blue said when he stepped back into the Del Morocco to meet Bless.

He felt like a fish that had flipped and flopped on the shore, nearly dead, and then somebody tossed it back into the water. He was back in his natural habitat; he could breathe again.

"What's shaking?" Bless said with a slap to his back to get his attention.

Blue laughed with relief and said, "Just glad to be back in civilization."

"Well, I missed you, my brother," Bless said sincerely. "Now what kind of trouble are you trying to get into tonight, looking like a hundred thousand dollar bill?"

"Right around that much, and I want my money's worth," Blue laughed.

"That's too high-class for me; I'd rather head down to the stomping grounds for regular folks at the Era to have a few beers."

"Give it a few minutes, and we'll check out."

They ordered another round of beers and Blue thought about what other trouble he could get into upstairs; but with Bless standing watch he decided to hold back.

"Let's go. I surrender," Blue said standing up. "You won't be satisfied until your ass hits a stool in the Era."

"I know something good when I find it, and then I stick with it," Bless said, taking the opportunity to drop a hint.

"You can preach at me all you want, I'm sitting in the amen section."

Content at the bar of the New Era, Bless got absorbed by the music, while Blue looked through the club for a woman who might be feeling lonely. But all the pretty ones were all paired-up, so he leaned back in his chair to enjoy the show. Memphis Slim was playing there, and he was singing, "Every day I have the Blues."

Blue raised his glass in salute and yelled, "Tell it, man!"

"Come on, brother, you don't know nothing about no blues. You got everything," Bless told him.

"There's always a first time," he answered.

"You not going to get me to shed one tear for you," Bless said and downed his beer. "Come on, it's late, and you got somebody to go home to."

"Go ahead, Bless, I'm right behind you after I get one more beer for the road," he said as he held out his hand to give him some skin.

Blue ordered another beer, but he didn't finish it. Fifteen minutes later, he was headed to Del Morocco to quench his thirst. He could always find what he wanted there. True to his word, marriage hadn't changed a thing.

***

"How's married life, Carol?" Cassy asked when she stopped by to see the new house.

"It could be better. Blue still prefers to hang in the streets," Carol said disappointed. "But I'm biding my time. This baby I'm carrying will plant his feet right where I want them."

"Oh my goodness! You're pregnant?" Cassy exclaimed in surprise.

"Yes, I am," Carol said happily. "I had planned to announce it over Christmas dinner here, but their parents want to be hosts again this year since it will be their last winter in Nashville."

Carol had played and replayed the scene in her mind, seeing Blue's joy at the precious gift she was giving him, him taking her in his arms and him pledging to be a new man, but she was upstaged.

"I have a special announcement this evening," Bless said, pounding the table and calling for everyone's attention. "Cassy and I are officially engaged."

"Congratulations, brother, you finally decided to join the club," Blue said, patting him firmly on the back.

Carol held her tongue, postponing her announcement, not being one who enjoyed sharing the spotlight. She would have her moment at her own table on for Caesar's birthday on New Year's Day.

"I want everything to be perfect," Carol said to the server for her New Year's Day dinner that had been catered for the occasion.

The family was already seated at the table when Carol floated into the dining room dressed in a pale pink velvet dress with an empire neckline. Looking every bit of the queen in her palace. Blue sat at the head of the table, poised to carve the rib roast, when Carol stood up.

"Before we begin eating, I would like to share the news that Blue and I are expecting our first baby," she said, glowing under the chandelier lights.

"Oh, I'm so happy!" Rainbow said, standing up to give Carol a hug.

"This has got to be one of the best birthday gifts I've gotten in my life," Caesar added.

"You're always up to something, Blue," Bless said, punching him in the arm.

The whole family, with the exception of Blue, was overjoyed with the news.

"I would have liked to have been told before anyone else," Blue grumbled, unhappy at the fact that she didn't tell him before the dinner.

Blue tried to swallow his resentment, not sure why he was so bothered, but he grew more irritable after the meal and walked out to get some air and didn't come back for hours.

***

Bless had put his $10,000 in the bank, but Blue put his to work immediately, leasing an office for his construction company.

"How's the business coming together?" Bless asked when he came by the store front on the lower end of Jefferson Street where Blue's company was located.

"It's going like clockwork, Bless. I've put together a crew of men that I worked with on other jobs over the years, and we are clicking."

"There's no shortage of work right now I bet, with the so-called urban renewal going down in the inner city putting poor black folks out of their houses."

"No, man, there's plenty money around for building housing projects. It's a lucrative business," Blue said. "I'm taking advantage of it. I've landed several big contracts."

"I'm happy for you, brother," Bless said with mixed feelings on his way out.

Blue was a perfectionist, and his craftsmanship was impeccable. His business grew with each passing month in parallel with Carol's belly.

"My husband is becoming a captain of industry in his own right," Carol bragged at one of the morning tea parties she held at her house.

She was enjoying the attention she got from her pregnancy, specifically from Blue. She occupied her days with teas and luncheons with her sorority sisters, a blue-vein social club, and was active in several church organizations. She felt fortunate to have the perfect life she always envisioned.

***

Bless and Cassy set their wedding for April 19, 1952, the height of the spring season. They planned a small ceremony at the Fisk Chapel. On his last night as a single man, Bless stopped by Blue's business after work at *The Nashville Globe*. Blue wanted to take him out on the town and show him a good time.

"You know we got to run these streets on your last night as a bachelor," Blue said to Bless on the evening before the wedding.

"Fine by me. Where are we headed?" Bless asked.

"Up to the Baron Club to hear to hear this new cat named Fats Domino play," Blue said eager to get the party started.

They got a table near the stage and ordered two beers.

"Only the best for my better half before his wedding day," Blue said as he pulled out four mini bottles of Remy Martin cognac out of his jacket.

"I'll drink to that," Bless said, and they screwed off the tops and downed the first bottles.

"Man, you remember how we used to rule the court when we were playing ball at Cameron?" Blues asked before he took another shot.

"Yeah, those were some fun times. I remember how you had the girls running around in circles at Pearl High," Bless said, laughing.

The two reminisced about the time when they were little boys to their early years in college, downing more of the tiny bottles of cognac. With each shot, they got louder, and a large table next to them started to complain.

Blue, full of himself and good liquor, began to talk shit. "Fuck you nigger!" and it set off a rally of curses that flew between the two tables and a few at the bar.

Bless knew it had passed the point of return, so he grabbed Blue's arm and pulled him into the men's room.

"Blue, we got a fight waiting out there; it might be five of them. Now, I can take one and maybe a second, so we are probably going to get our asses kicked tonight," Bless said.

"Here, man," Blue answered with a laugh as he passed Bless another mini bottle and drank the last one himself. "This should dull some of the knocks."

After he downed it, Blue reached in his pockets and pulled out all the empty bottles they had drunk. He placed one between each of his fingers on both hands, raised his arms and swiftly brought them down against the edge of the sink.

The clang of glass breaking ricocheted off the walls and adrenalin shot through their veins. They looked at each other for a moment, and then Blue said, "Let's do this."

They marched out the into the club ready for battle and as their eyes adjusted to the darkness in the room, they exhaled and their inflated chests came down.

"Well, Blue, seems like you dodged another bullet tonight," Bless said relieved.

"Seems so, my brother, seems so," Blue answered.

The club was practically empty, except for the musicians on the stage. Blue reached into his pocket and pulled out a handful of bills. He put half on the stage and half on the bar. Out in his car, he fell asleep while Bless drove him home. Then Bless went to spend the night at his mama and dad's house.

***

The wedding ceremony was simple and sweet, without a parade of bridesmaids or a long dress train. Caesar escorted Rainbow, and an usher walked Mrs. Philips to the front of the chapel. Cassy looked beautiful in a classic fitted gown and a short veil escorted by her father. Bless, with a sober Blue standing at his side, watched her approach and felt a flood of emotions that almost overflowed from eyes. He counted himself fortunate to have found such a sexy and smart woman to spend his life with. He took her hand and promised that he would never let it go.

Caesar and Rainbow had asked the Philips if they wouldn't mind having the wedding reception at The Storm's End. Mr. Philips was a mailman, and his wife, Cora, was teacher. They owned their home, raised and educated their children, but they didn't have money to splurge on a wedding and thankfully accepted the offer.

"I had to swallow nearly a bottle of aspirin to soothe the pain in my hands," Caesar said to Ed. "I put my heart and soul into the preparation of this food today."

"I know it must be a thrill to cook for your son and his new bride on their wedding day," Ed said, feeling sentimental.

"It's my swan song at the restaurant before I turn it over to you and Rose," Caesar said, clearing his throat of the lump of words that would have taken another lifetime to speak.

"I'm just relieved that I found a partner, and we were able to arrange a deal at the bank," Ed said, standing beside his friend.

Caesar had prepared a buffet with carved turkey, ham, and roast beef and a vast array of cold and hot side dishes. Rainbow got some help from the kitchen and prepared some of her famous mixed teas and cocktails. The wedding cake was red velvet, and there was homemade ice cream. Their guests included fellow students from A & I and colleagues at *The Nashville Globe*, but more well-wishers from all over Nashville came to congratulate Bless than the restaurant could hold. He was a person who never met a stranger and always made a friend.

Blue supplied them with fine champagne and a small band played, and they all danced until their feet throbbed. Caesar and Rainbow danced for one song and sat down at their table to watch the young people enjoy themselves.

"My vision was clearer this morning," Rainbow remarked. "Now I can't see my boy's eyes or his smile while he dances with his wife."

"Close your eyes and use your mind's eye. Imagine it, and you can see it just the way it is," Caesar said softly in her ear.

Rainbow leaned back in her chair with her eyes shut, after a moment, she grabbed Caesar's hand and gave it a gentle squeeze. He answered with a soft pat on her thigh.

"I'm so proud of these men that we've raised. They're strong and educated, and now they both will have families of their own," Rainbow said satisfied.

"It's a blessing. Leaving and traveling so far away will be bittersweet, but we can take comfort knowing that both of them are settled," Caesar said, watching them on the dance floor. "I still plan to give them both a share of the restaurant proceeds on their 25th birthday; I don't want them to have to wait until I die before they can realize their dreams."

"Blue is already doing well and doesn't need any more help," Rainbow said. "But we've always treated them equally, and that's not about to change."

"Blue might even put it up for the baby they're expecting in three months and any other children," Caesar told her. "He knows the difference it made."

Blue sat with Carol at the table next to them, watching Bless and Cassy out on the floor, happy, enjoying each other, and in love. They had something he didn't have, and he wondered what it was and why didn't he have it. He couldn't explain the feeling that something was always missing or what it was; he only knew that he wasn't satisfied. He tried everything--women, gambling, drinking, and making money--but none of it filled the void.

"You're just like your Grandma Diana," Caesar would say, chastising him whenever people put his business in the street. Blue gazed over at Carol, who was beginning to look tired after the long day, and then at her belly, which held their child, and decided that he would try to be more considerate of her feelings.

"This camera was given to me by my Dad almost forty years ago when I was just a boy," Caesar announced at the end of the evening. "I would like to pass this along to Bless and Cassy as a wedding gift."

"Thank you so much for everything, Dad," Bless said, exhausted when he and Cassy excused themselves from the party. "We've got to get up early for our honeymoon."

***

Bless and Cassy Portunus left for Highland Beach in Maryland the next day. Cassy hadn't had the opportunity to spend much time in Baltimore since she came to Nashville as a college freshman. They both wanted to have a chance to have some fun and relax before they got to work on their magazine.

"I can't wait to get to the beach," Bless said anxiously while they were getting settled in their cottage. "I've never seen the ocean before."

The beauty of the water took his breath away, and he was humbled by the power of the waves as they rushed in toward them. Over the next two weeks, Bless sat on the sand, taking in the grandness of the ocean. The water began to speak to him; and with each swell and surge, things became clearer to him, and the purpose of his life was more defined.

Lying in bed on their last night in Ocean City, Bless leaned up and said, "Cass, it's time now. A shift in the South is coming, and I want us to use our magazine as a force in this fight for equal rights. It's going to be something none of us have seen before, and I want us to document everything that happens."

Cassy pretended that she was drowsy and half sleep, but she was wide awake when she answered, "Go back to sleep, Bless. We got a lot to do in the morning." She knew what he was talking about: the commitment, the risks, the danger, and the sacrifice that they would have to make if they did that. On the train ride back to Nashville, Cassy proposed a compromise.

"I don't think that we should limit ourselves to being a protest paper. We need information about so many things: education, healthcare, housing, sports, and even entertainment. That's the way we'll survive, even after the campaign for equality is over."

Bless got lost in his thoughts for a while before he said, "I see your point. We'll call it the *"The Banquet of Knowledge."*

It was a hot day in May, but the sweat on Cassy's brow wasn't from the heat, it was from relief. The fever she felt since last night had broken, and they were going to be all right.

Chapter
Twenty-Four

The summer ended with new beginnings, except, a new beginning for one is many times the conclusion for another. Blue and Carol had a baby girl they named Josephine.

"The Storm's End deal is closed, honey," Caesar told Rainbow when he got home. "Ed found a silent partner to share the financing, and they became the restaurant's new owners today. Even though it was something that we planned, and it was inevitable, it was still shocking when it really came to pass. My dream and my livelihood no longer belong to me anymore."

"That's not true, C; nobody can ever take that away from you. It served its purpose. We raised our boys, and we were very happy here. Now it's time for us to move on."

"When I was packing up my office, the mementos and photographs of all the celebrities that had dined there, the last twenty-five years flashed before me. The opening, the preparation of so many meals, the boys running around, the events, and the parties--it seemed like it all happened in such a short time."

"It was, honey. Now the boys are grown men with lives of their own, and we need to focus on each other again. I had all those same feelings when I looked around the house and wondered what we should to take to California. Then I decided that I don't want to take anything except some clothes and our photo album; it's going to be a rebirth, a fresh beginning, a chance for us to experience new things together, including setting up house. Bless and Cassy will be living in the family house, I'll let them decide what they want to keep."

"I'm just happy we got to see our first grandbaby before we leave. She's a beauty."

"Yeah, Josephine is the only girl to wrap Blue around her finger. She's got him coming straight home from work every day."

"Rain, I wouldn't have believed it if I hadn't seen it for myself, but my son is truly in love. I think the baby is really what Blue and Carol needed to bring them closer."

Josephine brought out another side of Blue. He spent hours holding her and playing with her. It was the smile she gave him in exchange for the one he gave to her that he craved. It was magic, the way he was transformed; he whispered stories softly to her each night and sometimes sung to her before he tucked her in. This part of Blue was even more perplexing to Carol than the one she had come to know, and she wondered why he never showed her that gentleness. She had succeeded in getting her husband to spend more time at home, but only to watch him shower another female with his affection.

Rainbow and Caesar said their emotional goodbyes to Bless and Cassy, Blue and Carol, and sweet Josephine. They were ready to take the next step in their journey together. It was different from when they first started out; this time they boarded an airplane for the first time and headed out to Los Angeles.

"It's frightening and exhilarating at the same time," Caesar said to Rainbow. "We're flying through the air like a bird. This is truly amazing."

"I feel so free," Rainbow told him, peering out of the window of the plane and seeing the ground so far below them.

It was a freedom that neither had ever felt before. The pressure of finding your place in this wide world was over, raising a family was finished, and making a living was done. Every new morning would be their own.

They found a roomy condominium in Baldwin Hills, where they could enjoy the sights and smells of lush green trees and vibrant flowers. There they did the things that they did on their very first date; they enjoyed the aromas and tastes of good food and the sounds of good music.

Caesar was her eyes on her bad days, and Rainbow was his hands on his bad days. Feelings became so important: the silkiness of a rose petal, the prickly skin of a pineapple, and a warm hand to hold in the quiet hours of the night. They were enjoying the peace that they hadn't taken the time to relish. They often caught a ride to the beach, where they would take long walks and Rainbow could feel the brightness of the sun on her face and the foam of the ocean waves on her feet.

***

Bless and Cassy's strategy was to start the magazine small, publishing monthly, and allow it to grow on its own. They rented the office space above Blue's construction company, chose a printing company, and a local distributor. Once they'd registered the title, they had to accumulate a respectable number of permanent advertisers. The list began with the Empire Construction Company and The Storm's End, but Bless still had the support of the community he grew up in. Nightclubs, funeral homes, barber shops, and grocery stores bought space in *The Banquet of Knowledge*.

In their first publication, they ran stories about the bus boycott in Louisiana; the desegregation court case being heard by the Supreme Court; and interviews with the Tigerbelles, from Tennessee A & I, who were going to the Olympic Games. When Bless and Cassy got the copy from their first printing in November, it wasn't the only thing they had to celebrate and be thankful for. Cassy was pregnant.

Six months later, on May 24, 1954, the twins' twenty-fifth birthday, they both received a check for another $10,000 from their Mama and Dad.

"I'm going to put this in a trust for Josephine," Blue told Bless. "I want my children to have every opportunity that Mama and Dad gave us."

"I wish I could, too, but it's just what I need to expand the distribution of *The Banquet of Knowledge*," Bless said. "There's a building a few blocks away on Charlotte Avenue that would be a perfect headquarters for the magazine, and I need to hire a staff. With the baby due next month, I can't do all the work by myself."

Bless had become a member of the National Negro Publishers Association, and news flowed in from all over the country, but there were stories where he wanted his own perspective. So much was happening all over the South with the Civil Rights Movement, he needed reporters and photographers that he could put on the road.

Cassy's water broke after they got home from a Juneteenth celebration at Fisk University.

"Blue, Cassy's pains have started, and we're on our way to Meharry Hospital," Bless relayed in a quick phone call to Blue.

In the car, with each of the gasps of pain that Cassy made from the contractions, Bless grew more excited that they would soon have a child of their own. When they got to the hospital Blue, was already there waiting for them.

Cassy was taken into the delivery room, and Blue took Bless by the arm and said, "Come on, bro, I need to go outside for a smoke."

Blue lit up his cigar and took a long drag. When the smoke cleared, he smiled at Bless, who stood beside him, patting his foot to a quick rhythm that marked his nervousness.

"Relax, man, she'll be fine. And in a few hours, you'll have another mouth to feed," Blue said with a nudge to his shoulder.

"I know it. I just feel so lucky to have a good woman who's in there having our baby and to have the magazine growing," Bless said. "Both of us have been smiled on, bro."

"It's not all it's cracked up to be, Bless," Blue added.

"I know it's hard going home to a fine woman and a beautiful baby girl," Bless said with a laugh. "Plus all the business you got, I bet you cry all the way to the bank."

Blue nodded and took another long inhale just as a nurse came to the door and signaled for them to come back in.

"Congratulations, Mr. Portunus," the nurse said. "You have a healthy baby girl, and your wife is doing fine."

Blue turned to Bless and shook his hand and then hugged him with the other arm, "Congrats, man," he said. "Go see your wife and baby; I'm going to go get a drink to celebrate."

"You know, you can go home and have that drink," Bless said.

"I will," he answered. "First, I have to drink a toast to my niece with a few friends."

"Thanks for coming, man," Bless said as he turned and followed the nurse down the hall to see Cassy and their new baby.

Their baby girl was a perfect blend of her mama and daddy. She had thin smooth cap of hair, and her eyes were amber, the same color as her skin, and they twinkled when she tried to focus. When Bless held her, she looked like her daddy and when Cassy held her, she looked like her mama.

"I want to name her Venus. She's the bright light in our lives now," Bless said.

Bless thought the sun rose when the baby woke up in the morning and set when she went to sleep at night. He could hardly contain himself to make the long distance phone call.

"Mama, get Daddy on the phone. I've got good news! Cassy had a baby girl, and we named her Venus."

"That's wonderful, son," Rainbow said as she and Caesar felt his joy come through the receiver. "We're so happy for you, son, and proud of you, too."

"Congratulations," Caesar told him. "I wish I could be there."

They were ecstatic. They had raised two sons, and now they had two precious granddaughters. "We coming out there to see y'all as soon as we can," they said before they hung up.

The next afternoon, Carol came to the hospital to visit Cassy and see the new baby. They talked for a while and compared the details of their deliveries before Carol said, "You know you're very lucky."

"What do you mean?" Cassy asked, puzzled by her words.

"You got the one with the heart," Carol answered.

"Carol, you know that Blue loves you, and Josephine is his heart," Cassy said.

"How can you love somebody and hurt them like he hurts me, Cassy? He has never been faithful to me. I'm a woman, not one of his possessions that he keeps as a decoration," Carol said with her eyes welling up.

"Do you know how many women would trade places with you in a heartbeat?"

"No, who would want to have a man who would rather hang in the streets than come home to his wife and child."

"Blue is wild like a tiger," Cassy said. "He can't be penned in. Just remember, he chose you out of all the women. He wants you."

"That's no comfort to me while I'm sitting in the house all by myself. The world doesn't belong to him. What I want matters, too."

"You knew how he was. Did you think he would change?"

"After we got married, yes, I did. What's wrong with that?" Carol asked.

"Is that fair?"

"I don't know," Carol responded.

"Well, you still have the right to stay or leave. If you can deal with the situation, stay, if you can't, then leave."

***

It was the season of growth and expansion. Bless and Cassy reveled in every new milestone as Venus grew, while at the same time, they monitored the development of the magazine. They rented the building on the corner of 14th and Charlotte and recruited a professional staff. The number of color pictures doubled, the variety of articles increased, and the amount of local and national advertisers multiplied.

Blue's construction business continued to prosper. He had three full crews that worked nonstop contracted out to other companies. Hiring out his crews got him the work on projects that didn't do business with black companies. He was a master bricklayer and still loved to do the physical work with his top crew on special projects.

"It sounds like you've decided to stay," Cassy said to Carol after she announced her pregnancy at a family picnic on Labor Day.

"I think another baby will help solidify our marriage. Blue is always more considerate of me when I'm pregnant," Carol explained. "He's coming home at a decent hour and spending more time with the family."

"I'm happy for you Carol; let's pray it last a long time," Cassy said cautiously.

For Christmas, Blue brought Carol a huge diamond ring, which she wore to church and all her social functions. He took her to the movies to see Dorothy Dandridge and Harry Belafonte in *Carmen Jones* and bought her flowers on Valentine's Day.

"I'm happier than I have ever been since we were married," Carol told Cassy when she called to see how she was feeling. "I'm glad I weathered the storms, and now it's time for me to have my place in the sun."

"Prayers went up, and blessings came down," Cassy shouted. "Hallelujah."

"I'm so thankful," Carol said before they hung up.

Blue was sweet and caring. When Carol's feet began to swell at the end of her eighth month, he would carry her up and down the steps. After Josephine went to bed, they would sit and watch television with his arms around belly. Carol gave birth to a son on May 8, 1955, Mother's Day. He was warm brown like bourbon, lean and long, and they named him Anthony.

With that news, Caesar and Rainbow couldn't put off their visit back east any longer. They had two grandbabies they hadn't seen.

"I thought we would have gotten back here before now, but it sure is good to be home," Caesar said to Bless at the airport. "We plan to be here for the whole summer."

"Your timing couldn't have been better; Cassy and I need the extra help with Venus in the midst of all the breaking news black folks are making from coast to coast. Things are getting bad right now, the number of lynchings has picked up, unemployment is on the rise, and black gangs are gaining numbers in all the large metropolitan cities."

"Keep us all in the know, son. You sound like my grandy back in the days when he was protesting in Savannah."

"I wish I could have known him," Bless said.

"Me, too," Caesar said.

A season of upheaval was settling in. The preview of thunderstorms in the West, droughts in the Midwest, heatwaves in the South, and hurricanes on the East Coast gave signs of what was to come. It came to a head at the end of August when Emmett Till was murdered in Mississippi.

"I've got to go and cover this story myself," Bless said to Cassy.

"I know, and you're not going without me," Cassy informed him.

Caesar and Rainbow stayed at the family house, and Bless and Cassy drove down to the Delta to cover the story.

The brutal lynching of a fourteen-year-old boy, the vicious killers, the heartless white community, the ghastly body that lay in the open casket, and the injustice that followed in the Tallahatchie courtroom dominated the pages of the next two issues of *The Banquet of Knowledge*. Bless poured his heart and soul into the articles and Cassy captured the drama in vivid photographs on the cover, and the magazine sold a record numbers of copies.

"We had a good visit with the children," Rainbow said, satisfied as she and Caesar climbed the steps of the plane flying back to Los Angeles before the first chill.

"We leaving just in time," Caesar said, already beginning to feel the stiffness creeping into his joints and the growing pain that ran down his fingers. "Babies are for young people."

"It was good to see Bless and Blue busy doing the things they dreamed of doing and that they're happy in their homes," Rainbow said, content.

"I wanted to spoil my grandbabies some, so I enjoyed these months with Josephine, Venus, and Anthony; but I'm ready for us to get back to our own lives," Caesar said.

"You know, I'm more comfortable in our smaller place with my eyes acting up."

Rainbow's vision had narrowed down to shadows moving in a dense fog, and they missed the lazy mornings where they had nothing to do and the quiet time that you rarely experience in a house full of toddlers.

Chapter
Twenty-Five

The peaceful holiday season was upstaged by a woman who refused to give up her bus seat to a white man in Montgomery, Alabama. It was the snowfall that caused an avalanche when a bus boycott was organized, and a young black preacher named Martin Luther King Jr. was selected as the leader. The story kept Bless and Cassy on the road, back and forth to Alabama for months. They covered the bombing of black churches and the bombing of Dr. King's own home.

It was thrilling time. They followed the campaigns of the Civil Rights Movement, Floyd Patterson in the boxing ring, Willie Mays and Hank Aaron on the baseball field, and Althea Gibson on the tennis court. Even more so, stimulating interviews with Ralph Ellison and Sidney Poitier inspired them. The growing popularity of the magazine opened doors to meet people that they never thought they would encounter.

"I feel bad dragging you and Venus out on the road," Bless said to Cassy while all three of them sat in a car in Montgomery.

"It's not your fault, Bless," Cassy reassured him. "I want to be here, and Venus wants to be wherever we are."

"I understand that, but it's the baby's second birthday, and she can't even celebrate it with her cousins at home."

"Next year, we'll throw her a big party she'll never forget," Cassy said, giving Venus a kiss on the forehead.

The boycott was still dragging on; and they needed to tell the story of the struggle, the unity, and the violence that the campaign incited. They gave rides to as many folks walking as they could, and it gave them opportunities to interview the people and get an honest view of how difficult it was day after day. Venus sat in the front seat with Cassy while she took pictures in the heat and the rain. They picked up an older woman who had on a uniform of a domestic worker late one evening.

"You looked tired," Cassy said to the woman. "How are you making it?"

"I ain't gonna lie. It's been hell, but I've stuck it out this long, and I'm going to see it through to the end."

"I'm praying it won't have to go on much longer," Cassy said as they dropped her at home.

"God bless you," the older woman said.

The boycott went on to the end of the year before the magazine could print the news of a victory for the movement and the end of the boycott on December 20, 1956. Bless thought the next phase of the movement would focus on school desegregation. There were several public schools in Nashville that were integrating, but the real story developed in the fall of 1957, at the start of another school year in Little Rock, Arkansas.

"I can't believe we're doing this again," Bless said as he and Cassy loaded up the car with three-year-old Venus in tow to witness nine black students walk into Little Central High School.

"This is the first time that I have been afraid for yours and Venus's safety," Bless told Cassy when he saw the Arkansan National Guard armed with rifles lined up to block the students' entrance to the school. He watched Cassy take pictures of the scene, with Venus holding on to to her skirt and knew this was the last time that she would be with them on a story.

They hired a nanny named Ann for Venus, and Cassy continued to work. She felt she was too smart and too talented to waste herself staying at home.

"You knew when you married me that I wasn't going to be your housewife. I made it clear that I wanted to have a career," Cassy said in the car with Bless.

"It's no problem for me as long as Venus is being cared for properly," Bless said. "We started the magazine as partners, and that's the way I want it to stay."

"I love it when you say things like that," Cassy said, scooting over close to him. "It's like being on a good date with a cute guy that never ends."

When the spring came, Cassy was pregnant again. She was happy about it, but she also knew it would put a lull in her work on the magazine. She traveled with Bless until her doctor advised her to stop. Their son was born November 4, 1958, and they named him Alexander. Everyone said he would be lucky because he looked just like his mother.

***

In the meantime, Blue had become bored. He had done whatever Carol asked. He spent more time at home, ate dinner with his kids, and sat with them on the third pew every Sunday morning. He had done his best to behave as a prominent and respected member of Nashville's black society; but he'd had his fill of the fundraiser balls, the business luncheons, and drinking White Russians that soured on his stomach.

He was out for his own after-party when the celebration for his and Bless's thirtieth birthday at The Storm's End was over. He headed straight to the Del Morocco to check out the new show. The new competition on Jefferson Street compelled Uncle Teddy to take his entertainment to another level.

"Happy Birthday, Blue. I didn't expect to see you tonight," Uncle Teddy said, welcoming him in the club. "Slip me some skin."

"It wouldn't be my birthday if I didn't stop by here," Blue answered, slapping his hand and looking around the room.

"You better believe it," Uncle Teddy said. "I've got something special going on tonight."

"Point me in the right direction," Blue said eagerly.

Uncle Teddy had created a Vegas-type revue. Blue sat down, ordered a drink, turned to the stage, and laid eyes on Lola. Lola stood out among the long-legged dancers, not only because she was the prettiest, but because she was the darkest. She absorbed the spotlight and glowed on stage, and Blue was like a moth drawn to a flame. He wrote a note and asked the waiter to give it to her backstage.

He watched her glide over to his table in an emerald green satin dress and matching high heels after she changed.

Blue stood up and introduced himself. "Good evening, I'm Caesar Blue, and I enjoyed your performance in the show."

"Thank you," she answered, "I'm Lola, Lola Davis."

"Pleased to meet you, Miss Lola. May I buy you a drink?" he asked.

"Mrs. Lola," she said, looking straight at him with her dark eyes.

"Does that mean you don't get thirsty?" Blue asked, flashing his sexy smile.

"No, it's doesn't," she answered. Blue stood up, pulled out the chair for her, and motioned for the waiter to come over to the table.

"You blew me away up there. You're gorgeous," Blue told her.

"Thanks, I'm glad you enjoyed it," Lola said.

"By the way, where is Mr. Davis tonight?" Blue asked her seductively. "I wouldn't take my eyes off you if you were mine."

"He doesn't care to keep late hours," Lola replied.

"Just my luck," Blue said, moving his chair closer to hers. "Could I see you home or possibly to another spot where we can talk privately."

"It just so happens that I feel like talking," she said before she walked out with Blue following a few seconds behind her.

Lola was married to an older man who provided her with the readymade comforts of a home set up by his late wife, whatever she wanted to eat or drink, and a credit account for clothes from Harvey's Department Store. Lola's condition for accepting her husband Dean's proposal was that she be allowed to pursue her career as a dancer. Twenty-five years her senior, he was the father she never had, and she truly loved him. However, she was like Blue; she had everything and didn't know it. Neither of the two wanted to break up their marriages, it was the secrecy and the danger of their relationship fed them the excitement they both craved.

Blue and Lola were discreet with their affair. He watched her show on the three nights that the Del Morocco featured the dancers, but they never left the club together. Blue rented a small apartment in Haynes Manor, and they met there in the mornings as often as they could and stayed to the late hours of the afternoon.

Blue loved that she was an aggressive and adventurous lover. Lola loved touching a young, strong, and muscular body. They would take off their clothes when they got inside and leave them off until it was time to go. He was mesmerized by the firmness of her dancer's body and the darkness of her skin. She couldn't get enough of the curly hair on his chest and how he lifted her around like she was a doll and never got tired.

***

Bless and Cassy were grounded with the new baby since Bless was reluctant to do much traveling while Alex was so young. The

Civil Rights Movement was intensifying across the South, and the demonstrations were becoming more overt.

"I'm ready to join the protest and be more involved," Bless said to Cassy in their joint office at the magazine. "I'm tired of being on the outside looking in."

"I think it will be difficult to be a participant and be objective at the same time," she advised him. "Involving the magazine directly can put it in jeopardy and put us at risk for being bombed.

"I hadn't considered that as a possibility, but you're right,"

Bless said in agreement. "Any protest activities should be separate from the magazine. I can use our old office space over Blue's company as a place for working, writing, and organizing campaigns with the movement."

"I suppose that is as close to a compromise as I'm going to get," Cassy said, realizing he wasn't going to let it go.

Midsummer, nothing generated more heat than the documentary on the Nation of Islam called *The Hate That Hate Produced*. Bless was leaning toward the nonviolent method of protest, but he wanted to make sure *The Banquet of Knowledge* provided its readers with a well-rounded view of the black struggle for equality. He printed articles on the emerging leadership of Martin Luther King Jr. and his philosophies, as well as the controversial viewpoints of Malcolm X, the rising representative for the Nation of Islam.

Bless was particularly energized after meeting with James Lawson. James had come to Nashville from Ohio to educate the demonstrators on Ghandi's principle of nonviolence.

Young college students were impatient for change and were willing to get involved. In the fall, Bless made sure he was in attendance when James Lawson started his nonviolent training workshops that fall in the basement of First Baptist Church for students from Tennessee A&I, Fisk, Meharry, and American Baptist College. The first meeting for the sit-in campaign was on February 12, and more than 500 students showed up.

"All of you look good, neat, and clean-cut; that's the way I want to see you in every demonstration;" Lawson told them. "I don't want them to have any other reason to refuse us."

"How long before we get started on the campaign?" a tall and thin young man in the front asked. "I'm tired of waiting."

"Is tomorrow soon enough for you?" Lawson replied. "We are about to integrate the downtown lunch counters, but before I let you go, we need to practice some roleplaying to prepare yourselves for the name-calling and physical abuse that will come, without retaliating."

Lawson took the students through a number of different scenarios where they were yelled at and physical attacked.

Bless joined them the next day, armed with a camera to record the protest of segregated lunch counters. The well-dressed group flooded the downtown lunch venues with nothing but books in their hands. Bless accompanied several student to Woolworths. No sooner had they sat down before they were verbally assaulted, pushed over, spit on, beaten, and then arrested. Bless wrote it all down and took pictures as the same treatment was delivered to the next group of students. It was hard to see the young men and women be cursed, called niggers, and have food thrown on them; but the hardest part was to see them punched, kicked, burned with cigarettes, and hit with sticks and have to hold his peace.

At the end of the day, over 150 students had been arrested. The nonviolent campaign had taken off like a plane flying in an air show, speeding through steep climbs, quick turns, spins, and sweeping dives. The whole scene left Bless nauseated and disgusted. He went to his private office on Jefferson Street to decompress before he went home. He saw Blue coming out of his office door. They grabbed hands and leaned in close to greet each other. Blue was looking dapper in a dark brown wool suit, and Bless looked wrinkled and worn in a tan trench coat.

"You look tired, man. What you been up to?" Blue asked, concerned.

"Helluva day, Blue," Bless answered, not ready to talk it.

"Take it easy, brother. Life is short. We got to enjoy it," Blue said.

"Where you headed dressed to kill?" Bless asked.

"I'm going to Del Morocco to take everybody's money," he said, shaking his handful of imaginary dice.

"While you out here throwing caution to the wind, think about some of the other folks who are laying their lives down so somebody else can get a break."

"I hear you, brother, but right now, you blowing my buzz," Blue told him. "We'll talk."

"You messing up, Blue. You need to straighten up and fly right before your luck runs out," Bless warned.

"I will, but not tonight. Tonight I feel lucky," he said as he grabbed Bless's hand and leaned in again. "Later, man."

Bless shook his head in frustration with Blue. He knew his brother was taking too many chances, gambling with his marriage and his money. There were days he wished he could talk some sense into him; and other days, he wished he could care less and be more like Blue. After witnessing the sacrifice of the students today without any defense, Bless wasn't sure which way was the best. He knew he had a job to do, so he walked up the stairs to his office to put the day's events on paper.

This was the key difference between the twins. Bless didn't think of his life as his own. He saw his life as more of an extension of the people he loved and cared about. Blue saw his life as his own and was determined to live it as he saw fit without any apologies for putting his happiness first.

***

"I'm coming out with you today, Bless," Cassy told him when he headed toward the office exit one morning.

"Okay, but there's not going to be the regular sit-ins at Krege's and Walgreens lunch counters today," Bless said with some apprehension. "The students have scheduled a silent march on City Hall in protest of Councilman Z. Alexander Looby's house being bombed."

"What about the boycotts of downtown stores?" she asked.

"Those were organized by the parents and other folks who were upset about the brutal treatment of the students. I don't know what we'll run into before the day is out."

"I'm right behind you," Cassy said, grabbing her camera.

Councilman Z. Alexander Looby had been working at fever pitch to defend the student demonstrators, who were being arrested daily. More than 4,000 people, led by the students, were marching to show their outrage over his home being terrorized. At the end of the day, the mayor admitted that segregation was wrong, and they were all so proud of what they had accomplished.

"It feels good to be out here again," Cassy said to Bless. It was the first protest that she had photographed since Alexander was born, and she was glad to be back at work.

It was uplifting to see people organized and working toward a just cause. The highlight came the following day when they got a chance to meet Martin Luther King Jr. when he came to speak to the students at Fisk University. They quoted him in the magazine, *"I came to Nashville not to bring inspiration, but to gain inspiration from the great movement that has taken place in this community."* It was another victory. The June issue of *The Banquet of Knowledge* announced that the lunch counters in downtown Nashville were now serving negroes.

"It's encouraging to see positive results come from the suffering I've seen these students endure," Bless said to Cassy as they worked at the office. "It would have been easier for me to take the punishment myself than have to stand back and observe it all."

"You have to remember that the work that we do is extremely important to the success of the movement," Cassy said, trying to assure him that he was doing his part. "We should probably take a break from the heavy stories and lighten up for a couple of months. The Summer Olympics will be starting soon."

"You're always the voice of reason," Bless said, driving home. "I couldn't make it without you, Cass."

"Believe me, I'm not going to let you," she said, settling back in the seat.

A new focus came for them during the Summer Olympics when a number of black athletes entered the spotlight on the world's stage. Cassius Clay won the light heavyweight gold medal; but it was Wilma Rudolph who amazed the world with her performance, winning three gold medals and becoming the fastest woman in the world. She graced the cover of the magazine in the October issue.

It was a much needed break for Bless and Cassy. Stepping back from the civil rights campaigns and spending more time with the family gave Bless time to relax and renew.

"What's shaking, Blue?" Bless asked him over the telephone. "We need to hang out."

"I'm ready when you are," Blue answered, sounding upbeat. "It's been a few years since we've painted the town together."

"How about right now?" Bless asked.

"I'll be over there in an hour," Blue said.

Blue picked Bless up from the magazine office, and they went to the barbershop for fresh cuts and shaves. Bless let the tension evaporate with the steam under the hot towel, while he listened to the men talk shit and joke around.

"This is the plan, bro," Blue said when they were done. "Go home, have dinner, change clothes, kiss your wife, and then meet me at your spot around 9:00."

They met in the parking lot outside the New Era and walked in together. Bless couldn't deny it felt good to put on a nice suit and strut into the club with Blue. They were looking good and smelling good and basking in the attention like they used to when they were in college.

"Two beers," Blue said to the bartender.

Bless tapped his bottle against Blue's and drank. The beer went down cool and mellowed his insides. He ordered two more for them, and with the second one, he joined the other patrons in their quest to temporarily escape from everything that existed outside that room.

"It's just like old times," Bless said, listening to the band play.

At least it was until a young woman in a silver dress with a fur jacket came over to the table. Blue stood up and pulled a chair over to the table for her to sit down.

He smiled at her and said, "Lola, this is my brother, Bless."

"Nice to meet you, Bless," Lola said as she sat down next to Blue.

"Likewise," Bless said, taken aback.

The two sat as close together as two people could without sitting in the other's lap. Bless watched them hold hands and whisper intimately in each other's ears. Blue had his vices, and pretty women topped the list, but he always kept his two worlds well-divided. Bless had never met any of the women Blue fooled around with, and that's the way he liked it. Lola lit a cigarette, and the smooth groove that he had been feeling went up in the smoke. After a few more minutes of Blue pretending that he wasn't there, Bless spoke up as if Lola wasn't there.

"What in the hell do you think you are doing?"

Blue looked at him and said, "You tell me, and we'll both know."

"You got a wife, and you need to respect that. Since when have you started putting your business in the street?" Bless asked.

"I respect my wife by keeping it in the street. I've asked her to roll with me, and it's not her thing. So right now, I'm here with my lady, and there's no place she won't go with me," Blue answered.

Bless sat there and drank the rest of his beer, wondering what he could do to change the situation and with nothing coming to mind, he stood up and said, "This was nice," with all the sarcasm he could muster. Bless drove home pissed off. Blue was getting reckless, and no good would come from it. Cassy was still up watching TV in her night clothes when he got home.

"You're in early. Did you have a good time?" she asked.

"Now, how was I supposed to have good time if you weren't there?" he asked.

Cassy rewarded his sweet words with a kiss, turned off the television, and followed him upstairs to bed. She wondered what could have happened; he always held her extra tight whenever something was bothering him. But she knew better than to question him about anything that had to do with Blue.

Chapter Twenty-Six

Carol wanted to host the Christmas dinner. Her housekeeper was going to be with her family for the holidays, and Carol was looking forward to preparing all the food herself for a change. The kids were all playing in den, with Josephine thinking she was in charge; and Blue and Bless were in Blue's home office having a drink. Cassy was in the kitchen with Carol as she put the finishing touches on the meal.

"You look like you have a touch of holiday blues, girl," Cassy said, watching Carol work. "Let's turn on the radio."

Cassy thought the music would distract Carol from her thoughts. The new song by the Miracles, "Shop Around," was playing, and Cassy started to do the twist all the way to the floor and Carol couldn't help but smile.

"Come on, girl, let me see you churn it," Cassy said, pulling Carol away from the counter.

They twisted to the beat in the middle of the floor like young girls and the music seemed to cheer Carol up.

"Now, don't you feel better?" Cassy said as they sat down to catch their breath when the song ended.

Then, Tina Turner came on singing "A Fool in Love." The lyrics thumped out of the radio,

Oh, there's something on my mind
Won't somebody please, please tell me what's wrong?
You're just a fool, you know you're in love
You've got to face it to let it explode
You take the good along with the bad
Sometimes you're happy and sometimes you're sad
You know you love him, you can't understand
Why he treats you like he do, when he's such a good man?

The lyrics were just enough to crack Carol's fragile façade. Sitting in the chair, she bowed her head and sobbed as her body attempted to flush out the sadness.

Cassy slid over and put her arms around her. "What is it Carol? What's wrong?"

"I can't take it any more, Cassy. Everybody knows that Blue is running around on me with some slut from that club on Jefferson Street. I've done everything I know to do, and he still treats me like shit," Carol said through her tears.

"You might need to take the kids and leave him for a while, let him know you're not going to put up with his bullshit. He loves you, and he doesn't want to lose his family, he'll drop her like a hot potato," Cassy told her.

Cassy pat her on the shoulder until she composed herself. Then she got one of the dinner napkins and wet it in cold water at the sink and gave it to Carol to clean her face, saying, "You know both of them were spoiled rotten. Show him he can't have his cake and eat it, too."

Christmas dinner was a bit tense around the table, but the kids didn't seem to notice. Josephine, Venus, and Anthony talked among themselves while Cassy fed Alexander in the high-chair. Carol was quiet and looked down at her plate for most of the meal, and the conversation between Blue and Bless stayed on safe subjects like the weather, sports, and the presidential election. It was a perfect picture, two brothers with beautiful wives and healthy children, sitting before a delicious meal. There wasn't much more that life could offer to make someone happy. Unfortunately, it's never that simple.

Blue knew that he had gone too far. It wasn't his intention to hurt Carol. It just seemed that he couldn't make her happy and be happy himself at the same time.

When the three older children were finished eating, they were excused from the table.

Blue clapped his hands together to get their attention, and then he said, "I don't know if you all can tell, but my wife is upset with me and probably with good reason, but I want to take this time to tell her that I love her and give her something to show her how much I appreciate her."

Blue reached into his jacket pocket and pulled out a black velvet box. He opened it and took out a diamond and ruby necklace. It was stunning and very expensive. He stood up and placed it around Carol's neck. Carol was overwhelmed, Blue had never been apologetic for anything that he did, and she wasn't sure what it meant.

"It's beautiful," Cassy said, trying to fill the awkward silence.

"Thank you," Carol said.

"Well, I can't follow that, so we'll wait for you guys in the den with the kids," Bless said, picking up the baby and taking Cassy's hand to give Blue and Carol a minute to be alone.

"Baby, you and the kids mean the world to me, and I don't want you to ever doubt that," Blue said, holding her tight in his arms.

"I don't need any more jewelry, furs, or cars, Blue. I need to know that you don't want any other women," Carol replied.

"You're my queen, honey. Don't you know that?" Blue asked, looking her in the eyes.

"What I know is talk around town says you got another woman, and you're planning on leaving me for her."

"Don't believe any of the trash talk going around. Some folks are just jealous. You're my wife."

"If you can't be here at home with me instead of roaming the streets, I'm not going to sit here like a fool," she said angrily.

"Baby, I'm grown, and I'm not going to sit around here like I'm one of the children. You are well taken care of. What more do you want?" he asked, losing his patience.

"I guess I want a man who can be faithful to me," she answered.

Blue threw up his hands and walked out.

Blue worked harder in the new year and business was good. He was a skillful contract negotiator and usually underbid his competitors, but recently there had been some sabotage on his worksites. However, it wasn't enough to slow him down, and his insurance covered the damages. Naturally, he played harder. There were high-stakes poker games, late nights at the clubs, and his hot afternoons with Lola. Unfortunately, her husband, Dean, who had looked the other way at some of her dalliances, was keeping closer tabs on where she went.

***

"We're going to make some changes to stay more competitive," Bless said to Cassy. "Our national advertisers have picked up, but we're losing readers to white magazines, and now our best writer has quit."

"I been thinking about that. My idea is to shrink the size of the magazine down a few inches. That will save a lot of cost, and then we can add more color photos. Our readers love my photography," she said with a teasing grin.

"That's good because I'm worn out writing as well as editing," Bless replied.

"There's kind of a lull now in the Civil Rights Movement after the successes of the bus boycotts and sit-ins," Cassy added. "For the first part of the year, *The Banquet of Knowledge* should feature black actors and actresses who are rising in Hollywood and black athletes who are advancing in professional sports."

"I want to keep the struggle on everybody's mind. It's just beginning, and we have a long way to go."

"I know, but we don't want our readers to get burned out with the fight," she reminded him.

The momentum of the movement surged in the spring of 1961, with the Freedom Riders planning to ride buses from Washington, DC, to New Orleans to test the validity of the Supreme Court ruling that banned segregation on interstate bus travel in the South.

"Press releases are coming in every minute on the hour," Bless announced to his staff. "They say there was minimal conflict until the buses reached South Carolina; and en route to Birmingham, an angry mob of whites threw rocks at one of the buses and slashed its tires. When the bus driver walked away, some windows were busted out, and some type of burning object was thrown through the window and filled it with smoke. The bus caught fire, and in seconds after the riders burst through the door, it exploded."

"Where were the police or national guards?" Cassy asked.

"Who knows," Bless said. "When the bus arrived in Birmingham, there was another mob waiting, and those riders were viciously attacked. The latest release says that the riders suffered from smoke inhalation, and some were severely beaten."

A few hours later, James Lawson called Bless at the magazine office.

"How's it going down there?" Bless asked James over the phone.

"The riders are battle-weary and traumatized," James told him. "President Kennedy has advised us of the danger in proceeding further with the campaign, so we're flying down to New Orleans. It looks like the Freedom Ride will end in Birmingham."

"That's too bad, James," Bless said sadly. "What more could you do?"

It was the Nashville Student Movement that declared the Freedom Riders couldn't accept defeat. The campaign had to be continued. There were seven riders, three female and four male, Diane Nash would be the leader. They signed their last will and testaments and then traveled to Birmingham as fresh reinforcements who were more experienced with the bigotry and violence in the South.

"This is going to be an historical event, and I want a front seat to the proceedings," Bless said to Cassy. "I'm going to trail the buses with one of our writers and a photographer. I'm considering Marvin and Troy.

"I can't believe I'm going to have sit out a major story out at home again, pregnant," Cassy said disappointed.

"I know, babe, but I can't take a chance on you getting caught in any crossfire. It's not worth it," Bless told her.

If emotions could have been visualized, he would have seen her blow fire like a dragon and smoke come out of her head. That was the moment she made up her mind that this was their last baby. She loved her children and wanted a family, but she felt like she was missing out on her life at home having babies. Every time she got things moving forward, there was a baby and she had to get in the back seat. The best photographs she had ever taken were during the boycott, and that was over five years ago. She felt as if the bus was rolling and leaving her behind in more than one way.

Bless, Marvin, and Troy left for Birmingham on May, 17. When they got to Birmingham, the Freedom Riders were quickly arrested. Bless lost contact with them when they were released in the night, and he was afraid to even think about what could have happened to them.

"I can't tell you all how good it is to see you guys," Bless said when they came back to the station, "What a welcome relief."

"They just took us to the state line and put us out," Diane informed him.

No bus driver wanted the precarious job of driving the Freedom Riders out of the city, and the KKK even came to the bus station with their hoods hanging on the back of their robes and taunted them as they waited.

"This a powder keg waiting to blow," Bless said on the phone to Cassy.

"Maybe you should back off some, Bless. We need you to come back home you know."

"It's hard trying to stay out of the fray and still be close enough to know what was going on. But don't worry. I'm coming home."

Thankfully, the governor bowed to pressure from the media. Promises were given to the President, and state troopers escorted the riders to Montgomery, even though that was where the protection disappeared. A mob of hate-filled hoodlums came out of nowhere armed with whatever they could pick up when they left the house, and a riot broke out. Their first targets at the bus station were the reporters and camera men.

"We shall overcome," Bless sang with the group as he folded his arms over his head to fend off the blows.

Bless, Marvin, and Troy were pushed outside with the other reporters, and their cameras were thrown on the ground. Then the mob turned their attention to the riders, hitting them with pipes and bats, while the police watched. It seemed like forever before the police finally ended the melee, and the riders and the reporters took refuge in a church.

Later in the evening, the church was surrounded until the National Guard and State Police were called out. State police, troopers, and helicopters followed the bus as it traveled to the Mississippi border, and they all thought the worst had ended until they were arrested in the bus station in Jackson for breach of peace.

Bless sat in the back of the courtroom on May 24, the first birthday that he and Blue had ever spent apart.

"You all will be sent to prison for sixty days to do hard time. Maybe it'll teach you people a lesson," the judge said, turning his back to justice.

In spite of the consequences, more Freedom Riders--men and women, black and white, and all religions from all over the country--were boarding buses, trains, and planes going to Jackson.

"It's going to be a hot summer in Mississippi," Bless said to Marvin and Troy as they drove back to Nashville.

Danielle was born on September 29, a week after the Southern signs of segregation, "white and colored," were taken down. But it wasn't until November that the Interstate Commerce Commission issued rules prohibiting segregated transportation facilities.

Chapter
Twenty-Seven

A season of evaluation began with the new year in the Portunus families with them wondering if they were fulfilling their true destinies. It could have been a case of success breeding discontent more that dissatisfaction with the choices they had made, but they all had questions about the decisions they'd made for their lives and were contemplating whether the directions could be changed.

Bless wasn't sure he was making a difference for black people that he wanted to make with the magazine. Cassy was nursing Danielle and feeling like she had given up her own life to have the children and was desperate to get her career back on track. Blue was thinking about divorce. He didn't want his actions to torture Carol anymore, and he had to admit that it was unfair to have married her. Carol felt like a victim of her circumstances. She had tried to accept the cards that she had been dealt, but she was tired of the games.

"We need to fly out to Nashville," Caesar said to Rainbow, sensing the frustration in the phone calls with the twins.

"Why don't we go for their birthday in May?" Rainbow suggested, getting excited. "Why don't you talk to Ed about doing a big dinner at The Storm's End?"

"Dial him up on the phone for me, sweetie," he said, ready to get his plans together.

Business at the restaurant was slow since black folks could go and eat with white folks in their restaurants, and Ed was glad to have a chance for them all to get together before he had to close the doors.

The day of the dinner, Caesar and Rainbow went over to restaurant to help prepare the food. Despite the fact that Caesar's fingers had knots and some were twisted, he still had the magic in the kitchen. They prepared a simple menu of fried chicken and baked ham, with roasted corn and green bean casserole.

"I'll arrange the tables so you can all sit around it as a family like you used to," Ed told them when they arrived.

"This is such a blessing to sit at the head of my family again," Caesar said, and his eyes moistened as he looked at his sons, their wives, and their children.

"These eyes of mine won't let me see much more than shadows of color, but hearing the chatter and laughter of my grandbabies are priceless," Rainbow said to all of them.

The meal together was just what the doctor for all of them. It gave them the opportunity to stop thinking about themselves and their individual importance and appreciate that they were a part of a family.

After they'd eaten all they could stand, Caesar said, "Our gift to you gentlemen is a night out with your wives and no children. You guys go out and have some fun, and we'll take care of the rest."

"Right on. Let's go," Bless said. "I hear they have this guitarist they call Marbles playing at the Del Morocco. They say he's a musical genius. Let's go over to hear him."

"That's sounds like an offer I can't refuse," Cassy said, clapping her hands ecstatically. She needed some time to feel like a free woman for a little longer before she had to go home and be mama to the kids.

Blue was always ready to party, but Carol had her reservations. She wasn't comfortable around the kind of people who hung out in clubs.

The four of them walked into the Del Morocco, and when Uncle Teddy saw Blue, he led them to a reserved table close to the stage. It was a good crowd there, even for a Thursday night.

"What are you folks having to drink tonight?" Uncle Teddy asked.

"A couple of beers of us," Bless said, pointing to himself and Cassy.

"The usual cognac for me, Ted, and white wine for my wife," Blue added.

The disc jockey spun a few more records while the band set up.

"Good evening, ladies and gentlemen. Prepare yourselves for a soulful music extravaganza. Join me in welcoming the King Kasuals, featuring Jimmy Hendrix on guitar," Uncle Teddy said in his introduction.

The band was good, but it was the guitarist that took them to another level. He played loose and free like jazz, but it was loud with a rock feel. The crowd loved it.

"He's really feeling it," Cassy said, watching the guitarist play with all parts of his body, including his teeth.

"It's not the typical rhythm and blues that I groove to, but he's putting that guitar to work. The man's got talent," Bless remarked as he ordered another beer.

Carol even seemed to relax with her second glass of wine. Then a man came over to the table and spoke to Blue in his ear. Blue got up and followed him into another room.

"I hate to cut a good time short, but we're going to have to leave," Blue said, agitated when he came back to the table after twenty minutes.

"I don't get out much, so I'm staying until the band finishes their set," Cassy said, refusing to let Blue control the situation.

"I'll walk you guys out," Bless said, curious to know what the man said to Blue.

Before they got to Blue's car parked a few yards down the street, they could see that the driver's window was busted out.

Bless was shocked. "I'm going back in to call the police."

"Why, man? It's nothing they can do. They don't fix windows," Blue said.

"That's exactly why I don't like to come out to these places," Carol said, upset and feeling justified in her decision.

Bless watched the car drive away and tried to shake off the strange vibe he got when he saw the broken glass.

***

Caesar and Rainbow returned home after a two-week visit, and life for the Portunus families in Nashville quickly reverted to the familiar rhythm of working and raising children. Tensions and tempers were rising with the summer heat at work and at home for both of them.

"Blue, you been scarce lately," Bless said into the phone receiver, "I haven't gotten a chance to talk to you for more than a minute since the birthday party."

"The work is backing up on me, bro. My supplies are being affected by the lumber and sawmill worker strike, and I've had to lay off a few men."

"That's tough, but you always manage," Bless said. "I'm hoping I can talk you and Carol into bringing the kids and going up to Idlewild with us for a couple of weeks. It would give us all some time away from all the craziness of life around here."

"I do need some time to relax and catch up on what's been going on with you," Blue said, wondering if he could convince Carol to go. "I'll call you in a few days and let you know."

"All right, Blue, till then," Bless said.

It was a sweltering afternoon on June 19, and more than a week had passed, and Blue hadn't gotten back with him about the trip. Bless was under pressure trying to meet his own deadlines. Two of his top writers had left, one to *Life* magazine and the other to *Look*. He sat bowed over the typewriter in his office, struggling to finish his editorial on police brutality in Los Angeles, when he heard a thunderous explosion.

"What in the hell was that?" he hollered as he looked toward his open window and wondered what white man's vengeance had been acted out on this day.

Alarmed and shaken, he rose to his feet to investigate but found that his legs would barely move. He looked down at his shirt and moved his hands across his body, checking to see if he had possibly been hit by some debris. He didn't see any blood or signs of an injury and thought maybe he had been sitting too long. He stretched his legs and made his way to the window, feeling light-headed. He knew he had been pushing himself, but the steady stream of new developments in the Civil Rights Movement didn't allow time for a pause. He didn't see anything unusual out of the window, except for some other curious folks looking around and discussing the noise.

Bless hurried down the steps to see if Blue was in the office and if he knew what was going on. It would give him a chance to move around and get his blood flowing again. He stopped for a brief moment to take in a deep breath of air before he took the three strides that placed him at the Empire Construction Company's front door. He walked inside the front office, and there was no one there. Blue's secretary was out or had gone home early.

"Blue?" he called out as he walked through to his office in the back. "Did you hear that boom a few minutes ago?"

Bless stopped in his tracks when he walked through the door and saw his brother lying on the floor with the back of his suit soaked in blood and a pool surrounding him on the floor. Bless stood frozen at the sight and grappled with his mind to wake him from this horrible nightmare. His heart began to race, and he knew he wasn't dreaming. He dropped to his knees and crawled over to Blue. Bless looked at his face and the neat hairline of his fresh haircut. His eyes were open, but they looked past him, his lips were partially opened, as if he were speaking. It was surreal; it was if he was looking at himself lying there on the floor.

The numbness in Bless's body began to fade, and seething pain took its place when he realized that his brother was dead; somebody had come into his place of business and killed him. Bless pulled Blues body into his lap, trying to put the life back into his brother again. He needed to force him to breathe and his heart to beat, but it was no use.

Bless began to bellow and roar, "No, no, no!" over and over and over, unable to comprehend that his flesh and blood could be separated from him.

It took only a minute for a small crowd to gather at the front door, and someone called for an ambulance and the police. Bless had yelled his guts out to exhaustion and lay on the floor with Blue across his body. It was a heartbreaking scene, and not one of the onlookers had dared to approach the twins. When the police got there, they thought they were both dead. Once the police started asking questions, most of the crowd dissolved and went back to minding their own business.

The ambulance loaded up the body, and the uniformed police began searching inside and outside of the building. Two detectives in plainclothes began to question Bless.

"What's your name?" the plainclothes policeman asked.

"Caesar Portunus," Bless answered.

"Well, Mr. Portunus, I'm Sgt. Leonard, and this is my partner, Sgt. Philips. Can you tell us what happened here?"

Sick to his stomach, Bless explained, "I was upstairs in my office when I heard a loud boom. I looked out of my window, and I didn't see anybody. I walked down to ask my brother about it, and I found him lying on the floor."

"From what we can see, there isn't anything out of order here and your brother was wearing an expensive watch and ring, and they're not missing, so robbery wasn't the motive. Does your brother have any enemies, or do you know of anyone who would have a grudge against him?" Sgt. Leonard asked.

"No, Sgt, I can't think of anybody who would want to kill my brother," Bless answered, but in his mind, he was already going down a list of people that Blue had problems with.

"From what we can tell from the scene, it was someone that he knew well and trusted enough to turn his back on them. It looks like he was about to pour himself a drink when he was shot," Sgt. Philips said.

Bless went through his mental list and wondered who would be bold enough to come here and shoot Blue. He didn't know, but he promised himself he would find out.

When the questions for Bless were finished, the detectives left to go over to Blue's house to break the news to Carol and ask her the same questions. Bless knew the worst day of his life was nowhere near being over; he had to call his mama and dad with the news. None of it made sense. He had to go home, and he needed to see Cassy and the babies. The aches that he felt in his body were now centered heavily in his chest, but there was a catch or a cramp that was still in his left leg. Bless limped out as the police taped off the entrance of the Empire Construction Company. Bad news travels fast and the worst even faster.

Cassy stood at the door, with Danielle in her arms and Venus and Alexander on either side of her, waiting for him. Her face was already covered in tears, knowing how devastating this was going to be for Bless. The twins were connected in ways she didn't even understand. Yet, she felt encouraged with just the sight of him coming up the walkway. Cassy pushed the door open for him and locked her legs to brace herself under the weight of him when he fell into her arms sobbing. There were no words.

It was more than ten minutes before Bless could compose himself enough to call his folks in Los Angeles. It was impossible to soften a blow that was so destructive it would leave them damaged and dazed for life.

"I'll dial the number for you," Cassy said as she handed him the phone.

"Hello," Caesar said cheerfully when he answered the phone; he and Rainbow were having an early dinner on their balcony.

"Hello, Dad," Bless said in an effort to keep the trembling out of his voice, "I have bad news."

"What is it, son?" Caesar asked, holding his breath.

"Blue was shot today."

"O Lord, have mercy! Is he all right?" Caesar pleaded into the phone.

Those were the words that cut off Rainbow's breath, and she leaned on the edge of her chair to hear the call.

"No, Dad, he's not. He's dead," Bless said, holding back another flood of tears for the hurt of his mama and dad.

"How did this happen?" Caesar asked, begging for an explanation to the madness of it all.

"I was working upstairs at my magazine office, and somebody came in downstairs and shot him in the back," Bless answered. "I don't know who did it. But if the police don't find out, I will, and then I'll kill them myself," Bless declared as the anger began to surface.

"We're on our way, son," Caesar said over Rainbow's screams in the background.

Caesar and Rainbow held on to each other for dear life, the pain in each of them was unbearable, and they couldn't understand why they couldn't keep their son. A day that had started out so peaceful and beautiful for them had turned violent and ugly.

***

"I remember how panicked I felt when I first saw Blue's lifeless body on the day the twins were born," Rainbow said to Caesar on the airplane ride back to Nashville.

"I know, honey, I remember."

"Now I can't help but wonder if he had died that day, would I have hurt as much as I'm hurting now," she murmured as she sat on the plane, burning as if she existed in her own private hell.

"Don't torture yourself thinking about that, Rain," Caesar said, feeling his own agony.

"I can't see how that would be possible, mourning for a baby that I hadn't even held to my breast compared to the grief for a child I raised to a man."

"Stop it now," Caesar said. "You going to make yourself sick. You got to be strong for everybody, even me. I thank God he didn't die back then."

"I'm sorry, C," Rainbow said as she shook the thoughts out of her head, realizing that if he had died as an infant, she would never have been blessed with seeing him grow up or share his life. She silently asked the Lord to forgive her mind's wanderings and thanked Him for infinite wisdom and mercy that granted her the thirty-three years to be Blue's mother and for his presence in the family.

Bless met them at the airport, and they hugged each other tightly, with a fear that had never been real to them before, that they were vulnerable and could be separated for life at the drop of a hat. The house was crowded with all the children when they got there but somehow the noise and confusion distracted them and made everyone feel better.

"Cassy and I went to see Carol, but she was so hysterical that a doctor had to be called to sedate her," Bless informed them.

"Two of her sorority sisters are over there with her, and they said that Mrs. Jefferson would be there as soon as she could," Cassy added while they sat at the kitchen table. "They thought that it would be a good idea if we took Josephine and Anthony home with us until Carol could pull herself together. It broke my heart. Josephine cried all the way over here, clinging to Bless like he was the only thing she had left in the world and Anthony tried to sink down into the seat between Jo and me. Being with the kids here, they seem to have calmed down."

They were all caught in a cyclone of sadness that threatened to rip them apart. The only thing they could do was hold onto each other.

The Smith's Funeral Home did an excellent job. Blue was dressed in a midnight blue tuxedo and had his signature fresh haircut. He looked like he was sleeping and having a pleasant dream from which he didn't want to be awakened.

Carol sat in the front and was impeccably dressed. Her make-up was flawless, and every hair was in place. She was the picture of class and good taste, even at a time like this. Bless sat next to her, with Cassy on his other side. Caesar and Rainbow sat on the pew behind them with the children.

Reverend Sloan, a classmate and good friend of Blue's, gave the eulogy; he used the 23rd Psalm for his scripture to try to give the family some peace in this tragedy, and he likened Caesar Blue to Julius Caesar, who had too been struck down by his enemies. He closed with a passage from Shakespeare:

He only in a general honest thought and common good to all, made one of them.

His life was gentle, and the elements so mixed in him that
Nature might stand up and say to all the world, "This was
a man."

The burial at the cemetery was too much for Carol to bear; and
when the casket was lower into the ground, she slowly keeled
over in her chair. Her parents escorted her back to house, where
she received another dose of sedatives. Ed served the rest of the
Portunus family the repast at The Storm's End, but it only served to
bring more sadness to the occasion. It reminded them of the way it
once was and that it would never be that way again.

"We're going to take Carol back with us to New Orleans for a
rest," Mr. Jefferson said to Caesar. "She's sick with grief. Would it
be all right if the kids stayed here for a while?"

"Absolutely," Caesar answered. "I plan to be around for a while, at
least until the weather turns cold. I've missed the grandchildren so
much, and we want some extra time to spend with them."

That was the story Caesar told anyone who asked him, but the
real motivation was that he wanted to do some investigating of
his own. The police didn't have much to go on without witnesses
or a murder weapon. He didn't have any ambitions of catching
the killer himself and satisfying any need for vengeance. It was
more to keep Bless from doing something that would put him
in danger or ruin his life. Caesar couldn't stand it if something
happened to him.

***

Bless closed his office above Empire Construction and moved
over to the main headquarters of the magazine over on Charlotte
Ave. He couldn't work another day in the place where his brother
was killed. He was thankful for the invaluable staff that worked so
hard to put out a quality magazine because he was still preoccupied
with finding the killer.

Every hour Bless asked himself, "Who did it? Was it some white hoogie jealous of his success, someone he burned in business, a jealous husband, somebody who lost too much at the card table, a gambling debt?" The list was long. On the weekends, he would go wherever Blue hung out and look for any detection of guilt in the faces of everyone there.

A lead came in the case when a .44 Magnum gun was found in the trash bin behind the Del Morocco about a month after the murder. The bin was rarely used by the supper club because it wasn't emptied often enough, and Uncle Teddy didn't want to draw rats around his place of business. The police discovered the gun was registered to Caesar Blue Portunus, and ballistic tests determined that it was the murder weapon.

"I was with Blue when he bought the gun," Bless said told the police when they questioned him. "I know he kept it locked up in the desk of his home office."

"Could he have started carrying it because of some threat?" Sgt. Leonard asked.

"Not that I know of," Bless answered, thinking about the night at the Del Morocco.

"The real question is how the killer got it away from him," Sgt. Philips, the other detective, speculated. "The gun had been wiped clean, and there were no fingerprints to be found on it."

"There's no way anyone on this earth could have taken that gun from my brother," Bless told them. "They would have been the one lying there dead instead of him. I never knew him to carry it around; it may have been stolen from the house."

Bless used his set of keys to get into Blue and Carol's house and led Sgt. Leonard and Philips to Blue's office. Inside the desk drawer was the wooden gun case, and on top of the well-polished wood were four visible fingerprints.

The forensic lab lifted the prints, and they didn't belong to Blue. They checked the prints of Mabel, their housekeeper, and that wasn't a match. The police thought maybe the prints belonged to Carol.

***

"Hello, Carol. You look like you're feeling better. Hello, Mrs. Jefferson," Bless said when he picked them up from the airport. They had come back in town to pack up the house.

"I'm feeling better, thank you," Carol answered politely.

"I was wondering if you knew anything about Blue carrying a gun around with him?" Bless asked Carol on the ride to the house.

"Definitely not," she said. "He knew that I hated guns, and I didn't want one around the children."

"You do know that he bought a gun over a year ago and kept it in his office desk?" Bless added.

"No, I didn't. If I had, I would have made him get rid of it," she said.

Bless dropped them off and went back to the magazine office. He called Sgt. Leonard at the station and said, "I brought Carol home today, and those fingerprints could not have been hers. She didn't know that he even had the gun."

The detectives came out to the house to talk with Carol. She and her mother were busy packing up the dishes in the kitchen when they arrived.

"I don't see how I can be much help, Detective," Carol said. "I didn't know about the gun, and I never paid much attention to the business acquaintances that visited Blue at the house."

"Well, thank you anyway, Mrs. Portunus," Sgt. Leonard said, not wanting to offend her by asking her to come to the station to have her fingerprints compared to the ones on the gun case. But he wasn't above lifting one of the glasses she packed in the box on the table when her head was turned.

The forensic tests were mindboggling; Carol's prints from the glass were a match to those found on the case.

"Why would she lie and say she didn't know he had a gun?" Sgt. Leonard asked Philips. "Call Bless Portunus, and have Carol Portunus brought in for questioning.

Bless was at the door when she came into the station and asked her point blank, "Carol, did you kill my brother?"

She turned her head away from him with no answer and followed Sgt. Philips into the interrogation room. When the door was closed behind them, she took a seat at the table.

"I knew Blue had a gun, and I used it to shoot him," Carol said, admitting that she had lied. "But that is all I'm going to say."

She was willing to kill him but unwilling to air their dirty laundry. They were all shocked and disappointed that she could have done this to the father of her children.

"Carol just confessed to Blue's murder, and she's been arrested," a despondent Mrs. Jefferson told her husband on the phone from the police station.

"I'll be on the next plane with the best attorney for our baby that money can buy," Mr. Jefferson assured her.

The next pill to swallow was who would tell the children that their mama was the one who killed their daddy.

***

The district attorney's opening statement began with the courtship and marriage of Caesar Blue and Carol Portunus. During his commentary, he showed pictures of their stately home and photographs of their children. He spoke of the success of the Empire Construction Company and all the accomplishments that Blue had achieved in such a short time.

"Caesar Blue was a gregarious and self-directed individual, and Carol was a possessive and demanding wife. I declare that Carol Portunus plotted and killed her husband because of her obsessive jealousy and inability to control his actions. A devout Catholic, divorce was not a consideration for her; murder was a more acceptable solution to end the marriage. She willfully, without any thought for her children, walked into his office and cold-bloodedly shot him in his back as he poured a glass of water. And with his death, they did part."

The defense attorney rose to the stand and reiterated the loving courtship and wedding of Caesar Blue and Carol Portunus, but it was there that the two statements diverged.

"Caesar Blue was a self-absorbed and cruel husband, and Carol was a devoted and self-sacrificing wife. I declare that Carol Portunus shot Blue in self-defense of unrelenting psychological abuse. She was devoted to her marriage and family. In her understanding, she had been pushed until her back was against the wall, and only one of them could survive. In her desperation, she took the gun to Blue's office to compel him to listen, one last effort to appeal to his sensitivities. She professed her love, and he rejected her, degraded her, and it drove her to the point of insanity. She was no longer in control but acting under irresistible impulses. When he turned his back on her, she raised the gun and fired, not in viciousness, but in helplessness."

The prosecution put forth witnesses that testified about Caesar Blue, a man who loved and cared for his family. They bore witness to a man who escorted his wife to all of the events on her social calendar, a man who treated her like queen, and showered her with expensive gifts. He was a gentleman; he never raised his hand to her or spoke an ill word to her. However, none of it was enough. He was a free-spirit, and she resented every minute that he was out of her presence.

The defense put forth witnesses who testified about Blue's never-ending parade of disreputable women. No, he never laid a hand on her, but they communicated how many times she reeled from the blows of his infidelity, the humiliation she felt each time she heard about his scandalous exploits with other women. She had just come to the end of her rope. The closing arguments repeated the opening statement, and the jury was discharged for deliberation.

The families sat across from each other in the courtroom, not as enemies, but all victims of circumstance. Neither wished hardship on the other. Their common desire was to turn back time--the Portunus family, to the time before the shooting; the Jeffersons, to the time before Blue and Carol met.

They all watched in silence, barely breathing as the foreman of the jury passed the verdict to the judge.

"Will the defendant please rise?" the judge said.

Carol stood to her feet, as still as a mannequin.

"Carol Jefferson Portunus, the jury finds you are guilty of murder in the first-degree."

Carol showed no reaction, containing her emotions, as any self-respecting lady ought to do in public.

"Oh no! Not my baby!" Mrs. Jefferson cried out, no longer able to maintain her restraint as her backbone collapses and she falls against her husband.

"I can't believe this is happening!" Mr. Jefferson said as he shook his head in disbelief, unable to comprehend the legal defeat.

The bailiff led Carol out of the courtroom, and Caesar and Rainbow slowly walked out, with Bless and Cassy close behind. There were no words of comfort that could be offered or received that would bring consolation to either family. Carol was mercifully spared from the death penalty and sentenced to life in prison.

The cold winter months lay ahead, and the season of melancholy was upon them. The quiet after the chaos was torture. The trial had sustained them and given them a purpose for getting up every morning. Now that it was over, they had the painful task of living their lives incomplete with a void that could never be filled.

Caesar and Rainbow flew back to Los Angeles, praying the distance would ease their suffering. Mr. and Mrs. Jefferson quickly returned home to New Orleans without making any requests for custody of Josephine or Anthony. Bless and Cassy got the children settled in with them at the family home, praying that the preacher's words at the funeral would hold true when he said, "Weeping may endure for a night, but joy comes in the morning."

***

"I hated having to write this," Bless said to Cassy about the article in *The Banquet of Knowledge.*

"I know, honey, but who better could have told the story?" she asked.

On the cover was a collage of Caesar Blue, from him running in the grass beside Bless, a family picture at The Storm's End, to him playing on the football field, working his first construction job, sitting inside the Del Morocco, receiving his college diploma from Fisk, toasting his bride at the wedding, Josephine's christening, and receiving an award for business. The article read:

"It was a tragedy of the greatest proportion, causing unspeakable grief, heartache, and loss. Successful business magnate Caesar Blue Portunus was killed by his wife, socialite Carol Jefferson Portunus. In taking his life, she gave up her own, their children lost a father and a mother, a father and a mother lost a son, and I lost a brother. The reality that makes it so difficult to accept is that this misfortune need not have materialized. When I'm honest with myself, I must admit that I did foresee some catastrophic event on the horizon for some years. Small tremors of unrest that surround an active volcano shook in my core, but in my trepidation, I chose to ignore all the warnings and hoped against hope that all's well that ends well. Unfortunately, a bullet went through Blue's back and pierced the heart of my brother, and he died instantly.

"There are two faces of passion--love and hate--and the fragile line that separates them had been splintered by infidelity. It's useless to discuss the right or wrong or what Blue or Carol deserved, but what must be said is that Blue lived his life on his terms. He was a man's man by all definitions: successful, educated, athletic, stylish, a trustworthy businessman, and adventurous. He loved the women, and they loved him in return. He could hold his liquor and was a good sport, win or lose. His voracious appetite for life should aptly be blamed for his undoing. Inheriting a legacy of dignity, perseverance, and good fortune this story should have had the happy ending of a fairytale. Instead, it concludes as a Shakespearean tragedy. Opportunely, 'Cowards die many times before their death, the valiant never taste of death but once.'"

Bless held the copy of the magazine. It was light in his hands but heavy on his heart.

"You did a fine job, Bless. I know it wasn't easy," Cassy said proudly.

"No, it wasn't, although writing it provided me with a revelation."

"Why is it that your deepest thoughts always make me nervous?" she asked with reservation.

"It's about legacy and time, sweetheart. Blue's children need a fresh start, and I want to give them one. The history here is too heavy to bear on their lives. Besides, I don't think I can stay and raise these kids here after all that has happened. What kind of life do you think they can have in Nashville?"

"Well, where do you suggest we go with five children?"

"I'm thinking that we should go north, away from the past. We can move the magazine offices wherever we go."

"You don't have to convince me if it will give me a chance to be closer to my mama and daddy. The question is, where?"

"I was thinking about Philadelphia," Bless said wistfully. "In Greek, it means 'brotherly love.'"

www.ingramcontent.com/pod-product-compliance
Lightning Source LLC
Chambersburg PA
CBHW070112120726
47909CB00002B/571